IN OPAR, LOST OUTPOST OF ATLANTIS:

The brutish man was quite close now, creeping around the end of the altar, with clawlike hands extended toward La, priestess of the Flaming God of drowned Atlantis.

Tarzan strained at the bonds which pinioned him to the blood-stained altar. The woman did not see—she had forgotten him in the horror of the danger. As the brute leaped to clutch his victim, the ape-man gave one superhuman wrench at the thongs. The effort sent him rolling from the altar to the stone floor on the opposite side from where the priestess stood. As he sprang to his feet, the thongs dropped from his freed arms. At the same time, he realized that he was alone in the inner temple—the high priestess and the mad priest had disappeared.

And then a muffled scream came from the cavernous mouth of the dark hole beyond the sacrificial altar . . .

Edgar Rice Burroughs

TARZAN NOVELS

TARZAN OF THE APES (#1)
THE RETURN OF TARZAN (#2)
THE BEASTS OF TARZAN (#3)
THE SON OF TARZAN (#4)
TARZAN AND THE JEWELS OF OPAR (#5)
JUNGLE TALES OF TARZAN (#6)
TARZAN THE UNTAMED (#7)
TARZAN THE TERRIBLE (#8)
TARZAN AND THE GOLDEN LION (#9)
TARZAN AND THE ANT MEN (#10)
TARZAN, LORD OF THE JUNGLE (#11)
TARZAN AND THE LOST EMPIRE (#12)
TARZAN AT THE EARTH'S CORE (#13)
TARZAN THE INVINCIBLE (#14)
TARZAN TRIUMPHANT (#15)
TARZAN AND THE CITY OF GOLD (#16)
TARZAN AND THE LION MAN (#17)
TARZAN AND THE LEOPARD MEN (#18)
TARZAN'S QUEST (#19)
TARZAN AND THE FORBIDDEN CITY (#20)
TARZAN THE MAGNIFICENT (#21)
TARZAN AND THE FOREIGN LEGION (#22)
TARZAN AND THE MADMAN (#23)
TARZAN AND THE CASTAWAYS (#24)

COMPLETE AND UNABRIDGED!

THE RETURN OF TARZAN

Edgar Rice Burroughs

BALLANTINE BOOKS • NEW YORK

ISBN 0-345-31575-8

This authorized edition published by arrangement with Edgar Rice Burroughs, Inc.

Manufactured in the United States of America

First U.S. Printing: July 1963
Eighteenth Printing: February 1984

Cover art by Charles Ren

CONTENTS

1

The Affair on the Liner

"MAGNIFIQUE!" ejaculated the Countess de Coude, beneath her breath.

"Eh?" questioned the count, turning toward his young wife. "What is it that is magnificent?" and the count bent his eyes in various directions in quest of the object of her admiration.

"Oh, nothing at all, my dear," replied the countess, a slight flush momentarily coloring her already pink cheek. "I was but recalling with admiration those stupendous skyscrapers, as they call them, of New York," and the fair countess settled herself more comfortably in her steamer chair, and resumed the magazine which "nothing at all" had caused her to let fall upon her lap.

Her husband again buried himself in his book, but not without a mild wonderment that three days out from New York his countess should suddenly have realized an admiration for the very buildings she had but recently characterized as horrid.

Presently the count put down his book. "It is very tiresome, Olga," he said. "I think that I shall hunt up some others who may be equally bored, and see if we cannot find enough for a game of cards."

"You are not very gallant, my husband," replied the young woman, smiling, "but as I am equally bored I can forgive you. Go and play at your tiresome old cards, then, if you will."

When he had gone she let her eyes wander slyly to the figure of a tall young man stretched lazily in a chair not far distant.

"Magnifique!" she breathed once more.

The Countess Olga de Coude was twenty. Her husband forty. She was a very faithful and loyal wife, but as she had had nothing whatever to do with the selection of a husband, it is not at all unlikely that she was not wildly and passionately in love with the one that fate and her titled Russian father had selected for her. However, simply because she was surprised into a tiny exclamation of approval at sight of a splendid young stranger it must not be inferred therefrom that her thoughts were in any way disloyal to her spouse. She merely admired, as she might have admired a particularly fine specimen of any species. Furthermore, the young man was unquestionably good to look at.

As her furtive glance rested upon his profile he rose to leave the deck. The Countess de Coude beckoned to a passing steward.

"Who is that gentleman?" she asked.

"He is booked, madam, as Monsieur Tarzan, of Africa," replied the steward.

"Rather a large estate," thought the girl, but now her interest was still further aroused.

As Tarzan walked slowly toward the smoking-room he came unexpectedly upon two men whispering excitedly just without. He would have vouchsafed them not even a passing thought but for the strangely guilty glance that one of them shot in his direction. They reminded Tarzan of melodramatic villains he had seen at the theaters in Paris. Both were very dark, and this, in connection with the shrugs and stealthy glances that accompanied their palpable intriguing, lent still greater force to the similarity.

Tarzan entered the smoking-room, and sought a chair a little apart from the others who were there. He felt in no mood for conversation, and as he sipped his absinth he let his mind run rather sorrowfully over the past few weeks of his life. Time and again he had wondered if he had acted wisely in renouncing his birthright to a man to whom he owed nothing. It is true that he liked Clayton, but—ah, but that was not the question. It was not for William Cecil Clayton, Lord Greystoke, that he had denied his birth. It was for the woman whom both he and Clayton loved, and whom a strange freak of fate had given to Clayton instead of to him.

That she loved him made the thing doubly difficult to bear, yet he knew that he could have done nothing less than he did do that night within the little railway station in the far Wisconsin woods. To him her happiness was the first consideration of all, and his brief experience with civilization and civilized men had taught him that without money and position life to most of them was unendurable.

Jane Porter had been born to both, and had Tarzan taken them away from her future husband it would doubtless have plunged her into a life of misery and torture. That she would have spurned Clayton once he had been stripped of both his title and his estates never for once occurred to Tarzan, for he credited to others the same honest loyalty that was so inherent a quality in himself. Nor, in this instance, had he erred. Could any one thing have further bound Jane Porter to her promise to Clayton it would have been in the nature of some such misfortune as this overtaking him.

Tarzan's thoughts drifted from the past to the future. He tried to look forward with pleasurable sensations to his return to the jungle of his birth and boyhood; the cruel, fierce jungle in which he had spent twenty of his twenty-two years. But who or what of all the myriad jungle life would there be to welcome his return? Not one. Only Tantor, the elephant, could he call friend. The others would hunt him or flee from him as had been their way in the past.

Not even the apes of his own tribe would extend the hand of fellowship to him.

If civilization had done nothing else for Tarzan of the Apes, it had to some extent taught him to crave the society of his own kind, and to feel with genuine pleasure the congenial warmth of companionship. And in the same ratio had it made any other life distasteful to him. It was difficult to imagine a world without a friend—without a living thing who spoke the new tongues which Tarzan had learned to love so well. And so it was that Tarzan looked with little relish upon the future he had mapped out for himself.

As he sat musing over his cigarette his eyes fell upon a mirror before him, and in it he saw reflected a table at which four men sat at cards. Presently one of them rose to leave, and then another approached, and Tarzan could see that he courteously offered to fill the vacant chair, that the game might not be interrupted. He was the smaller of the two whom Tarzan had seen whispering just outside the smoking-room.

It was this fact that aroused a faint spark of interest in Tarzan, and so as he speculated upon the future he watched in the mirror the reflection of the players at the table behind him. Aside from the man who had but just entered the game Tarzan knew the name of but one of the other players. It was he who sat opposite the new player, Count Raoul de Coude, whom an over-attentive steward had pointed out as one of the celebrities of the passage, describing him as a man high in the official family of the French minister of war.

Suddenly Tarzan's attention was riveted upon the picture in the glass. The other swarthy plotter had entered, and was standing behind the count's chair. Tarzan saw him turn and glance furtively about the room, but his eyes did not rest for a sufficient time upon the mirror to note the reflection of Tarzan's watchful eyes. Stealthily the man withdrew something from his pocket. Tarzan could not discern what the object was, for the man's hand covered it.

Slowly the hand approached the count, and then, very deftly, the thing that was in it was transferred to the count's pocket. The man remained standing where he could watch the Frenchman's cards. Tarzan was puzzled, but he was all attention now, nor did he permit another detail of the incident to escape him.

The play went on for some ten minutes after this, until the count won a considerable wager from him who had last joined the game, and then Tarzan saw the fellow back of the count's chair nod his head to his confederate. Instantly the player arose and pointed a finger at the count.

"Had I known that monsieur was a professional card sharp I had not been so ready to be drawn into the game," he said.

Instantly the count and the two other players were upon their feet.

De Coude's face went white.

"What do you mean, sir?" he cried. "Do you know to whom you speak?"

"I know that I speak, for the last time, to one who cheats at cards," replied the fellow.

The count leaned across the table, and struck the man full in the mouth with his open palm, and then the others closed in between them.

"There is some mistake, sir," cried one of the other players. "Why, this is Count de Coude, of France."

"If I am mistaken," said the accuser, "I shall gladly apologize; but before I do so first let monsieur le count explain the extra cards which I saw him drop into his side pocket."

And then the man whom Tarzan had seen drop them there turned to sneak from the room, but to his annoyance he found the exit barred by a tall, gray-eyed stranger.

"Pardon," said the man brusquely, attempting to pass to one side.

"Wait," said Tarzan.

"But why, monsieur?" exclaimed the other petulantly. "Permit me to pass, monsieur."

"Wait," said Tarzan. "I think that there is a matter in here that you may doubtless be able to explain."

The fellow had lost his temper by this time, and with a low oath seized Tarzan to push him to one side. The ape-man but smiled as he twisted the big fellow about and, grasping him by the collar of his coat, escorted him back to the table, struggling, cursing, and striking in futile remonstrance. It was Nikolas Rokoff's first experience with the muscles that had brought their savage owner victorious through encounters with Numa, the lion, and Terkoz, the great bull ape.

The man who had accused De Coude, and the two others who had been playing, stood looking expectantly at the count. Several other passengers had drawn toward the scene of the altercation, and all awaited the dénouement.

"The fellow is crazy," said the count. "Gentlemen, I implore that one of you search me."

"The accusation is ridiculous." This from one of the players.

"You have but to slip your hand in the count's coat pocket and you will see that the accusation is quite serious," insisted the accuser. And then, as the others still hesitated to do so: "Come, I shall do it myself if no other will," and he stepped forward toward the count.

"No, monsieur," said De Coude. "I will submit to a search only at the hands of a gentleman."

"It is unnecessary to search the count. The cards are in his pocket. I myself saw them placed there."

All turned in surprise toward this new speaker, to behold a very well-built young man urging a resisting captive toward them by the scruff of his neck.

"It is a conspiracy," cried De Coude angrily. "There are no cards in my coat," and with that he ran his hand into his pocket. As he did so tense silence reigned in the little group. The count went dead white, and then very slowly he withdrew his hand, and in it were three cards.

He looked at them in mute and horrified surprise, and slowly the red of mortification suffused his face. Expressions of pity and contempt tinged the features of those who looked on at the death of a man's honor.

"It is a conspiracy, monsieur." It was the gray-eyed stranger who spoke. "Gentlemen," he continued, "monsieur le count did not know that those cards were in his pocket. They were placed there without his knowledge as he sat at play. From where I sat in that chair yonder I saw the reflection of it all in the mirror before me. This person whom I just intercepted in an effort to escape placed the cards in the count's pocket."

De Coude had glanced from Tarzan to the man in his grasp.

"*Mon Dieu,* Nikolas!" he cried. "You?"

Then he turned to his accuser, and eyed him intently for a moment.

"And you, monsieur, I did not recognize you without your beard. It quite disguises you, Paulvitch. I see it all now. It is quite clear, gentlemen."

"What shall we do with them, monsieur?" asked Tarzan. "Turn them over to the captain?"

"No, my friend," said the count hastily. "It is a personal matter, and I beg that you will let it drop. It is sufficient that I have been exonerated from the charge. The less we have to do with such fellows, the better. But, monsieur, how can I thank you for the great kindness you have done me? Permit me to offer you my card, and should the time come when I may serve you, remember that I am yours to command."

Tarzan had released Rokoff, who, with his confederate, Paulvitch, had hastened from the smoking-room. Just as he was leaving, Rokoff turned to Tarzan. "Monsieur will have ample opportunity to regret his interference in the affairs of others."

Tarzan smiled, and then, bowing to the count, handed him his own card.

The count read:

M. Jean C. Tarzan

"Monsieur Tarzan," he said, "may indeed wish that he had never befriended me, for I can assure him that he has won the enmity of two of the most unmitigated scoundrels in all Europe. Avoid them, monsieur, by all means."

"I have had more awe-inspiring enemies, my dear count," replied Tarzan, with a quiet smile, "yet I am still alive and unworried. I think that neither of these two will ever find the means to harm me."

"Let us hope not, monsieur," said De Coude; "but yet it will do no harm to be on the alert, and to know that you have made at least one enemy today who never forgets and never forgives, and in whose malignant brain there are always hatching new atrocities to perpetrate upon those who have thwarted or offended him. To say that Nikolas Rokoff is a devil would be to place a wanton affront upon his satanic majesty."

That night as Tarzan entered his cabin he found a folded note upon the floor that had evidently been pushed beneath the door. He opened it and read:

M. TARZAN:

Doubtless you did not realize the gravity of your offense, or you would not have done the thing you did today. I am willing to believe that you acted in ignorance and without any intention to offend a stranger. For this reason I shall gladly permit you to offer an apology, and on receiving your assurances that you will not again interfere in affairs that do not concern you, I shall drop the matter.

Otherwise—but I am sure that you will see the wisdom of adopting the course I suggest.

Very respectfully,

NIKOLAS ROKOFF.

Tarzan permitted a grim smile to play about his lips for a moment, then he promptly dropped the matter from his mind, and went to bed.

In a nearby cabin the Countess de Coude was speaking to her husband.

"Why so grave, my dear Raoul?" she asked. "You have been as glum as could be all evening. What worries you?"

"Olga, Nikolas is on board. Did you know it?"

"Nikolas!" she exclaimed. "But it is impossible, Raoul. It cannot be. Nikolas is under arrest in Germany."

"So I thought myself until I saw him today—him and that other arch scoundrel, Paulvitch. Olga, I cannot endure his persecution much longer. No, not even for you. Sooner or later I shall turn him over to the authorities. In fact, I am half minded to explain all to the captain before we land. On a French liner it were an easy matter, Olga, permanently to settle this Nemesis of ours."

"Oh, no, Raoul!" cried the countess, sinking to her knees before him as he sat with bowed head upon a divan. "Do not do that. Remember your promise to me. Tell me, Raoul, that you will not do that. Do not even threaten him, Raoul."

De Coude took his wife's hands in his, and gazed upon her pale and troubled countenance for some time before he spoke, as though he would wrest from those beautiful eyes the real reason which prompted her to shield this man.

"Let it be as you wish, Olga," he said at length. "I cannot understand. He has forfeited all claim upon your love, loyalty, or respect. He is a menace to your life and honor, and the life and honor of your husband. I trust you may never regret championing him."

"I do not champion him, Raoul," she interrupted vehemently. "I believe that I hate him as much as you do, but— Oh, Raoul, blood is thicker than water."

"I should today have liked to sample the consistency of his," growled De Coude grimly. "The two deliberately attempted to besmirch my honor, Olga," and then he told her of all that had happened in the smoking-room. "Had it not been for this utter stranger, they had succeeded, for who would have accepted my unsupported word against the damning evidence of those cards hidden on my person? I had almost begun to doubt myself when this Monsieur Tarzan dragged your precious Nikolas before us, and explained the whole cowardly transaction."

"Monsieur Tarzan?" asked the countess, in evident surprise.

"Yes. Do you know him, Olga?"

"I have seen him. A steward pointed him out to me."

"I did not know that he was a celebrity," said the count.

Olga de Coude changed the subject. She discovered suddenly that she might find it difficult to explain just why the steward had pointed out the handsome Monsieur Tarzan to her. Perhaps she flushed the least little bit, for was not the count, her husband, gazing at her with a strangely quizzical expression. "Ah," she thought, "a guilty conscience is a most suspicious thing."

2

Forging Bonds of Hate and —?

IT WAS not until late the following afternoon that Tarzan saw anything more of the fellow passengers into the midst of whose affairs his love of fair play had thrust him. And then he came most unexpectedly upon Rokoff and Paulvitch at a moment when of all others the two might least appreciate his company.

They were standing on deck at a point which was temporarily deserted, and as Tarzan came upon them they were in heated argument with a woman. Tarzan noted that she was richly appareled, and that her slender, well-modeled figure denoted youth; but as she was heavily veiled he could not discern her features.

The men were standing on either side of her, and the backs of all were toward Tarzan, so that he was quite close to them without their being aware of his presence. He noticed that Rokoff seemed to be threatening, the woman pleading; but they spoke in a strange tongue, and he could only guess from appearances that the girl was afraid.

Rokoff's attitude was so distinctly filled with the threat of physical violence that the ape-man paused for an instant just behind the trio, instinctively sensing an atmosphere of danger. Scarcely had he hesitated ere the man seized the woman roughly by the wrist, twisting it as though to wring a promise from her through torture. What would have happened next had Rokoff had his way we may only conjecture, since he did not have his way at all. Instead, steel fingers gripped his shoulder, and he was swung unceremoniously around, to meet the cold gray eyes of the stranger who had thwarted him on the previous day.

"*Sapristi!*" screamed the infuriated Rokoff. "What do you mean? Are you a fool that you thus again insult Nikolas Rokoff?"

"This is my answer to your note, monsieur," said Tarzan, in a low voice. And then he hurled the fellow from him with such force that Rokoff lunged sprawling against the rail.

"Name of a name!" shrieked Rokoff. "Pig, but you shall die for this," and, springing to his feet, he rushed upon Tarzan, tugging the meanwhile to draw a revolver from his hip pocket. The girl shrank back in terror.

"Nikolas!" she cried. "Do not—oh, do not do that. Quick, monsieur, fly, or he will surely kill you!" But instead of flying Tarzan advanced to meet the fellow. "Do not make a fool of yourself, monsieur," he said.

Rokoff, who was in a perfect frenzy of rage at the humiliation the stranger had put upon him, had at last succeeded in drawing the revolver. He had stopped, and now he deliberately raised it to Tarzan's breast and pulled the trigger. The hammer fell with a futile click on an empty chamber—the ape-man's hand shot out like the head of an angry python; there was a quick wrench, and the revolver sailed far out across the ship's rail, and dropped into the Atlantic.

For a moment the two men stood there facing one another. Rokoff had regained his self-possession. He was the first to speak.

"Twice now has monsieur seen fit to interfere in matters which do not concern him. Twice he has taken it upon himself to humiliate Nikolas Rokoff. The first offense was overlooked on the assumption that monsieur acted through ignorance, but this affair shall not be overlooked. If monsieur does not know who Nikolas Rokoff is, this last piece of effrontery will insure that monsieur later has good reason to remember him."

"That you are a coward and a scoundrel, monsieur," replied Tarzan, "is all that I care to know of you," and he turned to ask the girl if the man had hurt her, but she had disappeared. Then, without even a glance toward Rokoff and his companion, he continued his stroll along the deck.

Tarzan could not but wonder what manner of conspiracy was on foot, or what the scheme of the two men might be. There had been something rather familiar about the appearance of the veiled woman to whose rescue he had just come, but as he had not seen her face he could not be sure that he had ever seen her before. The only thing about her that he had particularly noticed was a ring of peculiar workmanship upon a finger of the hand that Rokoff had seized, and he determined to note the fingers of the women passengers he came upon thereafter, that he might discover the identity of her whom Rokoff was persecuting, and learn if the fellow had offered her further annoyance.

Tarzan had sought his deck chair, where he sat speculating on the numerous instances of human cruelty, selfishness, and spite that had fallen to his lot to witness since that day in the jungle four years since that his eyes had first fallen upon a human being other than himself—the sleek, black Kulonga, whose swift spear had that day found the vitals of Kala, the great she-ape, and robbed the youth, Tarzan, of the only mother he had ever known.

He recalled the murder of King by the rat-faced Snipes; the abandonment of Professor Porter and his party by the mutineers of the *Arrow;* the cruelty of the black warriors and women of Mbonga to their captives; the petty jealousies of the civil and military officers of the West Coast colony that had afforded him his first introduction to the civilized world.

"Mon Dieu!" he soliloquized, "but they are all alike. Cheating, murdering, lying, fighting, and all for things that the beasts of the jungle would not deign to possess—money to purchase the effeminate pleasures of weaklings. And yet withal bound down by silly customs that make them slaves to their unhappy lot while firm in the belief that they be the lords of creation enjoying the only real pleasures of existence. In the jungle one would scarcely stand supinely aside while another took his mate. It is a silly world, an idiotic world, and Tarzan of the Apes was a fool to renounce the freedom and the happiness of his jungle to come into it."

Presently, as he sat there, the sudden feeling came over him that eyes were watching from behind, and the old instinct of the wild beast broke through the thin veneer of civilization, so that Tarzan wheeled about so quickly that the eyes of the young woman who had been surreptitiously regarding him had not even time to drop before the gray eyes of the ape-man shot an inquiring look straight into them. Then, as they fell, Tarzan saw a faint wave of crimson creep swiftly over the now half-averted face.

He smiled to himself at the result of his very uncivilized and ungallant action, for he had not lowered his own eyes when they met those of the young woman. She was very young, and equally good to look upon. Further, there was something rather familiar about her that set Tarzan to wondering where he had seen her before. He resumed his former position, and presently he was aware that she had arisen and was leaving the deck. As she passed, Tarzan turned to watch her, in the hope that he might discover a clew to satisfy his mild curiosity as to her identity.

Nor was he disappointed entirely, for as she walked away she raised one hand to the black, waving mass at the nape of her neck—the peculiarly feminine gesture that admits cognizance of appraising eyes behind her—and Tarzan saw upon a finger of this hand the ring of strange workmanship that he had seen upon the finger of the veiled woman a short time before.

So it was this beautiful young woman Rokoff had been persecuting. Tarzan wondered in a lazy sort of way whom she might be, and what relations one so lovely could have with the surly, bearded Russian.

After dinner that evening Tarzan strolled forward, where he remained until after dark, in conversation with the second officer, and when that gentleman's duties called him elsewhere Tarzan lolled lazily by the rail watching the play of the moonlight upon the gently rolling waters. He was half hidden by a davit, so that two men who approached along the deck did not see him, and as they passed Tarzan caught enough of their conversation to cause him to fall in behind them, to follow and learn what deviltry they were up to. He had recognized the voice as that of Rokoff, and had seen that his companion was Paulvitch.

Tarzan had overheard but a few words: "And if she screams you may choke her until—" But those had been enough to arouse the spirit of adventure within him, and so he kept the two men in sight as they walked, briskly now, along the deck. To the smoking-room he followed them, but they merely halted at the doorway long enough, apparently, to assure themselves that one whose whereabouts they wished to establish was within.

Then they proceeded directly to the first-class cabins upon the promenade deck. Here Tarzan found greater difficulty in escaping detection, but he managed to do so successfully. As they halted before one of the polished hardwood doors, Tarzan slipped into the shadow of a passageway not a dozen feet from them.

To their knock a woman's voice asked in French: "Who is it?"

"It is I, Olga—Nikolas," was the answer, in Rokoff's now familiar guttural. "May I come in?"

"Why do you not cease persecuting me, Nikolas?" came the voice of the woman from beyond the thin panel. "I have never harmed you."

"Come, come, Olga," urged the man, in propitiatory tones; "I but ask a half dozen words with you. I shall not harm you, nor shall I enter your cabin; but I cannot shout my message through the door."

Tarzan heard the catch click as it was released from the inside. He stepped out from his hiding-place far enough to see what transpired when the door was opened, for he could not but recall the sinister words he had heard a few moments before upon the deck, "And if she screams you may choke her."

Rokoff was standing directly in front of the door. Paulvitch had flattened himself against the paneled wall of the corridor beyond. The door opened. Rokoff half entered the room, and stood with his back against the door, speaking in a low whisper to the woman, whom Tarzan could not see. Then Tarzan heard the woman's voice, level, but loud enough to distinguish her words.

"No, Nikolas," she was saying, "it is useless. Threaten as you will, I shall never accede to your demands. Leave the room, please; you have no right here. You promised not to enter."

"Very well, Olga, I shall not enter; but before I am done with you, you shall wish a thousand times that you had done at once the favor I have asked. In the end I shall win anyway, so you might as well save trouble and time for me, and disgrace for yourself and your—"

"Never, Nikolas!" interrupted the woman, and then Tarzan saw Rokoff turn and nod to Paulvitch, who sprang quickly toward the doorway of the cabin, rushing in past Rokoff, who held the door open for him. Then the latter stepped quickly out. The door closed. Tarzan heard the click of the lock as Paulvitch turned it from the inside. Rokoff remained standing before the door, with head bent, as though to catch the words of the two within. A nasty smile curled his bearded lip.

Tarzan could hear the woman's voice commanding the fellow to leave her cabin. "I shall send for my husband," she cried. "He will show you no mercy."

Paulvitch's sneering laugh came through the polished panels.

"The purser will fetch your husband, madame," said the man. "In fact, that officer has already been notified that you are entertaining a man other than your husband behind the locked door of your cabin."

"Bah!" cried the woman. "My husband will know!"

"Most assuredly your husband will know, but the purser will not; nor will the newspaper men who shall in some mysterious way hear of it on our landing. But they will think it a fine story, and so will all your friends when they read of it at breakfast on—let me see, this is Tuesday—yes, when they read of it at breakfast next Friday morning. Nor will it detract from the interest they will all feel when they learn that the man whom madame entertained is a Russian servant—her brother's valet, to be quite exact."

"Alexis Paulvitch," came the woman's voice, cold and fearless, "you are a coward, and when I whisper a certain name in your ear you will think better of your demands upon me and your threats against me, and then you will leave my cabin quickly, nor do I think that ever again will you, at least, annoy me," and there came a moment's silence in which Tarzan could imagine the woman leaning toward the scoundrel and whispering the thing she had hinted at into his ear. Only a moment of silence, and then a startled oath from the man—the scuffling of feet—a woman's scream—and silence.

But scarcely had the cry ceased before the ape-man had leaped from his hiding-place. Rokoff started to run, but Tarzan grasped him by the collar and dragged him back. Neither spoke, for both felt instinctively that murder was being done in that room, and Tarzan was confident that Rokoff had had no intention that his confederate should go that far—he felt that the man's aims were deeper than that—deeper and even more sinister than brutal, cold-blooded murder.

Without hesitating to question those within, the ape-man threw his giant shoulder against the frail panel, and in a shower of splintered wood he entered the cabin, dragging Rokoff after him. Before him, on a couch, the woman lay, and on top of her was Paulvitch, his fingers gripping the fair throat, while his victim's hands beat futilely at his face, tearing desperately at the cruel fingers that were forcing the life from her.

The noise of his entrance brought Paulvitch to his feet, where he stood glowering menacingly at Tarzan. The girl rose falteringly to a sitting posture upon the couch. One hand was at her throat, and her breath came in little gasps. Although disheveled and very pale, Tarzan recognized her as the young woman whom he had caught staring at him on deck earlier in the day.

"What is the meaning of this?" said Tarzan, turning to Rokoff, whom he intuitively singled out as the instigator of the outrage. The man remained silent, scowling. "Touch the button, please," continued the ape-man; "we will have one of the ship's officers here—this affair has gone quite far enough."

"No, no," cried the girl, coming suddenly to her feet. "Please do not do that. I am sure that there was no real intention to harm me. I angered this person, and he lost control of himself, that is all. I would not care to have the matter go further, please, monsieur," and there was such a note of pleading in her voice that Tarzan could not press the matter, though his better judgment warned him that there was something afoot here of which the proper authorities should be made cognizant.

"You wish me to do nothing, then, in the matter?" he asked.

"Nothing, please," she replied.

"You are content that these two scoundrels should continue persecuting you?"

She did not seem to know what answer to make, and looked very troubled and unhappy. Tarzan saw a malicious grin of triumph curl Rokoff's lip. The girl evidently was in fear of these two—she dared not express her real desires before them.

"Then," said Tarzan, "I shall act on my own responsibility. To you," he continued, turning to Rokoff, "and this includes your accomplice, I may say that from now on to the end of the voyage I shall take it upon myself to keep an eye on you, and should there chance to come to my notice any act of either one of you that might even remotely annoy this young woman you shall be called to account for it directly to me, nor shall the calling or the accounting be pleasant experiences for either of you.

"Now get out of here," and he grabbed Rokoff and Paulvitch each by the scruff of the neck and thrust them forcibly through the doorway, giving each an added impetus down the corridor with the toe of his boot. Then he turned back to the stateroom and the girl. She was looking at him in wide-eyed astonishment.

"And you, madame, will confer a great favor upon me if you will but let me know if either of those rascals troubles you further."

"Ah, monsieur," she answered, "I hope that you will not suffer for the kind deed you attempted. You have made a very wicked and resourceful enemy, who will stop at nothing to satisfy his hatred. You must be very careful indeed, Monsieur—"

"Pardon me, madame, my name is Tarzan."

"Monsieur Tarzan. And because I would not consent to notify the officers, do not think that I am not sincerely grateful to you for the brave and chivalrous protection you rendered me. Good night, Monsieur Tarzan. I shall never forget the debt I owe you," and, with a most winsome smile that displayed a row of perfect teeth, the girl curtsied to Tarzan, who bade her good night and made his way on deck.

It puzzled the man considerably that there should be two on board—this girl and Count de Coude—who suffered indignities at the hands of Rokoff and his companion, and yet would not permit the offenders to be brought to justice. Before he turned in that night his thoughts reverted many times to the beautiful young woman into the evidently tangled web of whose life fate had so strangely introduced him. It occurred to him that he had not learned her name. That she was married had been evidenced by the narrow gold band that encircled the third finger of her left hand. Involuntarily he wondered who the lucky man might be.

Tarzan saw nothing further of any of the actors in the little drama that he had caught a fleeting glimpse of until late in the afternoon of the last day of the voyage. Then he came suddenly face to face with the young woman as the two approached their deck chairs from opposite directions. She greeted him with a pleasant smile, speaking almost immediately of the affair he had witnessed in her cabin two nights before. It was as though she had been perturbed by a conviction that he might have construed her acquaintance with such men as Rokoff and Paulvitch as a personal reflection upon herself.

"I trust that monsieur has not judged me," she said, "by the unfortunate occurrence of Tuesday evening. I have suffered much on account of it—this is the first time that I have ventured from my cabin since; I have been ashamed," she concluded simply.

"One does not judge the gazelle by the lions that attack it," replied Tarzan. "I had seen those two work before—in the smoking-room the day prior to their attack on you, if I recollect it correctly, and so, knowing their methods, I am convinced that their enmity is a sufficient guarantee of the integrity of its object. Men such as they must cleave only to the vile, hating all that is noblest and best."

"It is very kind of you to put it that way," she replied, smiling. "I have already heard of the matter of the card game. My husband told me the entire story. He spoke especially of the strength and bravery of Monsieur Tarzan, to whom he feels that he owes an immense debt of gratitude."

"Your husband?" repeated Tarzan questioningly.

"Yes. I am the Countess de Coude."

"I am already amply repaid, madame, in knowing that I have rendered a service to the wife of the Count de Coude."

"Alas, monsieur, I already am so greatly indebted to you that I may never hope to settle my own account, so pray do not add further to my obligations," and she smiled so sweetly upon him that Tarzan felt that a man might easily attempt much greater things than he had accomplished, solely for the pleasure of receiving the benediction of that smile.

He did not see her again that day, and in the rush of landing on the following morning he missed her entirely, but there had been something in the expression of her eyes as they parted on deck the previous day that haunted him. It had been almost wistful as they had spoken of the strangeness of the swift friendships of an ocean crossing, and of the equal ease with which they are broken forever.

Tarzan wondered if he should ever see her again.

3

What Happened in the Rue Maule

On his arrival in Paris, Tarzan had gone directly to the apartments of his old friend, D'Arnot, where the naval lieutenant had scored him roundly for his decision to renounce the title and estates that were rightly his from his father, John Clayton, the late Lord Greystoke.

"You must be mad, my friend," said D'Arnot, "thus lightly to give up not alone wealth and position, but an opportunity to prove beyond doubt to all the world that in your veins flows the noble blood of two of England's most honored houses—instead of the blood of a savage she-ape. It is incredible that they could have believed you—Miss Porter least of all.

"Why, I never did believe it, even back in the wilds of your African jungle, when you tore the raw meat of your kills with mighty jaws, like some wild beast, and wiped your greasy hands upon your thighs. Even then, before there was the slightest proof to the contrary, I knew that you were mistaken in the belief that Kala was your mother.

"And now, with your father's diary of the terrible life led by him and your mother on that wild African shore; with the account of your birth, and, final and most convincing proof of all, your own baby finger prints upon the pages of it, it seems incredible to me that you are willing to remain a nameless, penniless vagabond."

"I do not need any better name than Tarzan," replied the ape-man; "and as for remaining a penniless vagabond, I have no intention of so doing. In fact, the next, and let us hope the last, burden that I shall be forced to put upon your unselfish friendship will be the finding of employment for me."

"Pooh, pooh!" scoffed D'Arnot. "You know that I did not mean that. Have I not told you a dozen times that I have enough for twenty men, and that half of what I have is yours? And if I gave it all to you, would it represent even the tenth part of the value I place upon your friendship, my Tarzan? Would it repay the services you did me in Africa? I do not forget, my friend, that but for you and your wondrous bravery I had died at the stake in the village of Mbonga's cannibals. Nor do I forget that to your self-sacrificing devotion I owe the fact that I recovered from the terrible wounds I received at their hands—I discovered later something of what it meant to you to remain with me in the amphitheater of apes while your heart was urging you on to the coast.

"When we finally came there, and found that Miss Porter and her party had left, I commenced to realize something of what you had done for an utter stranger. Nor am I trying to repay you with money, Tarzan. It is that just at present you need money; were it sacrifice that I might offer you it were the same—my friendship must always be yours, because our tastes are similar, and I admire you. That I cannot command, but the money I can and shall."

"Well," laughed Tarzan, "we shall not quarrel over the money. I must live, and so I must have it; but I shall be more contented with something to do. You cannot show me your friendship in a more convincing manner than to find employment for me—I shall die of inactivity in a short while. As for my birthright—it is in good hands. Clayton is not guilty of robbing me of it. He truly believes that he is the real Lord Greystoke, and the chances are that he will make a better English lord than a man who was born and raised in an African jungle. You know that I am but half civilized even now. Let me see red in anger but for a moment, and all the instincts of the savage beast that I really am, submerge what little I possess of the milder ways of culture and refinement.

"And then again, had I declared myself I should have robbed the woman I love of the wealth and position that her marriage to Clayton will now insure to her. I could not have done that—could I, Paul?

"Nor is the matter of birth of great importance to me," he went on, without waiting for a reply. "Raised as I have been, I see no worth in man or beast that is not theirs by virtue of their own mental or physical prowess. And so I am as happy to think of Kala as my mother as I would be to try to picture the poor, unhappy little English girl who passed away a year after she bore me. Kala was always kind of me in her fierce and savage way. I must have nursed at her hairy breast from the time that my own mother died. She fought for me against the wild denizens of the forest, and against the savage members of our tribe, with the ferocity of real mother love.

"And I, on my part, loved her, Paul. I did not realize how much until after the cruel spear and the poisoned arrow of Mbonga's black warrior had stolen her away from me. I was still a child when that occurred, and I threw myself upon her dead body and wept out my anguish as a child might for his own mother. To you, my friend, she would have appeared a hideous and ugly creature, but to me she was beautiful—so gloriously does love transfigure its object. And so I am perfectly content to remain forever the son of Kala, the she-ape."

"I do not admire you the less for your loyalty," said D'Arnot, "but the time will come when you will be glad to claim your own. Remember what I say, and let us hope that it will be as easy then as it is now. You must bear in mind that Professor Porter and Mr. Philander are the only people in the world who can swear that the little skeleton found in the cabin with those of your father and mother was that of an infant anthropoid ape, and not the offspring of Lord and Lady Greystoke. That evidence is most important. They are both old men. They may not live many years longer. And then, did it not occur to you that once Miss Porter knew the truth she would break her engagement with Clayton? You might easily have your title, your estates, and the woman you love, Tarzan. Had you not thought of that?"

Tarzan shook his head. "You do not know her," he said. "Nothing could bind her closer to her bargain than some misfortune to Clayton. She is from an old southern family in America, and southerners pride themselves upon their loyalty."

Tarzan spent the two following weeks renewing his former brief acquaintance with Paris. In the daytime he haunted the libraries and picture galleries. He had become an omnivorous reader, and the world of possibilities that were opened to him in this seat of culture and learning fairly appalled him when he contemplated the very infinitesimal crumb of the sum total of human knowledge that a single individual might hope to acquire even after a lifetime of study and research; but he learned what he could by day, and threw himself into a search for relaxation and amusement at night. Nor did he find Paris a whit less fertile field for his nocturnal avocation.

If he smoked too many cigarettes and drank too much absinth it was because he took civilization as he found it, and did the things that he found his civilized brothers doing. The life was a new and alluring one, and in addition he had a sorrow in his breast and a great longing which he knew could never be fulfilled, and so he sought in study and in dissipation—the two extremes—to forget the past and inhibit contemplation of the future.

He was sitting in a music hall one evening, sipping his absinth and admiring the art of a certain famous Russian dancer, when he caught a passing glimpse of a pair of evil black eyes upon him. The man turned and was lost in the crowd at the exit before Tarzan could catch a good look at him, but he was confident that he had seen those eyes before and that they had been fastened on him this evening through no passing accident. He had had the uncanny feeling for some time that he was being watched, and it was in response to this animal instinct that was strong within him that he had turned suddenly and surprised the eyes in the very act of watching him.

Before he left the music hall the matter had been forgotten, nor did he notice the swarthy individual who stepped deeper into the shadows of an opposite doorway as Tarzan emerged from the brilliantly lighted amusement hall.

Had Tarzan but known it, he had been followed many times from this and other places of amusement, but seldom if ever had he been alone. Tonight D'Arnot had had another engagement, and Tarzan had come by himself.

As he turned in the direction he was accustomed to taking from this part of Paris to his apartments, the watcher across the street ran from his hiding-place and hurried on ahead at a rapid pace.

Tarzan had been wont to traverse the Rue Maule on his way home at night. Because it was very quiet and very dark it reminded him more of his beloved African jungle than did the noisy and garish streets surrounding it. If you are familiar with your Paris you will recall the narrow, forbidding precincts of the Rue Maule. If you are not, you need but ask the police about it to learn that in all Paris there is no street to which you should give a wider berth after dark.

On this night Tarzan had proceeded some two squares through the dense shadows of the squalid old tenements which line this dismal way when he was attracted by screams and cries for help from the third floor of an opposite building. The voice was a woman's. Before the echoes of her first cries had died Tarzan was bounding up the stairs and through the dark corridors to her rescue.

At the end of the corridor on the third landing a door stood slightly ajar, and from within Tarzan heard again the same appeal that had lured him from the street. Another instant found him in the center of a dimly-lighted room. An oil lamp burned upon a high, old-fashioned mantel, casting its dim rays over a dozen repulsive figures. All but one were men. The other was a woman of about thirty. Her face, marked by low passions and dissipation, might once have been lovely. She stood with one hand at her throat, crouching against the farther wall.

"Help, monsieur," she cried in a low voice as Tarzan entered the room; "they were killing me."

As Tarzan turned toward the men about him he saw the crafty, evil faces of habitual criminals. He wondered that they had made no effort to escape. A movement behind him caused him to turn. Two things his eyes saw, and one of them caused him considerable wonderment. A man was sneaking stealthily from the room, and in the brief glance that Tarzan had of him he saw that it was Rokoff.

But the other thing that he saw was of more immediate interest. It was a great brute of a fellow tiptoeing upon him from behind with a huge bludgeon in his hand, and then, as the man and his confederates saw that he was discovered, there was a concerted rush upon Tarzan from all sides. Some of the men drew knives. Others picked up chairs, while the fellow with the bludgeon raised it high above his head in a mighty swing that would have crushed Tarzan's head had it ever descended upon it.

But the brain, and the agility, and the muscles that had coped with the mighty strength and cruel craftiness of Terkoz and Numa in the fastness of their savage jungle were not to be so easily subdued as these apaches of Paris had believed.

Selecting his most formidable antagonist, the fellow with the bludgeon, Tarzan charged full upon him, dodging the falling weapon, and catching the man a terrific blow on the point of the chin that felled him in his tracks.

Then he turned upon the others. This was sport. He was reveling in the joy of battle and the lust of blood. As though it had been but a brittle shell, to break at the least rough usage, the thin veneer of his civilization fell from him, and the ten burly villains found themselves penned in a small room with a wild and savage beast, against whose steel muscles their puny strength was less than futile.

At the end of the corridor without stood Rokoff, waiting the outcome of the affair. He wished to be sure that Tarzan was dead before he left, but it was not a part of his plan to be one of those within the room when the murder occurred.

The woman still stood where she had when Tarzan entered, but her face had undergone a number of changes with the few minutes which had elapsed. From the semblance of distress which it had worn when Tarzan first saw it, it had changed to one of craftiness as he had wheeled to meet the attack from behind; but the change Tarzan had not seen.

Later an expression of surprise and then one of horror superseded the others. And who may wonder. For the immaculate gentleman her cries had lured to what was to have been his death had been suddenly metamorphosed into a demon of revenge. Instead of soft muscles and a weak resistance, she was looking upon a veritable Hercules gone mad.

"Mon Dieu!" she cried; "he is a beast!" For the strong, white teeth of the ape-man had found the throat of one of his assailants, and Tarzan fought as he had learned to fight with the great bull apes of the tribe of Kerchak.

He was in a dozen places at once, leaping hither and thither about the room in sinuous bounds that reminded the woman of a panther she had seen at the zoo. Now a wristbone snapped in his iron grip, now a shoulder was wrenched from its socket as he forced a victim's arm backward and upward.

With shrieks of pain the men escaped into the hallway as quickly as they could; but even before the first one staggered, bleeding and broken, from the room, Rokoff had seen enough to convince him that Tarzan would not be the one to lie dead in that house this night, and so the Russian had hastened to a nearby den and telephoned the police that a man was committing murder on the third floor of Rue Maule, 27.

When the officers arrived they found three men groaning

on the floor, a frightened woman lying upon a filthy bed, her face buried in her arms, and what appeared to be a well-dressed young gentleman standing in the center of the room awaiting the reenforcements which he had thought the footsteps of the officers hurrying up the stairway had announced —but they were mistaken in the last; it was a wild beast that looked upon them through those narrowed lids and steel-gray eyes. With the smell of blood the last vestige of civilization had deserted Tarzan, and now he stood at bay, like a lion surrounded by hunters, awaiting the next overt act, and crouching to charge its author.

"What has happened here?" asked one of the policemen.

Tarzan explained briefly, but when he turned to the woman for confirmation of his statement he was appalled by her reply.

"He lies!" she screamed shrilly, addressing the policeman. "He came to my room while I was alone, and for no good purpose. When I repulsed him he would have killed me had not my screams attracted these gentlemen, who were passing the house at the time. He is a devil, monsieurs; alone he has all but killed ten men with his bare hands and his teeth."

So shocked was Tarzan by her ingratitude that for a moment he was struck dumb. The police were inclined to be a little skeptical, for they had had other dealings with this same lady and her lovely coterie of gentlemen friends. However, they were policemen, not judges, so they decided to place all the inmates of the room under arrest, and let another, whose business it was, separate the innocent from the guilty.

But they found that it was one thing to tell this well-dressed young man that he was under arrest, but quite another to enforce it.

"I am guilty of no offense," he said quietly. "I have but sought to defend myself. I do not know why the woman has told you what she has. She can have no enmity against me, for never until I came to this room in response to her cries for help had I seen her."

"Come, come," said one of the officers; "there are judges to listen to all that," and he advanced to lay his hand upon Tarzan's shoulder. An instant later he lay crumpled in a corner of the room, and then, as his comrades rushed in upon the ape-man, they experienced a taste of what the apaches had but recently gone through. So quickly and so roughly did he handle them that they had not even an opportunity to draw their revolvers.

During the brief fight Tarzan had noted the open window and, beyond, the stem of a tree, or a telegraph pole—he could not tell which. As the last officer went down, one of his fellows succeeded in drawing his revolver and, from where he lay on the floor, fired at Tarzan. The shot missed, and before the man could fire again Tarzan had swept the lamp from the mantel and plunged the room into darkness.

The next they saw was a lithe form spring to the sill of the open window and leap, panther-like, onto the pole across the walk. When the police gathered themselves together and reached the street their prisoner was nowhere to be seen.

They did not handle the woman and the men who had not escaped any too gently when they took them to the station; they were a very sore and humiliated detail of police. It galled them to think that it would be necessary to report that a single unarmed man had wiped the floor with the whole lot of them, and then escaped them as easily as though they had not existed.

The officer who had remained in the street swore that no one had leaped from the window or left the building from the time they entered until they had come out. His comrades thought that he lied, but they could not prove it.

When Tarzan found himself clinging to the pole outside the window, he followed his jungle instinct and looked below for enemies before he ventured down. It was well he did, for just beneath stood a policeman. Above, Tarzan saw no one, so he went up instead of down.

The top of the pole was opposite the roof of the building, so it was but the work of an instant for the muscles that had for years sent him hurtling through the treetops of his primeval forest to carry him across the little space between the pole and the roof. From one building he went to another, and so on, with much climbing, until at a cross street he discovered another pole, down which he ran to the ground.

For a square or two he ran swiftly; then he turned into a little all-night café and in the lavatory removed the evidences of his over-roof promenade from hands and clothes. When he emerged a few moments later it was to saunter slowly on toward his apartments.

Not far from them he came to a well-lighted boulevard which it was necessary to cross. As he stood directly beneath a brilliant arc light, waiting for a limousine that was approaching to pass him, he heard his name called in a sweet feminine voice. Looking up, he met the smiling eyes of Olga de Coude as she leaned forward upon the back seat of the machine. He bowed very low in response to her friendly greeting. When he straightened up the machine had borne her away.

"Rokoff and the Countess de Coude both in the same evening," he soliloquized; "Paris is not so large, after all."

4

The Countess Explains

"YOUR Paris is more dangerous than my savage jungles, Paul," concluded Tarzan, after narrating his adventures to his friend the morning following his encounter with the apaches and police in the Rue Maule. "Why did they lure me there? Were they hungry?"

D'Arnot feigned a horrified shudder, but he laughed at the quaint suggestion.

"It is difficult to rise above the jungle standards and reason by the light of civilized ways, is it not, my friend?" he queried banteringly.

"Civilized ways, forsooth," scoffed Tarzan. "Jungle standards do not countenance wanton atrocities. There we kill for food and for self-preservation, or in the winning of mates and the protection of the young. Always, you see, in accordance with the dictates of some great natural law. But here! Faugh, your civilized man is more brutal than the brutes. He kills wantonly, and, worse than that, he utilizes a noble sentiment, the brotherhood of man, as a lure to entice his unwary victim to his doom. It was in answer to an appeal from a fellow being that I hastened to that room where the assassins lay in wait for me.

"I did not realize, I could not realize for a long time afterward, that any woman could sink to such moral depravity as that one must have to call a would-be rescuer to death. But it must have been so—the sight of Rokoff there and the woman's later repudiation of me to the police make it impossible to place any other construction upon her acts. Rokoff must have known that I frequently passed through the Rue Maule. He lay in wait for me—his entire scheme worked out to the last detail, even to the woman's story in case a hitch should occur in the program such as really did happen. It is all perfectly plain to me."

"Well," said D'Arnot, "among other things, it has taught you what I have been unable to impress upon you—that the Rue Maule is a good place to avoid after dark."

"On the contrary," replied Tarzan, with a smile, "it has convinced me that it is the one worth-while street in all Paris. Never again shall I miss an opportunity to traverse it, for it has given me the first real entertainment I have had since I left Africa."

"It may give you more than you will relish even without another visit," said D'Arnot. "You are not through with the police yet, remember. I know the Paris police well enough to assure you that they will not soon forget what you did to them. Sooner or later they will get you, my dear Tarzan, and then they will lock the wild man of the woods up behind iron bars. How will you like that?"

"They will never lock Tarzan of the Apes behind iron bars," replied he, grimly.

There was something in the man's voice as he said it that caused D'Arnot to look up sharply at his friend. What he saw in the set jaw and the cold, gray eyes made the young Frenchman very apprehensive for this great child, who could recognize no law mightier than his own mighty physical prowess. He saw that something must be done to set Tarzan right with the police before another encounter was possible.

"You have much to learn, Tarzan," he said gravely. "The law of man must be respected, whether you relish it or no. Nothing but trouble can come to you and your friends should you persist in defying the police. I can explain it to them once for you, and that I shall do this very day, but hereafter you must obey the law. If its representatives say 'Come,' you must come; if they say 'Go,' you must go. Now we shall go to my great friend in the department and fix up this matter of the Rue Maule. Come!"

Together they entered the office of the police official a half hour later. He was very cordial. He remembered Tarzan from the visit the two had made him several months prior in the matter of finger prints.

When D'Arnot had concluded the narration of the events which had transpired the previous evening, a grim smile was playing about the lips of the policeman. He touched a button near his hand, and as he waited for the clerk to respond to its summons he searched through the papers on his desk for one which he finally located.

"Here, Joubon," he said as the clerk entered. "Summon these officers—have them come to me at once," and he handed the man the paper he had sought. Then he turned to Tarzan.

"You have committed a very grave offense, monsieur," he said, not unkindly, "and but for the explanation made by our good friend here I should be inclined to judge you harshly. I am, instead, about to do a rather unheard-of-thing. I have summoned the officers whom you maltreated last night. They shall hear Lieutenant D'Arnot's story, and then I shall leave it to their discretion to say whether you shall be prosecuted or not.

"You have much to learn about the ways of civilization. Things that seem strange or unnecessary to you, you must learn to accept until you are able to judge the motives behind them. The officers whom you attacked were but doing their duty. They had no discretion in the matter. Every day they risk their lives in the protection of the lives or property of others. They would do the same for you. They are very brave men, and they are deeply mortified that a single unarmed man bested and beat them.

"Make it easy for them to overlook what you did. Unless I am gravely in error you are yourself a very brave man, and brave men are proverbially magnanimous."

Further conversation was interrupted by the appearance of the four policemen. As their eyes fell on Tarzan, surprise was writ large on each countenance.

"My children," said the official, "here is the gentleman whom you met in the Rue Maule last evening. He has come voluntarily to give himself up. I wish you to listen attentively to Lieutenant D'Arnot, who will tell you a part of the story of monsieur's life. It may explain his attitude toward you of last night. Proceed, my dear lieutenant."

D'Arnot spoke to the policemen for half an hour. He told them something of Tarzan's wild jungle life. He explained the savage training that had taught him to battle like a wild beast in self-preservation. It became plain to them that the man had been guided by instinct rather than reason in his attack upon them. He had not understood their intentions. To him they had been little different from any of the various forms of life he had been accustomed to in his native jungle, where practically all were his enemies.

"Your pride has been wounded," said D'Arnot, in conclusion. "It is the fact that this man overcame you that hurts the most. But you need feel no shame. You would not make apologies for defeat had you been penned in that small room with an African lion, or with the great Gorilla of the jungles.

"And yet you were battling with muscles that have time and time again been pitted, and always victoriously, against these terrors of the dark continent. It is no disgrace to fall beneath the superhuman strength of Tarzan of the Apes."

And then, as the men stood looking first at Tarzan and then at their superior the ape-man did the one thing which was needed to erase the last remnant of animosity which they might have felt for him. With outstretched hand he advanced toward them.

"I am sorry for the mistake I made," he said simply. "Let us be friends." And that was the end of the whole matter, except that Tarzan became a subject of much conversation in the barracks of the police, and increased the number of his friends by four brave men at least.

On their return to D'Arnot's apartments the lieutenant found a letter awaiting him from an English friend, William Cecil Clayton, Lord Greystoke. The two had maintained a correspondence since the birth of their friendship on that ill-fated expedition in search of Jane Porter after her theft by Terkoz, the bull ape.

"They are to be married in London in about two months," said D'Arnot, as he completed his perusal of the letter. Tarzan did not need to be told who was meant by "they." He made no reply, but he was very quiet and thoughtful during the balance of the day.

That evening they attended the opera. Tarzan's mind was still occupied by his gloomy thoughts. He paid little or no attention to what was transpiring upon the stage. Instead he saw only the lovely vision of a beautiful American girl, and heard naught but a sad, sweet voice acknowledging that his love was returned. And she was to marry another!

He shook himself to be rid of his unwelcome thoughts, and at the same instant he felt eyes upon him. With the instinct that was his by virtue of training he looked up squarely into the eyes that were looking at him, to find that they were shining from the smiling face of Olga, Countess de Coude. As Tarzan returned her bow he was positive that there was an invitation in her look, almost a plea.

The next intermission found him beside her in her box.

"I have so much wished to see you," she was saying. "It

has troubled me not a little to think that after the services you rendered to both my husband and myself no adequate explanation was ever made you of what must have seemed ingratitude on our part in not taking the necessary steps to prevent a repetition of the attacks upon us by those two men."

"You wrong me," replied Tarzan. "My thoughts of you have been only the most pleasant. You must not feel that any explanation is due me. Have they annoyed you further?"

"They never cease," she replied sadly. "I feel that I must tell some one, and I do not know another who so deserves an explanation as you. You must permit me to do so. It may be of service to you, for I know Nikolas Rokoff quite well enough to be positive that you have not seen the last of him. He will find some means to be revenged upon you. What I wish to tell you may be of aid to you in combating any scheme of revenge he may harbor. I cannot tell you here, but tomorrow I shall be at home to Monsieur Tarzan at five."

"It will be an eternity until tomorrow at five," he said, as he bade her good night.

From a corner of the theater Rokoff and Paulvitch saw Monsieur Tarzan in the box of the Countess de Coude, and both men smiled.

At four-thirty the following afternoon a swarthy, bearded man rang the bell at the servants' entrance of the palace of the Count de Coude. The footman who opened the door raised his eyebrows in recognition as he saw who stood without. A low conversation passed between the two.

At first the footman demurred from some proposition that the bearded one made, but an instant later something passed from the hand of the caller to the hand of the servant. Then the latter turned and led the visitor by a roundabout way to a little curtained alcove off the apartment in which the countess was wont to serve tea of an afternoon.

A half hour later Tarzan was ushered into the room, and presently his hostess entered, smiling, and with outstretched hands.

"I am so glad that you came," she said.

"Nothing could have prevented," he replied.

For a few moments they spoke of the opera, of the topics that were then occupying the attention of Paris, of the pleasure of renewing their brief acquaintance which had had its inception under such odd circumstances, and this brought them to the subject that was uppermost in the minds of both.

"You must have wondered," said the countess finally,

"what the object of Rokoff's persecution could be. It is very simple. The count is intrusted with many of the vital secrets of the ministry of war. He often has in his possession papers that foreign powers would give a fortune to possess—secrets of state that their agents would commit murder and worse than murder to learn.

"There is such a matter now in his possession that would make the fame and fortune of any Russian who could divulge it to his government. Rokoff and Paulvitch are Russian spies. They will stop at nothing to procure this information. The affair on the liner—I mean the matter of the card game—was for the purpose of blackmailing the knowledge they seek from my husband.

"Had he been convicted of cheating at cards, his career would have been blighted. He would have had to leave the war department. He would have been socially ostracized. They intended to hold this club over him—the price of an avowal on their part that the count was but the victim of the plot of enemies who wished to besmirch his name was to have been the papers they seek.

"You thwarted them in this. Then they concocted the scheme whereby my reputation was to be the price, instead of the count's. When Paulvitch entered my cabin he explained it to me. If I would obtain the information for them he promised to go no farther, otherwise Rokoff, who stood without, was to notify the purser that I was entertaining a man other than my husband behind the locked doors of my cabin. He was to tell every one he met on the boat, and when we landed he was to have given the whole story to the newspaper men.

"Was it not too horrible? But I happened to know something of Monsieur Paulvitch that would send him to the gallows in Russia if it were known by the police of St. Petersburg. I dared him to carry out his plan, and then I leaned toward him and whispered a name in his ear. Like that"—and she snapped her fingers—"he flew at my throat as a madman. He would have killed me had you not interfered."

"The brutes!" muttered Tarzan.

"They are worse than that, my friend," she said. "They are devils. I fear for you because you have gained their hatred. I wish you to be on your guard constantly. Tell me that you will, for my sake, for I should never forgive myself should you suffer through the kindness you did me."

"I do not fear them," he replied. "I have survived grimmer enemies than Rokoff and Paulvitch." He saw that she knew nothing of the occurrence in the Rue Maule, nor did he mention it, fearing that it might distress her.

"For your own safety," he continued, "why do you not turn the scoundrels over to the authorities? They should make quick work of them."

She hesitated for a moment before replying.

"There are two reasons," she said finally. "One of them it is that keeps the count from doing that very thing. The other, my real reason for fearing to expose them, I have never told—only Rokoff and I know it. I wonder," and then she paused, looking intently at him for a long time.

"And what do you wonder?" he asked, smiling.

"I was wondering why it is that I want to tell you the thing that I have not dared tell even to my husband. I believe that you would understand, and that you could tell me the right course to follow. I believe that you would not judge me too harshly."

"I fear that I should prove a very poor judge, madame," Tarzan replied, "for if you had been guilty of murder I should say that the victim should be grateful to have met so sweet a fate."

"Oh, dear, no," she expostulated; "it is not so terrible as that. But first let me tell you the reason the count has for not prosecuting these men; then, if I can hold my courage, I shall tell you the real reason that I dare not. The first is that Nikolas Rokoff is my brother. We are Russians. Nikolas has been a bad man since I can remember. He was cashiered from the Russian army, in which he held a captaincy. There was a scandal for a time, but after a while it was partially forgotten, and my father obtained a position for him in the secret service.

"There have been many terrible crimes laid at Nikolas' door, but he has always managed to escape punishment. Of late he has accomplished it by trumped-up evidence convicting his victims of treason against the czar, and the Russian police, who are always only too ready to fasten guilt of this nature upon any and all, have accepted his version and exonerated him."

"Have not his attempted crimes against you and your husband forfeited whatever rights the bonds of kinship might have accorded him?" asked Tarzan. "The fact that you are his sister has not deterred him from seeking to besmirch your honor. You owe him no loyalty, madame."

"Ah, but there is that other reason. If I owe him no loyalty though he be my brother, I cannot so easily disavow the fear I hold him in because of a certain episode in my life of which he is cognizant.

"I might as well tell you all," she resumed after a pause, "for I see that it is in my heart to tell you sooner or later. I was educated in a convent. While there I met a man whom I supposed to be a gentleman. I knew little or nothing about men and less about love. I got it into my foolish head that I loved this man, and at his urgent request I ran away with him. We were to have been married.

"I was with him just three hours. All in the daytime and in public places—railroad stations and upon a train. When we reached our destination where we were to have been married, two officers stepped up to my escort as we descended from the train, and placed him under arrest. They took me also, but when I had told my story they did not detain me, other than to send me back to the convent under the care of a matron. It seemed that the man who had wooed me was no gentleman at all, but a deserter from the army as well as a fugitive from civil justice. He had a police record in nearly every country in Europe.

"The matter was hushed up by the authorities of the convent. Not even my parents knew of it. But Nikolas met the man afterward, and learned the whole story. Now he threatens to tell the count if I do not do just as he wishes me to."

Tarzan laughed. "You are still but a little girl. The story that you have told me cannot reflect in any way upon your reputation, and were you not a little girl at heart you would know it. Go to your husband tonight, and tell him the whole story, just as you have told it to me. Unless I am much mistaken he will laugh at you for your fears, and take immediate steps to put that precious brother of yours in prison where he belongs."

"I only wish that I dared," she said; "but I am afraid. I learned early to fear men. First my father, then Nikolas, then the fathers in the convent. Nearly all my friends fear their husbands—why should I not fear mine?"

"It does not seem right that women should fear men," said Tarzan, an expression of puzzlement on his face. "I am better acquainted with the jungle folk, and there it is more often the other way around, except among the black men, and they to my mind are in most ways lower in the scale than the beasts. No, I cannot understand why civilized women should fear men, the beings that are created to protect them. I should hate to think that any woman feared me."

"I do not think that any woman would fear you, my

friend," said Olga de Coude softly. "I have known you but a short while, yet though it may seem foolish to say it, you are the only man I have ever known whom I think that I should never fear—it is strange, too, for you are very strong. I wondered at the ease with which you handled Nikolas and Paulvitch that night in my cabin. It was marvelous."

As Tarzan was leaving her a short time later he wondered a little at the clinging pressure of her hand at parting, and the firm insistence with which she exacted a promise from him that he would call again on the morrow.

The memory of her half-veiled eyes and perfect lips as she had stood smiling up into his face as he bade her good-by remained with him for the balance of the day. Olga de Coude was a very beautiful woman, and Tarzan of the Apes a very lonely young man, with a heart in him that was in need of the doctoring that only a woman may provide.

As the countess turned back into the room after Tarzan's departure, she found herself face to face with Nikolas Rokoff.

"How long have you been here?" she cried, shrinking away from him.

"Since before your lover came," he answered, with a nasty leer.

"Stop!" she commanded. "How dare you say such a thing to me—your sister!"

"Well, my dear Olga, if he is not your lover, accept my apologies; but it is no fault of yours that he is not. Had he one-tenth the knowledge of women that I have you would be in his arms this minute. He is a stupid fool, Olga. Why, your every word and act was an open invitation to him, and he had not the sense to see it."

The woman put her hands to her ears.

"I will not listen. You are wicked to say such things as that. No matter what you may threaten me with, you know that I am a good woman. After tonight you will not dare to annoy me, for I shall tell Raoul all. He will understand, and then, Monsieur Nikolas, beware!"

"You shall tell him nothing," said Rokoff. "I have this affair now, and with the help of one of your servants whom I may trust it will lack nothing in the telling when the time comes that the details of the sworn evidence shall be poured into your husband's ears. The other affair served its purpose well —we now have something tangible to work on, Olga. A real *affair*—and you a trusted wife. Shame, Olga," and the brute laughed.

So the countess told her count nothing, and matters were worse than they had been. From a vague fear her mind was transferred to a very tangible one. It may be, too, that conscience helped to enlarge it out of all proportions.

5

The Plot That Failed

For a month Tarzan was a regular and very welcome devotee at the shrine of the beautiful Countess de Coude. Often he met other members of the select little coterie that dropped in for tea of an afternoon. More often Olga found devices that would give her an hour of Tarzan alone.

For a time she had been frightened by what Nikolas had insinuated. She had not thought of this big, young man as anything more than friend, but with the suggestion implanted by the evil words of her brother she had grown to speculate much upon the strange force which seemed to attract her toward the gray-eyed stranger. She did not wish to love him, nor did she wish his love.

She was much younger than her husband, and without having realized it she had been craving the haven of a friendship with one nearer her own age. Twenty is shy in exchanging confidences with forty. Tarzan was but two years her senior. He could understand her, she felt. Then he was clean and honorable and chivalrous. She was not afraid of him. That she could trust him she had felt instinctively from the first.

From a distance Rokoff had watched this growing intimacy with malicious glee. Ever since he had learned that Tarzan knew that he was a Russian spy there had been added to his hatred for the ape-man a great fear that he would expose him. He was but waiting now until the moment was propitious for a master stroke. He wanted to rid himself forever of Tarzan, and at the same time reap an ample revenge for the humiliations and defeats that he had suffered at his hands.

Tarzan was nearer to contentment than he had been since the peace and tranquility of his jungle had been broken in upon by the advent of the marooned Porter party.

He enjoyed the pleasant social intercourse with Olga's friends, while the friendship which had sprung up between the fair countess and himself was a source of never-ending delight. It broke in upon and dispersed his gloomy thoughts, and served as a balm to his lacerated heart.

Sometimes D'Arnot accompanied him on his visits to the De Coude home, for he had long known both Olga and the count. Occasionally De Coude dropped in, but the multitudinous affairs of his official position and the never-ending demands of politics kept him from home usually until late at night.

Rokoff spied upon Tarzan almost constantly, waiting for the time that he should call at the De Coude palace at night, but in this he was doomed to disappointment. On several occasions Tarzan accompanied the countess to her home after the opera, but he invariably left her at the entrance —much to the disgust of the lady's devoted brother.

Finding that it seemed impossible to trap Tarzan through any voluntary act of his own, Rokoff and Paulvitch put their heads together to hatch a plan that would trap the ape-man in all the circumstantial evidence of a compromising position.

For days they watched the papers as well as the movements of De Coude and Tarzan. At length they were rewarded. A morning paper made brief mention of a smoker that was to be given on the following evening by the German minister. De Coude's name was among those of the invited guests. If he attended this meant that he would be absent from his home until after midnight.

On the night of the banquet Paulvitch waited at the curb before the residence of the German minister, where he could scan the face of each guest that arrived. He had not long to wait before De Coude descended from his car and passed him. That was enough. Paulvitch hastened back to his quarters, where Rokoff awaited him. There they waited until after eleven, then Paulvitch took down the receiver of their telephone. He called a number.

"The apartments of Lieutenant D'Arnot?" he asked, when he had obtained his connection.

"A message for Monsieur Tarzan, if he will be so kind as to step to the telephone."

For a minute there was silence.

"Monsieur Tarzan?

"Ah, yes, monsieur, this is François—in the service of the Countess de Coude. Possibly monsieur does poor François the honor to recall him—yes?

"Yes, monsieur. I have a message, an urgent message from the countess. She asks that you hasten to her at once—she is in trouble, monsieur.

"No, monsieur, poor François does not know. Shall I tell madame that monsieur will be here shortly?

"Thank you, monsieur. The good God will bless you."

Paulvitch hung up the receiver and turned to grin at Rokoff.

"It will take him thirty minutes to get there. If you reach the German minister's in fifteen, De Coude should arrive at his home in about forty-five minutes. It all depends upon whether the fool will remain fifteen minutes after he finds that a trick has been played upon him; but unless I am mistaken Olga will be loath to let him go in so short a time as that. Here is the note for De Coude. Hasten!"

Paulvitch lost no time in reaching the German minister's. At the door he handed the note to a footman. "This is for the Count de Coude. It is very urgent. You must see that it is placed in his hands at once," and he dropped a piece of silver into the willing hand of the servant. Then he returned to his quarters.

A moment later De Coude was apologizing to his host as he tore open the envelope. What he read left his face white and his hand trembling.

MONSIEUR LE COUNT DE COUDE:

One who wishes to save the honor of your name takes this means to warn you that the sanctity of your home is this minute in jeopardy.

A certain man who for months has been a constant visitor there during your absence is now with your wife. If you go at once to your countess' boudoir you will find them together.

A FRIEND.

Twenty minutes after Paulvitch had called Tarzan, Rokoff obtained a connection with Olga's private line. Her maid answered the telephone which was in the countess' boudoir.

"But madame has retired," said the maid, in answer to Rokoff's request to speak with her.

"This is a very urgent message for the countess' ears alone," replied Rokoff. "Tell her that she must arise and slip something about her and come to the telephone. I shall call up again in five minutes." Then he hung up his receiver. A moment later Paulvitch entered.

"The count has the message?" asked Rokoff.

"He should be on his way to his home by now," replied Paulvitch.

"Good! My lady will be sitting in her boudoir, very much in negligee, about now. In a minute the faithful Jacques will escort Monsieur Tarzan into her presence without announcing him. It will take a few minutes for explanations. Olga will look very alluring in the filmy creation that is her nightdress, and the clinging robe which but half conceals the charms that the former does not conceal at all. Olga will be surprised, but not displeased.

"If there is a drop of red blood in the man the count will break in upon a very pretty love scene in about fifteen minutes from now. I think we have planned marvelously, my dear Alexis. Let us go out and drink to the very good health of Monsieur Tarzan in some of old Plancon's unparalleled absinth; not forgetting that the Count de Coude is one of the best swordsmen in Paris, and by far the best shot in all France."

When Tarzan reached Olga's, Jacques was awaiting him at the entrance.

"This way, Monsieur," he said, and led the way up the broad, marble staircase. In another moment he had opened a door, and, drawing aside a heavy curtain, obsequiously bowed Tarzan into a dimly lighted apartment. Then Jacques vanished.

Across the room from him Tarzan saw Olga seated before a little desk on which stood her telephone. She was tapping impatiently upon the polished surface of the desk. She had not heard him enter.

"Olga," he said, "what is wrong?"

She turned toward him with a little cry of alarm.

"Jean!" she cried. "What are you doing here? Who admitted you? What does it mean?"

Tarzan was thunderstruck, but in an instant he realized a part of the truth.

"Then you did not send for me, Olga?"

"Send for you at this time of night? *Mon Dieu!* Jean, do you think that I am quite mad?"

"François telephoned me to come at once; that you were in trouble and wanted me."

"François? Who in the world is François?"

"He said that he was in your service. He spoke as though I should recall the fact."

"There is no one by that name in my employ. Some one has played a joke upon you, Jean," and Olga laughed.

"I fear that it may be a most sinister 'joke,' Olga," he replied. "There is more back of it than humor."

"What do you mean? You do not think that—"

"Where is the count?" he interrupted.

"At the German ambassador's."

"This is another move by your estimable brother. Tomorrow the count will hear of it. He will question the servants. Everything will point to—to what Rokoff wishes the count to think."

"The scoundrel!" cried Olga. She had arisen, and come close to Tarzan, where she stood looking up into his face. She was very frightened. In her eyes was an expression that the hunter sees in those of a poor, terrified doe—puzzled—questioning. She trembled, and to steady herself raised her hands to his broad shoulders. "What shall we do, Jean?" she whispered. "It is terrible. Tomorrow all Paris will read of it—he will see to that."

Her look, her attitude, her words were eloquent of the age-old appeal of defenseless woman to her natural protector—man. Tarzan took one of the warm little hands that lay on his breast in his own strong one. The act was quite involuntary, and almost equally so was the instinct of protection that threw a sheltering arm around the girl's shoulders.

The result was electrical. Never before had he been so close to her. In startled guilt they looked suddenly into each other's eyes, and where Olga de Coude should have been strong she was weak, for she crept closer into the man's arms, and clasped her own about his neck. And Tarzan of the Apes? He took the panting figure into his mighty arms, and covered the hot lips with kisses.

Raoul de Coude made hurried excuses to his host after he had read the note handed him by the ambassador's butler. Never afterward could he recall the nature of the excuses he made. Everything was quite a blur to him up to the time that he stood on the threshold of his own home. Then he became very cool, moving quietly and with caution. For some inexplicable reason Jacques had the door open before he was halfway to the steps. It did not strike him at the time as being unusual, though afterward he remarked it.

Very softly he tiptoed up the stairs and along the gallery to the door of his wife's boudoir. In his hand was a heavy walking stick—in his heart, murder.

Olga was the first to see him. With a horrified shriek she tore herself from Tarzan's arms, and the ape-man turned just in time to ward with his arm a terrific blow that De Coude had aimed at his head. Once, twice, three times the heavy stick fell with lightning rapidity, and each blow aided in the transition of the ape-man back to the primordial.

With the low, guttural snarl of the bull ape he sprang for the Frenchman. The great stick was torn from his grasp and broken in two as though it had been matchwood, to be flung aside as the now infuriated beast charged for his adversary's throat.

Olga de Coude stood a horrified spectator of the terrible scene which ensued during the next brief moment, then she sprang to where Tarzan was murdering her husband—choking the life from him—shaking him as a terrier might shake a rat.

Frantically she tore at his great hands. "Mother of God!" she cried. "You are killing him, you are killing him! Oh, Jean, you are killing my husband!"

Tarzan was deaf with rage. Suddenly he hurled the body to the floor, and, placing his foot upon the upturned breast, raised his head. Then through the palace of the Count de Coude rang the awesome challenge of the bull ape that has made a kill. From cellar to attic the horrid sound searched out the servants, and left them blanched and trembling. The woman in the room sank to her knees beside the body of her husband, and prayed.

Slowly the red mist faded from before Tarzan's eyes. Things began to take form—he was regaining the perspective of civilized man. His eyes fell upon the figure of the kneeling woman. "Olga," he whispered. She looked up, expecting to see the maniacal light of murder in the eyes above her. Instead she saw sorrow and contrition.

"Oh, Jean!" she cried. "See what you have done. He was my husband. I loved him, and you have killed him."

Very gently Tarzan raised the limp form of the Count de Coude and bore it to a couch. Then he put his ear to the man's breast.

"Some brandy, Olga," he said.

She brought it, and together they forced it between his lips. Presently a faint gasp came from the white lips. The head turned, and De Coude groaned.

"He will not die," said Tarzan. "Thank God!"

"Why did you do it, Jean?" she asked.

"I do not know. He struck me, and I went mad. I have seen the apes of my tribe do the same thing. I have never told you my story, Olga. It would have been better had you known it—this might not have happened. I never saw my father. The only mother I ever knew was a ferocious she-ape. Until I was fifteen I had never seen a human being. I was twenty before I saw a white man. A little more than a year ago I was a naked beast of prey in an African jungle.

"Do not judge me too harshly. Two years is too short a time in which to attempt to work the change in an individual that it has taken countless ages to accomplish in the white race."

"I do not judge you at all, Jean. The fault is mine. You must go now—he must not find you here when he regains consciousness. Good-by."

It was a sorrowful Tarzan who walked with bowed head from the palace of the Count de Coude.

Once outside his thoughts took definite shape, to the end that twenty minutes later he entered a police station not far from the Rue Maule. Here he soon found one of the officers with whom he had had the encounter several weeks previous. The policeman was genuinely glad to see again the man who had so roughly handled him. After a moment of conversation Tarzan asked if he had ever heard of Nikolas Rokoff or Alexis Paulvitch.

"Very often, indeed, monsieur. Each has a police record, and while there is nothing charged against them now, we make it a point to know pretty well where they may be found should the occasion demand. It is only the same precaution that we take with every known criminal. Why does monsieur ask?"

"They are known to me," replied Tarzan. "I wish to see Monsieur Rokoff on a little matter of business. If you can direct me to his lodgings I shall appreciate it."

A few minutes later he bade the policeman adieu, and, with a slip of paper in his pocket bearing a certain address in a semirespectable quarter, he walked briskly toward the nearest taxi stand.

Rokoff and Paulvitch had returned to their rooms, and were sitting talking over the probable outcome of the evening's events. They had telephoned to the offices of two of the morning papers from which they momentarily expected representatives to hear the first report of the scandal that was to stir social Paris on the morrow.

A heavy step sounded on the stairway. "Ah, but these newspaper men are prompt," exclaimed Rokoff, and as a knock fell upon the door of their room: "Enter, monsieur."

The smile of welcome froze upon the Russian's face as he looked into the hard, gray eyes of his visitor.

"Name of a name!" he shouted, springing to his feet. "What brings you here?"

"Sit down!" said Tarzan, so low that the men could barely catch the words, but in a tone that brought Rokoff to his chair, and kept Paulvitch in his.

"You know what has brought me here," he continued, in the same low tone. "It should be to kill you, but because you are Olga de Coude's brother I shall not do that—now.

"I shall give you a chance for your lives. Paulvitch does not count much—he is merely a stupid, foolish little tool, and so I shall not kill him so long as I permit you to live. Before I leave you two alive in this room you will have done two things. The first will be to write a full confession of your connection with tonight's plot—and sign it.

"The second will be to promise me upon pain of death that you will permit no word of this affair to get into the newspapers. If you do not do both, neither of you will be alive when I pass next through that doorway. Do you understand?" And, without waiting for a reply: "Make haste; there is ink before you, and paper and a pen."

Rokoff assumed a truculent air, attempting by bravado to show how little he feared Tarzan's threats. An instant later he felt the ape-man's steel fingers at his throat, and Paulvitch, who attempted to dodge them and reach the door, was lifted completely off the floor, and hurled senseless into a corner. When Rokoff commenced to blacken about the face Tarzan released his hold and shoved the fellow back into his chair. After a moment of coughing Rokoff sat sullenly glaring at the man standing opposite him. Presently Paulvitch came to himself, and limped painfully back to his chair at Tarzan's command.

"Now write," said the ape-man. "If it is necessary to handle you again I shall not be so lenient."

Rokoff picked up a pen and commenced to write.

"See that you omit no detail, and that you mention every name," cautioned Tarzan.

Presently there was a knock at the door. "Enter," said Tarzan.

A dapper young man came in. "I am from the *Matin,*" he announced. "I understand that Monsieur Rokoff has a story for me."

"Then you are mistaken, monsieur," replied Tarzan. "You have no story for publication, have you, my dear Nikolas."

Rokoff looked up from his writing with an ugly scowl upon his face.

"No," he growled, "I have no story for publication—now."

"Nor ever, my dear Nikolas," and the reporter did not see the nasty light in the ape-man's eye; but Nikolas Rokoff did.

"Nor ever," he repeated hastily.

"It is too bad that monsieur has been troubled," said Tarzan, turning to the newspaper man. "I bid monsieur good evening," and he bowed the dapper young man out of the room, and closed the door in his face.

An hour later Tarzan, with a rather bulky manuscript in his coat pocket, turned at the door leading from Rokoff's room.

"Were I you I should leave France," he said, "for sooner or later I shall find an excuse to kill you that will not in any way compromise your sister."

6

A Duel

D'ARNOT was asleep when Tarzan entered their apartments after leaving Rokoff's. Tarzan did not disturb him, but the following morning he narrated the happenings of the previous evening, omitting not a single detail.

"What a fool I have been," he concluded. "De Coude and his wife were both my friends. How have I returned their friendship? Barely did I escape murdering the count. I have cast a stigma on the name of a good woman. It is very probable that I have broken up a happy home."

"Do you love Olga de Coude?" asked D'Arnot.

"Were I not positive that she does not love me I could not answer your question, Paul; but without disloyalty to her I tell you that I do not love her, nor does she love me. For an instant we were the victims of a sudden madness—it was not love—and it would have left us, unharmed, as suddenly as it had come upon us even though De Coude had not returned. As you know, I have had little experience of women. Olga de Coude is very beautiful; that, and the dim light and the seductive surroundings, and the appeal of the defenseless for protection, might have been resisted by a more civilized man, but my civilization is not even skin deep—it does not go deeper than my clothes.

"Paris is no place for me. I will but continue to stumble into more and more serious pitfalls. The man-made restrictions are irksome. I feel always that I am a prisoner. I cannot endure it, my friend, and so I think that I shall go back to my own jungle, and lead the life that God intended that I should lead when He put me there."

"Do not take it so to heart, Jean," responded D'Arnot. "You have acquitted yourself much better than most 'civilized' men would have under similar circumstances. As to leaving Paris at this time, I rather think that Raoul de Coude may be expected to have something to say on that subject before long."

Nor was D'Arnot mistaken. A week later on Monsieur Flaubert was announced about eleven in the morning, as D'Arnot and Tarzan were breakfasting. Monsieur Flaubert was an impressively polite gentleman. With many low bows he delivered Monsieur le Count de Coude's challenge to Monsieur Tarzan. Would monsieur be so very kind as to arrange to have a friend meet Monsieur Flaubert at as early an hour as convenient, that the details might be arranged to the mutual satisfaction of all concerned?

Certainly. Monsieur Tarzan would be delighted to place his interests unreservedly in the hands of his friend, Lieutenant D'Arnot. And so it was arranged that D'Arnot was to call on Monsieur Flaubert at two that afternoon, and the polite Monsieur Flaubert, with many bows, left them.

When they were again alone D'Arnot looked quizzically at Tarzan.

"Well?" he said.

"Now to my sins I must add murder, or else myself be killed," said Tarzan. "I am progressing rapidly in the ways of my civilized brothers."

"What weapons shall you select?" asked D'Arnot. "De

Coude is accredited with being a master with the sword, and a splendid shot."

"I might then choose poisoned arrows at twenty paces, or spears at the same distance," laughed Tarzan. "Make it pistols, Paul."

"He will kill you, Jean."

"I have no doubt of it," replied Tarzan. "I must die some day."

"We had better make it swords," said D'Arnot. "He will be satisfied with wounding you, and there is less danger of a mortal wound."

"Pistols," said Tarzan, with finality.

D'Arnot tried to argue him out of it, but without avail, so pistols it was.

D'Arnot returned from his conference with Monsieur Flaubert shortly after four.

"It is all arranged," he said. "Everything is satisfactory. Tomorrow morning at daylight—there is a secluded spot on the road not far from Etamps. For some personal reason Monsieur Flaubert preferred it. I did not demur."

"Good!" was Tarzan's only comment. He did not refer to the matter again even indirectly. That night he wrote several letters before he retired. After sealing and addressing them he placed them all in an envelope addressed to D'Arnot. As he undressed D'Arnot heard him humming a music-hall ditty.

The Frenchman swore under his breath. He was very unhappy, for he was positive that when the sun rose the next morning it would look down upon a dead Tarzan. It grated upon him to see Tarzan so unconcerned.

"This is a most uncivilized hour for people to kill each other," remarked the ape-man when he had been routed out of a comfortable bed in the blackness of the early morning hours. He had slept well, and so it seemed that his head scarcely touched the pillow ere his man deferentially aroused him. His remark was addressed to D'Arnot, who stood fully dressed in the doorway of Tarzan's bedroom.

D'Arnot had scarcely slept at all during the night. He was nervous, and therefore inclined to be irritable.

"I presume you slept like a baby all night," he said.

Tarzan laughed. "From your tone, Paul, I infer that you rather harbor the fact against me. I could not help it, really."

"No, Jean; it is not that," replied D'Arnot, himself smiling. "But you take the entire matter with such infernal indifference—it is exasperating. One would think that you were going out to shoot at a target, rather than to face one of the best shots in France."

Tarzan shrugged his shoulders. "I am going out to expiate a great wrong, Paul. A very necessary feature of the expiation is the marksmanship of my opponent. Wherefore, then, should I be dissatisfied? Have you not yourself told me that Count de Coude is a splendid marksman?"

"You mean that you hope to be killed?" exclaimed D'Arnot, in horror.

"I cannot say that I hope to be; but you must admit that there is little reason to believe that I shall not be killed."

Had D'Arnot known the thing that was in the ape-man's mind—that had been in his mind almost from the first intimation that De Coude would call him to account on the field of honor—he would have been even more horrified than he was.

In silence they entered D'Arnot's great car, and in similar silence they sped over the dim road that leads to Etamps. Each man was occupied with his own thoughts. D'Arnot's were very mournful, for he was genuinely fond of Tarzan. The great friendship which had sprung up between these two men whose lives and training had been so widely different had but been strengthened by association, for they were both men to whom the same high ideals of manhood, of personal courage, and of honor appealed with equal force. They could understand one another, and each could be proud of the friendship of the other.

Tarzan of the Apes was wrapped in thoughts of the past; pleasant memories of the happier occasions of his lost jungle life. He recalled the countless boyhood hours that he had spent cross-legged upon the table in his dead father's cabin, his little brown body bent over one of the fascinating picture books from which, unaided, he had gleaned the secret of the printed language long before the sounds of human speech fell upon his ears. A smile of contentment softened his strong face as he thought of that day of days that he had had alone with Jane Porter in the heart of his primeval forest.

Presently his reminiscences were broken in upon by the stopping of the car—they were at their destination. Tarzan's mind returned to the affairs of the moment. He knew that he was about to die, but there was no fear of death in him. To a denizen of the cruel jungle death is a commonplace. The first law of nature compels them to cling tenaciously to life—to fight for it; but it does not teach them to fear death.

D'Arnot and Tarzan were first upon the field of honor. A moment later De Coude, Monsieur Flaubert, and a third gentleman arrived. The last was introduced to D'Arnot and Tarzan; he was a physician.

D'Arnot and Monsieur Flaubert spoke together in whispers for a brief time. The Count de Coude and Tarzan stood apart at opposite sides of the field. Presently the seconds summoned them. D'Arnot and Monsieur Flaubert had examined both pistols. The two men who were to face each other a moment later stood silently while Monsieur Flaubert recited the conditions they were to observe.

They were to stand back to back. At a signal from Monsieur Flaubert they were to walk in opposite directions, their pistols hanging by their sides. When each had proceeded ten paces D'Arnot was to give the final signal—then they were to turn and fire at will until one fell, or each had expended the three shots allowed.

While Monsieur Flaubert spoke Tarzan selected a cigarette from his case, and lighted it. De Coude was the personification of coolness—was he not the best shot in France?

Presently Monsieur Flaubert nodded to D'Arnot, and each man placed his principal in position.

"Are you quite ready, gentlemen?" asked Monsieur Flaubert.

"Quite," replied De Coude.

Tarzan nodded. Monsieur Flaubert gave the signal. He and D'Arnot stepped back a few paces to be out of the line of fire as the men paced slowly apart. Six! Seven! Eight! There were tears in D'Arnot's eyes. He loved Tarzan very much. Nine! Another pace, and the poor lieutenant gave the signal he so hated to give. To him it sounded the doom of his best friend.

Quickly De Coude wheeled and fired. Tarzan gave a little start. His pistol still dangled at his side. De Coude hesitated, as though waiting to see his antagonist crumple to the ground. The Frenchman was too experienced a marksman not to know that he had scored a hit. Still Tarzan made no move to raise his pistol. De Coude fired once more, but the attitude of the ape-man—the utter indifference that was so apparent in every line of the nonchalant ease of his giant figure, and the even, unruffled puffing of his cigarette—had disconcerted the best marksman in France. This time Tarzan did not start, but again De Coude knew that he had hit.

Suddenly the explanation leaped to his mind—his antagonist was coolly taking these terrible chances in the hope that he would receive no staggering wound from any of

De Coude's three shots. Then he would take his own time about shooting De Coude down deliberately, coolly, and in cold blood. A little shiver ran up the Frenchman's spine. It was fiendish—diabolical. What manner of creature was this that could stand complacently with two bullets in him, waiting for the third?

And so De Coude took careful aim this time, but his nerve was gone, and he made a clean miss. Not once had Tarzan raised his pistol hand from where it hung beside his leg.

For a moment the two stood looking straight into each other's eyes. On Tarzan's face was a pathetic expression of disappointment. On De Coude's a rapidly growing expression of horror—yes, of terror.

He could endure it no longer.

"Mother of God! Monsieur—shoot!" he screamed.

But Tarzan did not raise his pistol. Instead, he advanced toward De Coude, and when D'Arnot and Monsieur Flaubert, misinterpreting his intention, would have rushed between them, he raised his left hand in a sign of remonstrance.

"Do not fear," he said to them, "I shall not harm him."

It was most unusual, but they halted. Tarzan advanced until he was quite close to De Coude.

"There must have been something wrong with monsieur's pistol," he said. "Or monsieur is unstrung. Take mine, monsieur, and try again," and Tarzan offered his pistol, butt foremost, to the astonished De Coude.

"*Mon Dieu,* monsieur!" cried the latter. "Are you mad?"

"No, my friend," replied the ape-man; "but I deserve to die. It is the only way in which I may atone for the wrong I have done a very good woman. Take my pistol and do as I bid."

"It would be murder," replied De Coude. "But what wrong did you do my wife? She swore to me that—"

"I do not mean that," said Tarzan quickly. "You saw all the wrong that passed between us. But that was enough to cast a shadow upon her name, and to ruin the happiness of a man against whom I had no enmity. The fault was all mine, and so I hoped to die for it this morning. I am disappointed that monsieur is not so wonderful a marksman as I had been led to believe."

"You say that the fault was all yours?" asked De Coude eagerly.

"All mine, monsieur. Your wife is a very pure woman. She loves only you. The fault that you saw was all mine. The thing that brought me there was no fault of either the Countess de Coude or myself. Here is a paper which will quite positively demonstrate that," and Tarzan drew from his pocket the statement Rokoff had written and signed.

De Coude took it and read. D'Arnot and Monsieur Flaubert had drawn near. They were interested spectators of this strange ending of a strange duel. None spoke until De Coude had quite finished, then he looked up at Tarzan.

"You are a very brave and chivalrous gentleman," he said. "I thank God that I did not kill you."

De Coude was a Frenchman. Frenchmen are impulsive. He threw his arms about Tarzan and embraced him. Monsieur Flaubert embraced D'Arnot. There was no one to embrace the doctor. So possibly it was pique which prompted him to interfere, and demand that he be permitted to dress Tarzan's wounds.

"This gentleman was hit once at least," he said. "Possibly thrice."

"Twice," said Tarzan. "Once in the left shoulder, and again in the left side—both flesh wounds, I think." But the doctor insisted upon stretching him upon the sward, and tinkering with him until the wounds were cleansed and the flow of blood checked.

One result of the duel was that they all rode back to Paris together in D'Arnot's car, the best of friends. De Coude was so relieved to have had this double assurance of his wife's loyalty that he felt no rancor at all toward Tarzan. It is true that the latter had assumed much more of the fault than was rightly his, but if he lied a little he may be excused, for he lied in the service of a woman, and he lied like a gentleman.

The ape-man was confined to his bed for several days. He felt that it was foolish and unnecessary, but the doctor and D'Arnot took the matter so to heart that he gave in to please them, though it made him laugh to think of it.

"It is droll," he said to D'Arnot. "To lie abed because of a pin prick! Why, when Bolgani, the king gorilla, tore me almost to pieces, while I was still but a little boy, did I have a nice soft bed to lie on? No, only the damp, rotting vegetation of the jungle. Hidden beneath some friendly bush I lay for days and weeks with only Kala to nurse me—poor, faithful Kala, who kept the insects from my wounds and warned off the beasts of prey.

"When I called for water she brought it to me in her own mouth—the only way she knew to carry it. There was no sterilized gauze, there was no antiseptic bandage—there was nothing that would not have driven our dear doctor mad to have seen. Yet I recovered—recovered to lie in bed because of a tiny scratch that one of the jungle folk would scarce realize unless it were upon the end of his nose."

But the time was soon over, and before he realized it Tarzan found himself abroad again. Several times De Coude had called, and when he found that Tarzan was anxious for employment of some nature he promised to see what could be done to find a berth for him.

It was the first day that Tarzan was permitted to go out that he received a message from De Coude requesting him to call at the count's office that afternoon.

He found De Coude awaiting him with a very pleasant welcome, and a sincere congratulation that he was once more upon his feet. Neither had ever mentioned the duel or the cause of it since that morning upon the field of honor.

"I think that I have found just the thing for you, Monsieur Tarzan," said the count. "It is a position of much trust and responsibility, which also requires considerable physical courage and prowess. I cannot imagine a man better fitted than you, my dear Monsieur Tarzan, for this very position. It will necessitate travel, and later it may lead to a very much better post—possibly in the diplomatic service.

"At first, for a short time only, you will be a special agent in the service of the ministry of war. Come, I will take you to the gentleman who will be your chief. He can explain the duties better than I, and then you will be in a position to judge if you wish to accept or no."

De Coude himself escorted Tarzan to the office of General Rochere, the chief of the bureau to which Tarzan would be attached if he accepted the position. There the count left him, after a glowing description to the general of the many attributes possessed by the ape-man which should fit him for the work of the service.

A half hour later Tarzan walked out of the office the possessor of the first position he had ever held. On the morrow he was to return for further instructions, though General Rochere had made it quite plain that Tarzan might prepare to leave Paris for an almost indefinite period, possibly on the morrow.

It was with feelings of the keenest elation that he hastened home to bear the good news to D'Arnot. At last he was to be of some value in the world. He was to earn money, and, best of all, to travel and see the world.

He could scarcely wait to get well inside D'Arnot's sitting

room before he burst out with the glad tidings. D'Arnot was not so pleased.

"It seems to delight you to think that you are to leave Paris, and that we shall not see each other for months, perhaps. Tarzan, you are a most ungrateful beast!" and D'Arnot laughed.

"No, Paul; I am a little child. I have a new toy, and I am tickled to death."

And so it came that on the following day Tarzan left Paris en route for Marseilles and Oran.

7

The Dancing Girl of Sidi Aissa

TARZAN's first mission did not bid fair to be either exciting or vastly important. There was a certain lieutenant of *spahis* whom the government had reason to suspect of improper relations with a great European power. This Lieutenant Gernois, who was at present stationed at Sidi-bel-Abbes, had recently been attached to the general staff, where certain information of great military value had come into his possession in the ordinary routine of his duties. It was this information which the government suspected the great power was bartering for with the officer.

It was at most but a vague hint dropped by a certain notorious Parisienne in a jealous mood that had caused suspicion to rest upon the lieutenant. But general staffs are jealous of their secrets, and treason so serious a thing that even a hint of it may not be safely neglected. And so it was that Tarzan had come to Algeria in the guise of an American hunter and traveler to keep a close eye upon Lieutenant Gernois.

He had looked forward with keen delight to again seeing his beloved Africa, but this northern aspect of it was so different from his tropical jungle home that he might as well have been back in Paris for all the heart thrills of home-coming that he experienced. At Oran he spent a day wandering through the narrow, crooked alleys of the Arab quarter enjoying the strange, new sights. The next day found him at Sidi-bel-Abbes, where he presented his letters of introduction to both civil and military authorities—letters which gave no clew to the real significance of his mission.

Tarzan possessed a sufficient command of English to enable him to pass among Arabs and Frenchmen as an American, and that was all that was required of it. When he met an Englishman he spoke French in order that he might not betray himself, but occasionally talked in English to foreigners who understood that tongue, but could not note the slight imperfections of accent and pronunciation that were his.

Here he became acquainted with many of the French officers, and soon became a favorite among them. He met Gernois, whom he found to be a taciturn, dyspeptic-looking man of about forty, having little or no social intercourse with his fellows.

For a month nothing of moment occurred. Gernois apparently had no visitors, nor did he on his occasional visits to the town hold communication with any who might even by the wildest flight of imagination be construed into secret agents of a foreign power. Tarzan was beginning to hope that, after all, the rumor might have been false, when suddenly Gernois was ordered to Bou Saada in the Petit Sahara far to the south.

A company of *spahis* and three officers were to relieve another company already stationed there. Fortunately one of the officers, Captain Gerard, had become an excellent friend of Tarzan's, and so when the ape-man suggested that he should embrace the opportunity of accompanying him to Bou Saada, where he expected to find hunting, it caused not the slightest suspicion.

At Bouira the detachment detrained, and the balance of the journey was made in the saddle. As Tarzan was dickering at Bouira for a mount he caught a brief glimpse of a man in European clothes eying him from the doorway of a native coffeehouse, but as Tarzan looked the man turned and entered the little, low-ceilinged mud hut, and but for a haunting impression that there had been something familiar about the face or figure of the fellow, Tarzan gave the matter no further thought.

The march to Aumale was fatiguing to Tarzan, whose equestrian experiences hitherto had been confined to a course of riding lessons in a Parisian academy, and so it was that he quickly sought the comforts of a bed in the Hotel Grossat, while the officers and troops took up their quarters at the military post.

Although Tarzan was called early the following morning, the company of *spahis* was on the march before he had finished his breakfast. He was hurrying through his meal that the soldiers might not get too far in advance of him when he glanced through the door connecting the dining room with the bar.

To his surprise, he saw Gernois standing there in conversation with the very stranger he had seen in the coffeehouse at Bouira the day previous. He could not be mistaken, for there was the same strangely familiar attitude and figure, though the man's back was toward him.

As his eyes lingered on the two, Gernois looked up and caught the intent expression on Tarzan's face. The stranger was talking in a low whisper at the time, but the French officer immediately interrupted him, and the two at once turned away and passed out of the range of Tarzan's vision.

This was the first suspicious occurrence that Tarzan had ever witnessed in connection with Gernois' actions, but he was positive that the men had left the barroom solely because Gernois had caught Tarzan's eyes upon them; then there was the persistent impression of familiarity about the stranger to further augment the ape-man's belief that here at length was something which would bear watching.

A moment later Tarzan entered the barroom, but the men had left, nor did he see aught of them in the street beyond, though he found a pretext to ride to various shops before he set out after the column which had now considerable start of him. He did not overtake them until he reached Sidi Aissa shortly after noon, where the soldiers had halted for an hour's rest. Here he found Gernois with the column, but there was no sign of the stranger.

It was market day at Sidi Aissa, and the numberless caravans of camels coming in from the desert, and the crowds of bickering Arabs in the market place, filled Tarzan with a consuming desire to remain for a day that he might see more of these sons of the desert. Thus it was that the company of *spahis* marched on that afternoon toward Bou Saada without him. He spent the hours until dark wandering about the market in company with a youthful Arab, one Abdul, who had been recommended to him by the innkeeper as a trustworthy servant and interpreter.

Here Tarzan purchased a better mount than the one he had selected at Bouira, and, entering into conversation with the stately Arab to whom the animal had belonged, learned that the seller was Kadour ben Saden, sheik of a desert tribe far south of Djelfa. Through Abdul, Tarzan invited his new acquaintance to dine with him. As the three were making their way through the crowds of marketers, camels, donkeys, and horses that filled the market place with a confusing babel of sounds, Abdul plucked at Tarzan's sleeve.

"Look, master, behind us," and he turned, pointing at a figure which disappeared behind a camel as Tarzan turned. "He has been following us about all afternoon," continued Abdul.

"I caught only a glimpse of an Arab in a dark-blue burnoose and white turban," replied Tarzan. "Is it he you mean?"

"Yes. I suspected him because he seems a stranger here, without other business than following us, which is not the way of the Arab who is honest, and also because he keeps the lower part of his face hidden, only his eyes showing. He must be a bad man, or he would have honest business of his own to occupy his time."

"He is on the wrong scent then, Abdul," replied Tarzan, "for no one here can have any grievance against me. This is my first visit to your country, and none knows me. He will soon discover his error, and cease to follow us."

"Unless he be bent on robbery," returned Abdul.

"Then all we can do is wait until he is ready to try his hand upon us," laughed Tarzan, "and I warrant that he will get his bellyful of robbing now that we are prepared for him," and so he dismissed the subject from his mind, though he was destined to recall it before many hours through a most unlooked-for occurrence.

Kadour ben Saden, having dined well, prepared to take leave of his host. With dignified protestations of friendship, he invited Tarzan to visit him in his wild domain, where the antelope, the stag, the boar, the panther, and the lion might still be found in sufficient numbers to tempt an ardent huntsman.

On his departure the ape-man, with Abdul, wandered again into the streets of Sidi Aissa, where he was soon attracted by the wild din of sound coming from the open doorway of one of the numerous *cafés maures*. It was after eight, and the dancing was in full swing as Tarzan entered. The room was filled to repletion with Arabs. All were smoking, and drinking their thick, hot coffee.

Tarzan and Abdul found seats near the center of the room,

though the terrific noise produced by the musicians upon their Arab drums and pipes would have rendered a seat farther from them more acceptable to the quiet-loving ape-man. A rather good-looking Ouled-Nail was dancing, and, perceiving Tarzan's European clothes, and scenting a generous gratuity, she threw her silken handkerchief upon his shoulder, to be rewarded with a franc.

When her place upon the floor had been taken by another the bright-eyed Abdul saw her in conversation with two Arabs at the far side of the room, near a side door that let upon an inner court, around the gallery of which were the rooms occupied by the girls who danced in this café.

At first he thought nothing of the matter, but presently he noticed from the corner of his eye one of the men nod in their direction, and the girl turn and shoot a furtive glance at Tarzan. Then the Arabs melted through the doorway into the darkness of the court.

When it came again the girl's turn to dance she hovered close to Tarzan, and for the ape-man alone were her sweetest smiles. Many an ugly scowl was cast upon the tall European by swarthy, dark-eyed sons of the desert, but neither smiles nor scowls produced any outwardly visible effect upon him. Again the girl cast her handkerchief upon his shoulder, and again was she rewarded with a franc piece. As she was sticking it upon her forehead, after the custom of her kind, she bent low toward Tarzan, whispering a quick word in his ear.

"There are two without in the court," she said quickly, in broken French, "who would harm m'sieur. At first I promised to lure you to them, but you have been kind, and I cannot do it. Go quickly, before they find that I have failed them. I think that they are very bad men."

Tarzan thanked the girl, assuring her that he would be careful, and, having finished her dance, she crossed to the little doorway and went out into the court. But Tarzan did not leave the café as she had urged.

For another half hour nothing unusual occurred, then a surly-looking Arab entered the café from the street. He stood near Tarzan, where he deliberately made insulting remarks about the European, but as they were in his native tongue Tarzan was entirely innocent of their purport until Abdul took it upon himself to enlighten him.

"This fellow is looking for trouble," warned Abdul. "He is not alone. In fact, in case of a disturbance, nearly every man here would be against you. It would be better to leave quietly, master."

"Ask the fellow what he wants," commanded Tarzan.

"He says that 'the dog of a Christian' insulted the Ouled-Nail, who belongs to him. He means trouble, m'sieur."

"Tell him that I did not insult his or any other Ouled-Nail, that I wish him to go away and leave me alone. That I have no quarrel with him, nor has he any with me."

"He says," replied Abdul, after delivering this message to the Arab, "that besides being a dog yourself that you are the son of one, and that your grandmother was a hyena. Incidentally you are a liar."

The attention of those near by had now been attracted by the altercation, and the sneering laughs that followed this torrent of invective easily indicated the trend of the sympathies of the majority of the audience.

Tarzan did not like being laughed at, neither did he relish the terms applied to him by the Arab, but he showed no sign of anger as he arose from his seat upon the bench. A half smile played about his lips, but of a sudden a mighty fist shot into the face of the scowling Arab, and back of it were the terrible muscles of the ape-man.

At the instant that the man fell a half dozen fierce plainsmen sprang into the room from where they had apparently been waiting for their cue in the street before the café. With cries of "Kill the unbeliever!" and "Down with the dog of a Christian!" they made straight for Tarzan.

A number of the younger Arabs in the audience sprang to their feet to join in the assault upon the unarmed white man. Tarzan and Abdul were rushed back toward the end of the room by the very force of numbers opposing them. The young Arab remained loyal to his master, and with drawn knife fought at his side.

With tremendous blows the ape-man felled all who came within reach of his powerful hands. He fought quietly and without a word, upon his lips the same half smile they had worn as he rose to strike down the man who had insulted him. It seemed impossible that either he or Abdul could survive the sea of wicked-looking swords and knives that surrounded them, but the very numbers of their assailants proved the best bulwark of their safety. So closely packed was the howling, cursing mob that no weapon could be wielded to advantage, and none of the Arabs dared use a firearm for fear of wounding one of his compatriots.

Finally Tarzan succeeded in seizing one of the most persistent of his attackers. With a quick wrench he disarmed the fellow, and then, holding him before them as a shield, he backed slowly beside Abdul toward the little door which led into the inner courtyard. At the threshold he paused for an instant, and, lifting the struggling Arab above his head, hurled him, as though from a catapult, full in the faces of his on-pressing fellows.

Then Tarzan and Abdul stepped into the semidarkness of the court. The frightened Ouled-Nails were crouching at the tops of the stairs which led to their respective rooms, the only light in the courtyard coming from the sickly candles which each girl had stuck with its own grease to the woodwork of her door-frame, the better to display her charms to those who might happen to traverse the dark inclosure.

Scarcely had Tarzan and Abdul emerged from the room ere a revolver spoke close at their backs from the shadows beneath one of the stairways, and as they turned to meet this new antagonist, two muffled figures sprang toward them, firing as they came. Tarzan leaped to meet these two new assailants. The foremost lay, a second later, in the trampled dirt of the court, disarmed and groaning from a broken wrist. Abdul's knife found the vitals of the second in the instant that the fellow's revolver missed fire as he held it to the faithful Arab's forehead.

The maddened horde within the café were now rushing out in pursuit of their quarry. The Ouled-Nails had extinguished their candles at a cry from one of their number, and the only light within the yard came feebly from the open and half-blocked door of the café. Tarzan had seized a sword from the man who had fallen before Abdul's knife, and now he stood waiting for the rush of men that was coming in search of them through the darkness.

Suddenly he felt a light hand upon his shoulder from behind, and a woman's voice whispering, "Quick, m'sieur; this way. Follow me."

"Come, Abdul," said Tarzan, in a low tone, to the youth; "we can be no worse off elsewhere than we are here."

The woman turned and led them up the narrow stairway that ended at the door of her quarters. Tarzan was close beside her. He saw the gold and silver bracelets upon her bare arms, the strings of gold coin that depended from her hair ornaments, and the gorgeous colors of her dress. He saw that she was a Ouled-Nail, and instinctively he knew that she was the same who had whispered the warning in his ear earlier in the evening.

As they reached the top of the stairs they could hear the angry crowd searching the yard beneath.

"Soon they will search here," whispered the girl. "They must not find you, for, though you fight with the strength of many men, they will kill you in the end. Hasten; you can drop from the farther window of my room to the street beyond. Before they discover that you are no longer in the court of the buildings you will be safe within the hotel."

But even as she spoke, several men had started up the stairway at the head of which they stood. There was a sudden cry from one of the searchers. They had been discovered. Quickly the crowd rushed for the stairway. The foremost assailant leaped quickly upward, but at the top he met the sudden sword that he had not expected—the quarry had been unarmed before.

With a cry, the man toppled back upon those behind him. Like tenpins they rolled down the stairs. The ancient and rickety structure could not withstand the strain of this unwonted weight and jarring. With a creaking and rending of breaking wood it collapsed beneath the Arabs, leaving Tarzan, Abdul, and the girl alone upon the frail platform at the top.

"Come!" cried the Ouled-Nail. "They will reach us from another stairway through the room next to mine. We have not a moment to spare."

Just as they were entering the room Abdul heard and translated a cry from the yard below for several to hasten to the street and cut off escape from that side.

"We are lost now," said the girl simply.

"We?" questioned Tarzan.

"Yes, m'sieur," she responded; "they will kill me as well. Have I not aided you?"

This put a different aspect on the matter. Tarzan had rather been enjoying the excitement and danger of the encounter. He had not for an instant supposed that either Abdul or the girl could suffer except through accident, and he had only retreated just enough to keep from being killed himself. He had had no intention of running away until he saw that he was hopelessly lost were he to remain.

Alone he could have sprung into the midst of that close-packed mob, and, laying about him after the fashion of Numa, the lion, have struck the Arabs with such consternation that escape would have been easy. Now he must think entirely of these two faithful friends.

He crossed to the window which overlooked the street. In a minute there would be enemies below. Already he could hear the mob clambering the stairway to the next quarters—

they would be at the door beside him in another instant. He put a foot upon the sill and leaned out, but he did not look down. Above him, within arm's reach, was the low roof of the building. He called to the girl. She came and stood beside him. He put a great arm about her and lifted her across his shoulder.

"Wait here until I reach down for you from above," he said to Abdul. "In the meantime shove everything in the room against that door—it may delay them long enough." Then he stepped to the sill of the narrow window with the girl upon his shoulders. "Hold tight," he cautioned her. A moment later he had clambered to the roof above with the ease and dexterity of an ape. Setting the girl down, he leaned far over the roof's edge, calling softly to Abdul. The youth ran to the window.

"Your hand," whispered Tarzan. The men in the room beyond were battering at the door. With a sudden crash it fell splintering in, and at the same instant Abdul felt himself lifted like a feather onto the roof above. They were not a moment too soon, for as the men broke into the room which they had just quitted a dozen more rounded the corner in the street below and came running to a spot beneath the girl's window.

8

The Fight in the Desert

As THE three squatted upon the roof above the quarters of the Ouled-Nails they heard the angry cursing of the Arabs in the room beneath. Abdul translated from time to time to Tarzan.

"They are berating those in the street below now," said Abdul, "for permitting us to escape so easily. Those in the street say that we did not come that way—that we are still within the building, and that those above, being too cowardly to attack us, are attempting to deceive them into believing that we have escaped. In a moment they will have fighting of their own to attend to if they continue their brawling."

Presently those in the building gave up the search, and returned to the café. A few remained in the street below, smoking and talking.

Tarzan spoke to the girl, thanking her for the sacrifice she had made for him, a total stranger.

"I liked you," she said simply. "You were unlike the others who come to the café. You did not speak coarsely to me—the manner in which you gave me money was not an insult."

"What shall you do after tonight?" he asked. "You cannot return to the café. Can you even remain with safety in Sidi Aissa?"

"Tomorrow it will be forgotten," she replied. "But I should be glad if it might be that I need never return to this or another café. I have not remained because I wished to; I have been a prisoner."

"A prisoner!" ejaculated Tarzan incredulously.

"A slave would be the better word," she answered. "I was stolen in the night from my father's *douar* by a band of marauders. They brought me here and sold me to the Arab who keeps this café. It has been nearly two years now since I saw the last of mine own people. They are very far to the south. They never come to Sidi Aissa."

"You would like to return to your people?" asked Tarzan. "Then I shall promise to see you safely so far as Bou Saada at least. There we can doubtless arrange with the commandant to send you the rest of the way."

"Oh, m'sieur," she cried, "how can I ever repay you! You cannot really mean that you will do so much for a poor Ouled-Nail. But my father can reward you, and he will, for is he not a great sheik? He is Kadour ben Saden."

"Kadour ben Saden!" ejaculated Tarzan. "Why, Kadour ben Saden is in Sidi Aissa this very night. He dined with me but a few hours since."

"My father in Sidi Aissa?" cried the amazed girl. "Allah be praised then, for I am indeed saved."

"Hssh!" cautioned Abdul. "Listen."

From below came the sound of voices, quite distinguishable upon the still night air. Tarzan could not understand the words, but Abdul and the girl translated.

"They have gone now," said the latter. "It is you they want, m'sieur. One of them said that the stranger who had offered money for your slaying lay in the house of Akmed din Soulef with a broken wrist, but that he had offered a still greater reward if some would lay in wait for you upon the road to Bou Saada and kill you."

"It is he who followed m'sieur about the market today," exclaimed Abdul. "I saw him again within the café—him and another; and the two went out into the inner court after talking with this girl here. It was they who attacked and fired upon us as we came out of the café. Why do they wish to kill you, m'sieur?"

"I do not know," replied Tarzan, and then, after a pause: "Unless—" But he did not finish, for the thought that had come to his mind, while it seemed the only reasonable solution of the mystery, appeared at the same time quite improbable.

Presently the men in the street went away. The courtyard and the café were deserted. Cautiously Tarzan lowered himself to the sill of the girl's window. The room was empty. He returned to the roof and let Abdul down, then he lowered the girl to the arms of the waiting Arab.

From the window Abdul dropped the short distance to the street below, while Tarzan took the girl in his arms and leaped down as he had done on so many other occasions in his own forest with a burden in his arms. A little cry of alarm was startled from the girl's lips, but Tarzan landed in the street with but an imperceptible jar, and lowered her in safety to her feet.

She clung to him for a moment.

"How strong m'sieur is, and how active," she cried. "*El adrea,* the black lion, himself is not more so."

"I should like to meet this *el adrea* of yours," he said. "I have heard much about him."

"And you come to the *douar* of my father you shall see him," said the girl. "He lives in a spur of the mountains north of us, and comes down from his lair at night to rob my father's *douar*. With a single blow of his mighty paw he crushes the skull of a bull, and woe betide the belated wayfarer who meets *el adrea* abroad at night."

Without further mishap they reached the hotel. The sleepy landlord objected strenuously to instituting a search for Kadour ben Saden until the following morning, but a piece of gold put a different aspect on the matter, so that a few moments later a servant had started to make the rounds of the lesser native hostelries where it might be expected that a desert sheik would find congenial associations. Tarzan had felt it necessary to find the girl's father that night, for fear he might start on his homeward journey too early in the morning to be intercepted.

They had waited perhaps half an hour when the messenger returned with Kadour ben Saden. The old sheik entered the room with a questioning expression upon his proud face.

"Monsieur has done me the honor to—" he commenced, and then his eyes fell upon the girl. With outstretched arms he crossed the room to meet her. "My daughter!" he cried. "Allah is merciful!" and tears dimmed the martial eyes of the old warrior.

When the story of her abduction and her final rescue had been told to Kadour ben Saden he extended his hand to Tarzan.

"All that is Kadour ben Saden's is thine, my friend, even to his life," he said very simply, but Tarzan knew that those were no idle words.

It was decided that although three of them would have to ride after practically no sleep, it would be best to make an early start in the morning, and attempt to ride all the way to Bou Saada in one day. It would have been comparatively easy for the men, but for the girl it was sure to be a fatiguing journey.

She, however, was the most anxious to undertake it, for it seemed to her that she could not quickly enough reach the family and friends from whom she had been separated for two years.

It seemed to Tarzan that he had not closed his eyes before he was awakened, and in another hour the party was on its way south toward Bou Saada. For a few miles the road was good, and they made rapid progress, but suddenly it became only a waste of sand, into which the horses sank fetlock deep at nearly every step. In addition to Tarzan, Abdul, the sheik, and his daughter were four of the wild plainsmen of the sheik's tribe who had accompanied him upon the trip to Sidi Aissa. Thus, seven guns strong, they entertained little fear of attack by day, and if all went well they should reach Bou Saada before nightfall.

A brisk wind enveloped them in the blowing sand of the desert, until Tarzan's lips were parched and cracked. What little he could see of the surrounding country was far from alluring—a vast expanse of rough country, rolling in little, barren hillocks, and tufted here and there with clumps of dreary shrub. Far to the south rose the dim lines of the Saharan Atlas range. How different, thought Tarzan, from the gorgeous Africa of his boyhood!

Abdul, always on the alert, looked backward quite as often as he did ahead. At the top of each hillock that they mounted he would draw in his horse and, turning, scan the country to the rear with utmost care. At last his scrutiny was rewarded.

"Look!" he cried. "There are six horsemen behind us."

"Your friends of last evening, no doubt, monsieur," remarked Kadour ben Saden dryly to Tarzan.

"No doubt," replied the ape-man. "I am sorry that my society should endanger the safety of your journey. At the next village I shall remain and question these gentlemen, while you ride on. There is no necessity for my being at Bou Saada tonight, and less still why you should not ride in peace."

"If you stop we shall stop," said Kadour ben Saden. "Until you are safe with your friends, or the enemy has left your trail, we shall remain with you. There is nothing more to say."

Tarzan but nodded his head. He was a man of few words, and possibly it was for this reason as much as any that Kadour ben Saden had taken to him, for if there be one thing that an Arab despises it is a talkative man.

All the balance of the day Abdul caught glimpses of the horsemen in their rear. They remained always at about the same distance. During the occasional halts for rest, and at the longer halt at noon, they approached no closer.

"They are waiting for darkness," said Kadour ben Saden.

And darkness came before they reached Bou Saada. The last glimpse that Abdul had of the grim, white-robed figures that trailed them, just before dusk made it impossible to distinguish them, had made it apparent that they were rapidly closing up the distance that intervened between them and their intended quarry. He whispered this fact to Tarzan, for he did not wish to alarm the girl. The ape-man drew back beside him.

"You will ride ahead with the others, Abdul," said Tarzan. "This is my quarrel. I shall wait at the next convenient spot, and interview these fellows."

"Then Abdul shall wait at thy side," replied the young Arab, nor would any threats or commands move him from his decision.

"Very well, then," replied Tarzan. "Here is as good a place as we could wish. Here are rocks at the top of this hillock. We shall remain hidden here and give an account of ourselves to these gentlemen when they appear."

They drew in their horses and dismounted. The others riding ahead were already out of sight in the darkness. Beyond them shone the lights of Bou Saada. Tarzan removed his rifle from its boot and loosened his revolver in its holster. He ordered Abdul to withdraw behind the rocks with the horses, so that they should be shielded from the enemies' bullets should they fire. The young Arab pretended to do as he was bid, but when he had fastened the two animals securely to a low shrub he crept back to lie on his belly a few paces behind Tarzan.

The ape-man stood erect in the middle of the road, waiting. Nor did he have long to wait. The sound of galloping horses came suddenly out of the darkness below him, and a moment later he discerned the moving blotches of lighter color against the solid background of the night.

"Halt," he cried, "or we fire!"

The white figures came to a sudden stop, and for a moment there was silence. Then came the sound of a whispered council, and like ghosts the phantom riders dispersed in all directions. Again the desert lay still about him, yet it was an ominous stillness that foreboded evil.

Abdul raised himself to one knee. Tarzan cocked his jungle-trained ears, and presently there came to him the sound of horses walking quietly through the sand to the east of him, to the west, to the north, and to the south. They had been surrounded. Then a shot came from the direction in which he was looking, a bullet whirred through the air above his head, and he fired at the flash of the enemy's gun.

Instantly the soundless waste was torn with the quick staccato of guns upon every hand. Abdul and Tarzan fired only at the flashes—they could not yet see their foemen. Presently it became evident that the attackers were circling their position, drawing closer and closer in as they began to realize the paltry numbers of the party which opposed them.

But one came too close, for Tarzan was accustomed to using his eyes in the darkness of the jungle night, than which there is no more utter darkness this side the grave, and with a cry of pain a saddle was emptied.

"The odds are evening, Abdul," said Tarzan, with a low laugh.

But they were still far too one-sided, and when the five remaining horsemen whirled at a signal and charged full upon them it looked as if there would be a sudden ending of the battle. Both Tarzan and Abdul sprang to the shelter of the rocks, that they might keep the enemy in front of them.

There was a mad clatter of galloping hoofs, a volley of shots from both sides, and the Arabs withdrew to repeat the maneuver; but there were now only four against the two.

For a few moments there came no sound from out of the surrounding blackness. Tarzan could not tell whether the Arabs, satisfied with their losses, had given up the fight, or were waiting farther along the road to waylay them as they proceeded on toward Bou Saada. But he was not left long in doubt, for now all from one direction came the sound of a new charge. But scarcely had the first gun spoken ere a dozen shots rang out behind the Arabs. There came the wild shouts of a new party to the controversy, and the pounding of the feet of many horses from down the road to Bou Saada.

The Arabs did not wait to learn the identity of the oncomers. With a parting volley as they dashed by the position which Tarzan and Abdul were holding, they plunged off along the road toward Sidi Aissa. A moment later Kadour ben Saden and his men dashed up.

The old sheik was much relieved to find that neither Tarzan nor Abdul had received a scratch. Not even had their horses been wounded. They sought out the two men who had fallen before Tarzan's shots, and, finding that both were dead, left them where they lay.

"Why did you not tell me that you contemplated ambushing those fellows?" asked the sheik in a hurt tone. "We might have had them all if the seven of us had stopped to meet them."

"Then it would have been useless to stop at all," replied Tarzan, "for had we simply ridden on toward Bou Saada they would have been upon us presently, and all could have been engaged. It was to prevent the transfer of my own quarrel to another's shoulders that Abdul and I stopped off to question them. Then there is your daughter—I could not be the cause of exposing her needlessly to the marksmanship of six men."

Kadour ben Saden shrugged his shoulders. He did not relish having been cheated out of a fight.

The little battle so close to Bou Saada had drawn out a company of soldiers. Tarzan and his party met them just outside the town. The officer in charge halted them to learn the significance of the shots.

"A handful of marauders," replied Kadour ben Saden. "They attacked two of our number who had dropped behind, but when we returned to them the fellows soon dispersed. They left two dead. None of my party was injured."

This seemed to satisfy the officer, and after taking the names of the party he marched his men on toward the scene of the skirmish to bring back the dead men for purposes of identification, if possible.

Two days later, Kadour ben Saden, with his daughter and followers, rode south through the pass below Bou Saada, bound for their home in the far wilderness. The sheik had urged Tarzan to accompany him, and the girl had added her entreaties to those of her father; but, though he could not explain it to them, Tarzan's duties loomed particularly large after the happenings of the past few days, so that he could not think of leaving his post for an instant. But he promised to come later if it lay within his power to do so, and they had to content themselves with that assurance.

During these two days Tarzan had spent practically all his time with Kadour ben Saden and his daughter. He was keenly interested in this race of stern and dignified warriors, and embraced the opportunity which their friendship offered to learn what he could of their lives and customs. He even commenced to acquire the rudiments of their language under the pleasant tutorage of the brown-eyed girl. It was with real regret that he saw them depart, and he sat his horse at the opening to the pass, as far as which he had accompanied them, gazing after the little party as long as he could catch a glimpse of them.

Here were people after his own heart! Their wild, rough lives, filled with danger and hardship, appealed to this half-savage man as nothing had appealed to him in the midst of the effeminate civilization of the great cities he had visited. Here was a life that excelled even that of the jungle, for here he might have the society of men—real men whom he could honor and respect, and yet be near to the wild nature that he loved. In his head revolved an idea that when he had completed his mission he would resign and return to live for the remainder of his life with the tribe of Kadour ben Saden.

Then he turned his horse's head and rode slowly back to Bou Saada.

The front of the Hotel du Petit Sahara, where Tarzan stopped in Bou Saada, is taken up with the bar, two dining-rooms, and the kitchens. Both of the dining-rooms open directly off the bar, and one of them is reserved for the use of the officers of the garrison. As you stand in the barroom you may look into either of the dining-rooms if you wish.

It was to the bar that Tarzan repaired after speeding Kadour ben Saden and his party on their way. It was yet early in the morning, for Kadour ben Saden had elected to ride far that day, so that it happened that when Tarzan returned there were guests still at breakfast.

As his casual glance wandered into the officers' dining-room, Tarzan saw something which brought a look of interest to his eyes. Lieutenant Gernois was sitting there, and as Tarzan looked a white-robed Arab approached and, bending, whispered a few words into the lieutenant's ear. Then he passed on out of the building through another door.

In itself the thing was nothing, but as the man had stooped to speak to the officer, Tarzan had caught sight of something which the accidental parting of the man's burnoose had revealed—he carried his left arm in a sling.

9

Numa "El Adrea"

ON THE same day that Kadour ben Saden rode south the diligence from the north brought Tarzan a letter from D'Arnot which had been forwarded from Sidi-bel-Abbes. It opened the old wound that Tarzan would have been glad to have forgotten; yet he was not sorry that D'Arnot had written, for one at least of his subjects could never cease to interest the ape-man. Here is the letter:

MY DEAR JEAN:

Since last I wrote you I have been across to London on a matter of business. I was there but three days. The very first day I came upon an old friend of yours—quite unexpectedly—in Henrietta Street. Now you never in the world would guess whom. None other than Mr. Samuel T. Philander. But it is true. I can see your look of incredulity. Nor is this all. He insisted that I return to the hotel with him, and there I found the others—Professor Archimedes Q. Porter, Miss Porter, and that enormous black woman, Miss Porter's maid

—Esmeralda, you will recall. While I was there Clayton came in. They are to be married soon, or rather sooner, for I rather suspect that we shall receive announcements almost any day. On account of his father's death it is to be a very quiet affair—only blood relatives.

While I was alone with Mr. Philander the old fellow became rather confidential. Said Miss Porter had already postponed the wedding on three different occasions. He confided that it appeared to him that she was not particularly anxious to marry Clayton at all; but this time it seems that it is quite likely to go through.

Of course they all asked after you, but I respected your wishes in the matter of your true origin, and only spoke to them of your present affairs.

Miss Porter was especially interested in everything I had to say about you, and asked many questions. I am afraid I took a rather unchivalrous delight in picturing your desire and resolve to go back eventually to your native jungle. I was sorry afterward, for it did seem to cause her real anguish to contemplate the awful dangers to which you wished to return. "And yet," she said, "I do not know. There are more unhappy fates than the grim and terrible jungle presents to Monsieur Tarzan. At least his conscience will be free from remorse. And there are moments of quiet and restfulness by day, and vistas of exquisite beauty. You may find it strange that I should say it, who experienced such terrifying experiences in that frightful forest, yet at times I long to return, for I cannot but feel that the happiest moments of my life were spent there."

There was an expression of ineffable sadness on her face as she spoke, and I could not but feel that she knew that I knew her secret, and that this was her way of transmitting to you a last tender message from a heart that might still enshrine your memory, though its possessor belonged to another.

Clayton appeared nervous and ill at ease while you were the subject of conversation. He wore a worried and harassed expression. Yet he was very kindly in his expressions of interest in you. I wonder if he suspects the truth about you?

Tennington came in with Clayton. They are great friends, you know. He is about to set out upon one of his interminable cruises in that yacht of his, and was urging the entire party to accompany him. Tried to inveigle me into it, too. Is thinking of circumnavigating Africa this time. I told him that his precious toy would take him and some of his friends to the bottom of the ocean one of these days if he didn't get it out of his head that she was a liner or a battleship.

I returned to Paris day before yesterday, and yesterday I met the Count and Countess de Coude at the races. They inquired after you. De Coude really seems quite fond of you. Doesn't appear to harbor the least ill will. Olga is as beautiful as ever, but a trifle subdued. I imagine that she learned a lesson through her acquaintance with you that will serve her in good stead during the balance of her life. It is fortunate for her, and for De Coude as well, that it was you and not another man more sophisticated.

Had you really paid court to Olga's heart I am afraid that there would have been no hope for either of you.

She asked me to tell you that Nikolas had left France. She paid him twenty thousand francs to go away, and stay. She is congratulating herself that she got rid of him before he tried to carry out a threat he recently made her that he should kill you at the first opportunity. She said that she should hate to think that her brother's blood was on your hands, for she is very fond of you, and made no bones in saying so before the count. It never for a moment seemed to occur to her that there might be any possibility of any other outcome of a meeting between you and Nikolas. The count quite agreed with her in that. He added that it would take a regiment of Rokoffs to kill you. He has a most healthy respect for your prowess.

Have been ordered back to my ship. She sails from Havre in two days under sealed orders. If you will address me in her care, the letters will find me eventually. I shall write you as soon as another opportunity presents.

Your sincere friend,

PAUL D'ARNOT.

"I fear," mused Tarzan, half aloud, "that Olga has thrown away her twenty thousand francs."

He read over that part of D'Arnot's letter several times in which he had quoted from his conversation with Jane Porter. Tarzan derived a rather pathetic happiness from it, but it was better than no happiness at all.

The following three weeks were quite uneventful. On several occasions Tarzan saw the mysterious Arab, and once again he had been exchanging words with Lieutenant Gernois; but no amount of espionage or shadowing by Tarzan revealed the Arab's lodgings, the location of which Tarzan was anxious to ascertain.

Gernois, never cordial, had kept more than ever aloof from Tarzan since the episode in the dining-room of the hotel at Aumale. His attitude on the few occasions that they had been thrown together had been distinctly hostile.

That he might keep up the appearance of the character he was playing, Tarzan spent considerable time hunting in the vicinity of Bou Saada. He would spend entire days in the foothills, ostensibly searching for gazelle, but on the few occasions that he came close enough to any of the beautiful little animals to harm them he invariably allowed them to escape without so much as taking his rifle from its boot. The ape-man could see no sport in slaughtering the most harmless and defenseless of God's creatures for the mere pleasure of killing.

In fact, Tarzan had never killed for "pleasure," nor to him was there pleasure in killing. It was the joy of righteous battle that he loved—the ecstasy of victory. And the keen and successful hunt for food in which he pitted his skill and craftiness against the skill and craftiness of another; but to come out of a town filled with food to shoot down a soft-eyed, pretty gazelle—ah, that was crueller than the deliberate and cold-blooded murder of a fellow man. Tarzan would have none of it, and so he hunted alone that none might discover the sham that he was practicing.

And once, probably because of the fact that he rode alone, he was like to have lost his life. He was riding slowly through a little ravine when a shot sounded close behind him, and a bullet passed through the cork helmet he wore. Although he turned at once and galloped rapidly to the top of the ravine, there was no sign of any enemy, nor did he see aught of another human being until he reached Bou Saada.

"Yes," he soliloquized, in recalling the occurrence, "Olga has indeed thrown away her twenty thousand francs."

That night he was Captain Gerard's guest at a little dinner.

"Your hunting has not been very fortunate?" questioned the officer.

"No," replied Tarzan; "the game hereabout is timid, nor do I care particularly about hunting game birds or antelope. I think I shall move on farther south, and have a try at some of your Algerian lions."

"Good!" exclaimed the captain. "We are marching toward Djelfa on the morrow. You shall have company that far at least. Lieutenant Gernois and I, with a hundred men, are ordered south to patrol a district in which the marauders are giving considerable trouble. Possibly we may have the pleasure of hunting the lion together—what say you?"

Tarzan was more than pleased, nor did he hesitate to say so; but the captain would have been astonished had he known the real reason of Tarzan's pleasure. Gernois was sitting opposite the ape-man. He did not seem so pleased with his captain's invitation.

"You will find lion hunting more exciting than gazelle shooting," remarked Captain Gerard, "and more dangerous."

"Even gazelle shooting has its dangers," replied Tarzan. "Especially when one goes alone. I found it so today. I also found that while the gazelle is the most timid of animals, it is not the most cowardly."

He let his glance rest only casually upon Gernois after he had spoken, for he did not wish the man to know that he was under suspicion, or surveillance, no matter what he might think. The effect of his remark upon him, however, might tend to prove his connection with, or knowledge of, certain recent happenings. Tarzan saw a dull red creep up from beneath Gernois' collar. He was satisfied, and quickly changed the subject.

When the column rode south from Bou Saada the next morning there were half a dozen Arabs bringing up the rear.

"They are not attached to the command," replied Gerard in response to Tarzan's query. "They merely accompany us on the road for companionship."

Tarzan had learned enough about Arab character since he had been in Algeria to know that this was no real motive, for the Arab is never overfond of the companionship of strangers, and especially of French soldiers. So his suspicions were aroused, and he decided to keep a sharp eye on the little party that trailed behind the column at a distance of about a quarter of a mile. But they did not come close enough even during the halts to enable him to obtain a close scrutiny of them.

He had long been convinced that there were hired assassins on his trail, nor was he in great doubt but that Rokoff was at the bottom of the plot. Whether it was to be revenge for the several occasions in the past that Tarzan had defeated the Russian's purposes and humiliated him, or was in some way connected with his mission in the Gernois affair, he could not determine. If the latter, and it seemed probable since the evidence he had had that Gernois suspected him, then he had two rather powerful enemies to contend with, for there would be many opportunities in the wilds of Algeria, for which they were bound, to dispatch a suspected enemy quietly and without attracting suspicion.

After camping at Djelfa for two days the column moved to the southwest, from whence word had come that the marauders were operating against the tribes whose *douars* were situated at the foot of the mountains.

The little band of Arabs who had accompanied them from Bou Saada had disappeared suddenly the very night that orders had been given to prepare for the morrow's march from Djelfa. Tarzan made casual inquiries among the men, but none could tell him why they had left, or in what direction they had gone. He did not like the looks of it, especially in view of the fact that he had seen Gernois in conversation with one of them some half hour after Captain Gerard had issued his instructions relative to the new move. Only Gernois and Tarzan knew the direction of the proposed march. All the soldiers knew was that they were to be prepared to break camp early the next morning. Tarzan wondered if Gernois could have revealed their destination to the Arabs.

Late that afternoon they went into camp at a little oasis in which was the *douar* of a sheik whose flocks were being stolen, and whose herdsmen were being killed. The Arabs came out of their goatskin tents, and surrounded the soldiers, asking many questions in the native tongue, for the soldiers were themselves natives. Tarzan, who, by this time, with the assistance of Abdul, had picked up quite a smattering of Arab, questioned one of the younger men who had accompanied the sheik while the latter paid his respects to Captain Gerard.

No, he had seen no party of six horsemen riding from the direction of Djelfa. There were other oases scattered about—possibly they had been journeying to one of these. Then there were the marauders in the mountains above —they often rode north to Bou Saada in small parties, and even as far as Aumale and Bouira. It might indeed have been a few marauders returning to the band from a pleasure trip to one of these cities.

Early the next morning Captain Gerard split his command in two, giving Lieutenant Gernois command of one party, while he headed the other. They were to scour the mountains upon opposite sides of the plain.

"And with which detachment will Monsieur Tarzan ride?" asked the captain. "Or maybe it is that monsieur does not care to hunt marauders?"

"Oh, I shall be delighted to go," Tarzan hastened to explain. He was wondering what excuse he could make to accompany Gernois. His embarrassment was short-lived, and was relieved from a most unexpected source. It was Gernois himself who spoke.

"If my captain will forego the pleasure of Monsieur Tarzan's company for this once, I shall esteem it an honor indeed to have monsieur ride with me today," he said, nor was his tone lacking in cordiality. In fact, Tarzan imagined that he had overdone it a trifle, but, even so, he was both astounded and pleased, hastening to express his delight at the arrangement.

And so it was that Lieutenant Gernois and Tarzan rode off side by side at the head of the little detachment of *spahis*. Gernois' cordiality was short-lived. No sooner had they ridden out of sight of Captain Gerard and his men than he lapsed once more into his accustomed taciturnity. As they advanced the ground became rougher. Steadily it ascended toward the mountains, into which they filed through a narrow cañon close to noon. By the side of a little rivulet Gernois called the midday halt. Here the men prepared and ate their frugal meal, and refilled their canteens.

After an hour's rest they advanced again along the cañon, until they presently came to a little valley, from which several rocky gorges diverged. Here they halted, while Gernois minutely examined the surrounding heights from the center of the depression.

"We shall separate here," he said, "several riding into each of these gorges," and then he commenced to detail his various squads and issue instructions to the non-commissioned officers who were to command them. When he had done he turned to Tarzan. "Monsieur will be so good as to remain here until we return."

Tarzan demurred, but the officer cut him short. "There may be fighting for one of these sections," he said, "and troops cannot be embarrassed by civilian noncombatants during action."

"But, my dear lieutenant," expostulated Tarzan, "I am most ready and willing to place myself under command of yourself or any of your sergeants or corporals, and to fight in the ranks as they direct. It is what I came for."

"I should be glad to think so," retorted Gernois, with a sneer he made no attempt to disguise. Then shortly: "You are under my orders, and they are that you remain here until we return. Let that end the matter," and he turned and spurred away at the head of his men. A moment later Tarzan found himself alone in the midst of a desolate mountain fastness.

The sun was hot, so he sought the shelter of a nearby tree, where he tethered his horse, and sat down upon the ground to smoke. Inwardly he swore at Gernois for the trick he had played upon him. A mean little revenge, thought Tarzan, and then suddenly it occurred to him that the man would not be such a fool as to antagonize him through a trivial annoyance of so petty a description. There must be something deeper than this behind it. With the thought he arose and removed his rifle from its boot. He looked to its loads and saw that the magazine was full. Then he inspected his revolver. After this preliminary precaution he scanned the surrounding heights and the mouths of the several gorges —he was determined that he should not be caught napping.

The sun sank lower and lower, yet there was no sign of returning *spahis*. At last the valley was submerged in shadow. Tarzan was too proud to go back to camp until he had given the detachment ample time to return to the valley, which he thought was to have been their rendezvous. With the closing in of night he felt safer from attack, for he was at home in the dark. He knew that none might approach him so cautiously as to elude those alert and sensitive ears of his; then there were his eyes, too, for he could see well at night; and his nose, if they came toward him from up-wind, would apprise him of the approach of an enemy while they were still a great way off.

So he felt that he was in little danger, and thus lulled to a sense of security he fell asleep, with his back against the tree.

He must have slept for several hours, for when he was suddenly awakened by the frightened snorting and plunging of his horse the moon was shining full upon the little valley, and there, not ten paces before him, stood the grim cause of the terror of his mount.

Superb, majestic, his graceful tail extended and quivering, and his two eyes of fire riveted full upon his prey, stood Numa *el adrea*, the black lion. A little thrill of joy tingled through Tarzan's nerves. It was like meeting an old friend after years of separation. For a moment he sat rigid to enjoy the magnificent spectacle of this lord of the wilderness.

But now Numa was crouching for the spring. Very slowly Tarzan raised his gun to his shoulder. He had never killed a large animal with a gun in all his life—heretofore he had depended upon his spear, his poisoned arrows, his rope, his knife, or his bare hands. Instinctively he wished that he had his arrows and his knife—he would have felt surer with them.

Numa was lying quite flat upon the ground now, presenting only his head. Tarzan would have preferred to fire a little from one side, for he knew what terrific damage the lion could do if he lived two minutes, or even a minute after he was hit. The horse stood trembling in terror at Tarzan's back. The ape-man took a cautious step to one side—Numa but followed him with his eyes. Another step he took, and then another. Numa had not moved. Now he could aim at a point between the eye and the ear.

His finger tightened upon the trigger, and as he fired Numa sprang. At the same instant the terrified horse made a last frantic effort to escape—the tether parted, and he went careening down the cañon toward the desert.

No ordinary man could have escaped those frightful claws when Numa sprang from so short a distance, but Tarzan was no ordinary man. From earliest childhood his muscles had been trained by the fierce exigencies of his existence to act with the rapidity of thought. As quick as was *el adrea,* Tarzan of the Apes was quicker, and so the great beast crashed against a tree where he had expected to feel the soft flesh of man, while Tarzan, a couple of paces to the right, pumped another bullet into him that brought him clawing and roaring to his side.

Twice more Tarzan fired in quick succession, and then *el adrea* lay still and roared no more. It was no longer Monsieur Jean Tarzan; it was Tarzan of the Apes that put a savage foot upon the body of his savage kill, and, raising his face to the full moon, lifted his mighty voice in the weird and terrible challenge of his kind—a bull ape had made his kill. And the wild things in the wild mountains stopped in their hunting, and trembled at this new and awful voice, while down in the desert the children of the wilderness came out of their goatskin tents and looked toward the mountains, wondering what new and savage scourge had come to devastate their flocks.

A half mile from the valley in which Tarzan stood, a score of white-robed figures, bearing long, wicked-looking guns, halted at the sound, and looked at one another with questioning eyes. But presently, as it was not repeated, they took up their silent, stealthy way toward the valley.

Tarzan was now confident that Gernois had no intention

of returning for him, but he could not fathom the object that had prompted the officer to desert him, yet leave him free to return to camp. His horse gone, he decided that it would be foolish to remain longer in the mountains, so he set out toward the desert.

He had scarcely entered the confines of the cañon when the first of the white-robed figures emerged into the valley upon the opposite side. For a moment they scanned the little depression from behind sheltering bowlders, but when they had satisfied themselves that it was empty they advanced across it. Beneath the tree at one side they came upon the body of *el adrea.* With muttered exclamations they crowded about it. Then, a moment later, they hurried down the cañon which Tarzan was threading a brief distance in advance of them. They moved cautiously and in silence, taking advantage of shelter, as men do who are stalking man.

10

Through the Valley of the Shadow

As Tarzan walked down the wild cañon beneath the brilliant African moon the call of the jungle was strong upon him. The solitude and the savage freedom filled his heart with life and buoyancy. Again he was Tarzan of the Apes—every sense alert against the chance of surprise by some jungle enemy—yet treading lightly and with head erect, in proud consciousness of his might.

The nocturnal sounds of the mountains were new to him, yet they fell upon his ears like the soft voice of a half-forgotten love. Many he intuitively sensed—ah, there was one that was familiar indeed; the distant coughing of Sheeta, the leopard; but there was a strange note in the final wail which made him doubt. It was a panther he heard.

Presently a new sound—a soft, stealthy sound—obtruded itself among the others. No human ears other than the ape-man's would have detected it. At first he did not translate it, but finally he realized that it came from the bare feet of a number of human beings. They were behind him, and they were coming toward him quietly. He was being stalked.

In a flash he knew why he had been left in that little valley by Gernois; but there had been a hitch in the arrangements—the men had come too late. Closer and closer came the footsteps. Tarzan halted and faced them, his rifle ready in his hand. Now he caught a fleeting glimpse of a white burnoose. He called aloud in French, asking what they would of him. His reply was the flash of a long gun, and with the sound of the shot Tarzan of the Apes plunged forward upon his face.

The Arabs did not rush out immediately; instead, they waited to be sure that their victim did not rise. Then they came rapidly from their concealment, and bent over him. It was soon apparent that he was not dead. One of the men put the muzzle of his gun to the back of Tarzan's head to finish him, but another waved him aside. "If we bring him alive the reward is to be greater," explained the latter.

So they bound his hands and feet, and, picking him up, placed him on the shoulders of four of their number. Then the march was resumed toward the desert. When they had come out of the mountains they turned toward the south, and about daylight came to the spot where their horses stood in care of two of their number.

From here on their progress was more rapid. Tarzan, who had regained consciousness, was tied to a spare horse, which they evidently had brought for the purpose. His wound was but a slight scratch, which had furrowed the flesh across his temple. It had stopped bleeding, but the dried and clotted blood smeared his face and clothing. He had said no word since he had fallen into the hands of these Arabs, nor had they addressed him other than to issue a few brief commands to him when the horses had been reached.

For six hours they rode rapidly across the burning desert, avoiding the oases near which their way led. About noon they came to a *douar* of about twenty tents. Here they halted, and as one of the Arabs was releasing the alfa-grass ropes which bound him to his mount they were surrounded by a mob of men, women, and children. Many of the tribe, and more especially the women, appeared to take delight in heaping insults upon the prisoner, and some had even gone so far as to throw stones at him and strike him with sticks, when an old sheik appeared and drove them away.

"Ali-ben-Ahmed tells me," he said, "that this man sat alone in the mountains and slew *el adrea*. What the business of the stranger who sent us after him may be, I know not, and what he may do with this man when we turn him over to him, I care not; but the prisoner is a brave man, and while he is in our hands he shall be treated with the respect that be due one who hunts *the lord with the large head* alone and by night—and slays him."

Tarzan had heard of the respect in which Arabs held a lion-killer, and he was not sorry that chance had played into his hands thus favorably to relieve him of the petty tortures of the tribe. Shortly after this he was taken to a goatskin tent upon the upper side of the *douar*. There he was fed, and then, securely bound, was left lying on a piece of native carpet, alone in the tent.

He could see a guard sitting before the door of his frail prison, but when he attempted to force the stout bonds that held him he realized that any extra precaution on the part of his captors was quite unnecessary; not even his giant muscles could part those numerous strands.

Just before dusk several men approached the tent where he lay, and entered it. All were in Arab dress, but presently one of the number advanced to Tarzan's side, and as he let the folds of cloth that had hidden the lower half of his face fall away the ape-man saw the malevolent features of Nikolas Rokoff. There was a nasty smile on the bearded lips.

"Ah, Monsieur Tarzan," he said, "this is indeed a pleasure. But why do you not rise and greet your guest?" Then, with an ugly oath, "Get up, you dog!" and, drawing back his booted foot, he kicked Tarzan heavily in the side. "And here is another, and another, and another," he continued, as he kicked Tarzan about the face and side. "One for each of the injuries you have done me."

The ape-man made no reply—he did not even deign to look upon the Russian again after the first glance of recognition. Finally the sheik, who had been standing a mute and frowning witness of the cowardly attack, intervened.

"Stop!" he commanded. "Kill him if you will, but I will see no brave man subjected to such indignities in my presence. I have half a mind to turn him loose, that I may see how long you would kick him then."

This threat put a sudden end to Rokoff's brutality, for he had no craving to see Tarzan loosed from his bonds while he was within reach of those powerful hands.

"Very well," he replied to the Arab; "I shall kill him presently."

"Not within the precincts of my *douar*," returned the

sheik. "When he leaves here he leaves alive. What you do with him in the desert is none of my concern, but I shall not have the blood of a Frenchman on the hands of my tribe on account of another man's quarrel—they would send soldiers here and kill many of my people, and burn our tents and drive away our flocks."

"As you say," growled Rokoff. "I'll take him out into the desert below the *douar,* and dispatch him."

"You will take him a day's ride from my country," said the sheik, firmly, "and some of my children shall follow you to see that you do not disobey me—otherwise there may be two dead Frenchmen in the desert."

Rokoff shrugged. "Then I shall have to wait until the morrow—it is already dark."

"As you will," said the sheik. "But by an hour after dawn you must be gone from my *douar*. I have little liking for unbelievers, and none at all for a coward."

Rokoff would have made some kind of retort, but he checked himself, for he realized that it would require but little excuse for the old man to turn upon him. Together they left the tent. At the door Rokoff could not resist the temptation to turn and fling a parting taunt at Tarzan.

"Sleep well, monsieur," he said, "and do not forget to pray well, for when you die tomorrow it will be in such agony that you will be unable to pray for blaspheming."

No one had bothered to bring Tarzan either food or water since noon, and consequently he suffered considerably from thirst. He wondered if it would be worth while to ask his guard for water, but after making two or three requests without receiving any response, he decided that it would not.

Far up in the mountains he heard a lion roar. How much safer one was, he soliloquized, in the haunts of wild beasts than in the haunts of men. Never in all his jungle life had he been more relentlessly tracked down than in the past few months of his experience among civilized men. Never had he been any nearer death.

Again the lion roared. It sounded a little nearer. Tarzan felt the old, wild impulse to reply with the challenge of his kind. His kind? He had almost forgotten that he was a man and not an ape. He tugged at his bonds. God, if he could but get them near those strong teeth of his. He felt a wild wave of madness sweep over him as his efforts to regain his liberty met with failure.

Numa was roaring almost continually now. It was quite evident that he was coming down into the desert to hunt. It was the roar of a hungry lion. Tarzan envied him, for he was free. No one would tie him with ropes and slaughter him like a sheep. It was that which galled the ape-man. He did not fear to die, no—it was the humiliation of defeat before death, without even a chance to battle for his life.

It must be near midnight, thought Tarzan. He had several hours to live. Possibly he would yet find a way to take Rokoff with him on the long journey. He could hear the savage lord of the desert quite close by now. Possibly he sought his meat from among the penned animals within the *douar*.

For a long time silence reigned, then Tarzan's trained ears caught the sound of a stealthily moving body. It came from the side of the tent nearest the mountains—the back. Nearer and nearer it came. He waited, listening intently, for it to pass. For a time there was silence without, such a terrible silence that Tarzan was surprised that he did not hear the breathing of the animal he felt sure must be crouching close to the back wall of his tent.

There! It is moving again. Closer it creeps. Tarzan turns his head in the direction of the sound. It is very dark within the tent. Slowly the back rises from the ground, forced up by the head and shoulders of a body that looks all black in the semi-darkness. Beyond is a faint glimpse of the dimly starlit desert.

A grim smile plays about Tarzan's lips. At least Rokoff will be cheated. How mad he will be! And death will be more merciful than he could have hoped for at the hands of the Russian.

Now the back of the tent drops into place, and all is darkness again—whatever it is is inside the tent with him. He hears it creeping close to him—now it is beside him. He closes his eyes and waits for the mighty paw. Upon his upturned face falls the gentle touch of a soft hand groping in the dark, and then a girl's voice in a scarcely audible whisper pronounces his name.

"Yes, it is I," he whispers in reply. "But in the name of Heaven who are you?"

"The Ouled-Nail of Sisi Aissa," came the answer. While she spoke Tarzan could feel her working about his bonds. Occasionally the cold steel of a knife touched his flesh. A moment later he was free.

"Come!" she whispered.

On hands and knees he followed her out of the tent by the way she had come. She continued crawling thus flat to the ground until she reached a little patch of shrub. There she halted until he gained her side. For a moment he looked at her before he spoke.

"I cannot understand," he said at last. "Why are you here? How did you know that I was a prisoner in that tent? How does it happen that it is you who have saved me?"

She smiled. "I have come a long way tonight," she said, "and we have a long way to go before we shall be out of danger. Come; I shall tell you all about it as we go."

Together they rose and set off across the desert in the direction of the mountains.

"I was not quite sure that I should ever reach you," she said at last. "*El adrea* is abroad tonight, and after I left the horses I think he winded me and was following—I was terribly frightened."

"What a brave girl," he said. "And you ran all that risk for a stranger—an alien—an unbeliever?"

She drew herself up very proudly.

"I am the daughter of the Sheik Kabour ben Saden," she answered. "I should be no fit daughter of his if I would not risk my life to save that of the man who saved mine while he yet thought that I was but a common Ouled-Nail."

"Nevertheless," he insisted, "you are a very brave girl. But how did you know that I was a prisoner back there?"

"Achmet-din-Taieb, who is my cousin on my father's side, was visiting some friends who belong to the tribe that captured you. He was at the *douar* when you were brought in. When he reached home he was telling us about the big Frenchman who had been captured by Ali-ben-Ahmed for another Frenchman who wished to kill him. From the description I knew that it must be you. My father was away. I tried to persuade some of the men to come and save you, but they would not do it, saying: 'Let the unbelievers kill one another if they wish. It is none of our affair, and if we go and interfere with Ali-ben-Ahmed's plans we shall only stir up a fight with our own people.'

"So when it was dark I came alone, riding one horse and leading another for you. They are tethered not far from here. By morning we shall be within my father's *douar*. He should be there himself by now—then let them come and try to take Kadour ben Saden's friend."

For a few moments they walked on in silence.

"We should be near the horses," she said. "It is strange that I do not see them here."

Then a moment later she stopped, with a little cry of consternation.

"They are gone!" she exclaimed. "It is here that I tethered them."

Tarzan stooped to examine the ground. He found that a large shrub had been torn up by the roots. Then he found something else. There was a wry smile on his face as he rose and turned toward the girl.

"*El adrea* has been here. From the signs, though, I rather think that his prey escaped him. With a little start they would be safe enough from him in the open."

There was nothing to do but continue on foot. The way led them across a low spur of the mountains, but the girl knew the trail as well as she did her mother's face. They walked in easy, swinging strides, Tarzan keeping a hand's breadth behind the girl's shoulder, that she might set the pace, and thus be less fatigued. As they walked they talked, occasionally stopping to listen for sounds of pursuit.

It was now a beautiful, moonlit night. The air was crisp and invigorating. Behind them lay the interminable vista of the desert, dotted here and there with an occasional oasis. The date palms of the little fertile spot they had just left, and the circle of goatskin tents, stood out in sharp relief against the yellow sand—a phantom paradise upon a phantom sea. Before them rose the grim and silent mountains. Tarzan's blood leaped in his veins. This was life! He looked down upon the girl beside him—a daughter of the desert walking across the face of a dead world with a son of the jungle. He smiled at the thought. He wished that he had had a sister, and that she had been like this girl. What a bully chum she would have been!

They had entered the mountains now, and were progressing more slowly, for the trail was steeper and very rocky.

For a few minutes they had been silent. The girl was wondering if they would reach her father's *douar* before the pursuit had overtaken them. Tarzan was wishing that they might walk on thus forever. If the girl were only a man they might. He longed for a friend who loved the same wild life that he loved. He had learned to crave companionship, but it was his misfortune that most of the men he knew preferred immaculate linen and their clubs to nakedness and the jungle. It was, of course, difficult to understand, yet it was very evident that they did.

The two had just turned a projecting rock around which the trail ran when they were brought to a sudden stop. There, before them, directly in the middle of the path, stood Numa, *el adrea,* the black lion. His green eyes looked very wicked, and he bared his teeth, and lashed his bay-black sides with his angry tail. Then he roared—the fearsome, terror-inspiring roar of the hungry lion which is also angry.

"Your knife," said Tarzan to the girl, extending his hand. She slipped the hilt of the weapon into his waiting palm. As his fingers closed upon it he drew her back and pushed her behind him. "Walk back to the desert as rapidly as you can. If you hear me call you will know that all is well, and you may return."

"It is useless," she replied, resignedly. "This is the end."

"Do as I tell you," he commanded. "Quickly! He is about to charge." The girl dropped back a few paces, where she stood watching for the terrible sight that she knew she should soon witness.

The lion was advancing slowly toward Tarzan, his nose to the ground, like a challenging bull, his tail extended now and quivering as though with intense excitement.

The ape-man stood, half crouching, the long Arab knife glistening in the moonlight. Behind him the tense figure of the girl, motionless as a carven statue. She leaned slightly forward, her lips parted, her eyes wide. Her only conscious thought was wonder at the bravery of the man who dared face with a puny knife the lord with the large head. A man of her own blood would have knelt in prayer and gone down beneath those awful fangs without resistance. In either case the result would be the same—it was inevitable; but she could not repress a thrill of admiration as her eyes rested upon the heroic figure before her. Not a tremor in the whole giant frame—his attitude as menacing and defiant as that of *el adrea* himself.

The lion was quite close to him now—but a few paces intervened—he crouched, and then, with a deafening roar, he sprang.

11

John Caldwell, London

As NUMA *el adrea* launched himself with widespread paws and bared fangs he looked to find this puny man as easy prey as the score who had gone down beneath him in the past. To him man was a clumsy, slow-moving, defenseless creature—he had little respect for him.

But this time he found that he was pitted against a creature as agile and as quick as himself. When his mighty frame struck the spot where the man had been he was no longer there.

The watching girl was transfixed by astonishment at the ease with which the crouching man eluded the great paws. And now, O Allah! He had rushed in behind *el adrea's* shoulder even before the beast could turn, and had grasped him by the mane. The lion reared upon his hind legs like a horse—Tarzan had known that he would do this, and he was ready. A giant arm encircled the black-maned throat, and once, twice, a dozen times a sharp blade darted in and out of the bay-black side behind the left shoulder.

Frantic were the leaps of Numa—awful his roars of rage and pain; but the giant upon his back could not be dislodged or brought within reach of fangs or talons in the brief interval of life that remained to the lord with the large head. He was quite dead when Tarzan of the Apes released his hold and arose. Then the daughter of the desert witnessed a thing that terrified her even more than had the presence of *el adrea*. The man placed a foot upon the carcass of his kill, and, with his handsome face raised toward the full moon, gave voice to the most frightful cry that ever had smote upon her ears.

With a little cry of fear she shrank away from him—she thought that the fearful strain of the encounter had driven him mad. As the last note of that fiendish challenge died out in the diminishing echoes of the distance the man dropped his eyes until they rested upon the girl.

Instantly his face was lighted by the kindly smile that was ample assurance of his sanity, and the girl breathed freely once again, smiling in response.

"What manner of man are you?" she asked. "The thing you have done is unheard of. Even now I cannot believe that it is possible for a lone man armed only with a knife to have fought hand to hand with *el adrea* and conquered him, unscathed—to have conquered him at all. And that cry—it was not human. Why did you do that?"

Tarzan flushed. "It is because I forget," he said, "sometimes, that I am a civilized man. When I kill it must be that I am another creature." He did not try to explain further, for it always seemed to him that a woman must look with loathing upon one who was yet so nearly a beast.

Together they continued their journey. The sun was an hour high when they came out into the desert again beyond the mountains. Beside a little rivulet they found the girl's horses grazing. They had come this far on their way home, and with the cause of their fear no longer present had stopped to feed.

With little trouble Tarzan and the girl caught them, and, mounting, rode out into the desert toward the *douar* of Sheik Kadour ben Saden.

No sign of pursuit developed, and they came in safety about nine o'clock to their destination. The sheik had but just returned. He was frantic with grief at the absence of his daughter, whom he thought had been again abducted by the marauders. With fifty men he was already mounted to go in search of her when the two rode into the *douar*.

His joy at the safe return of his daughter was only equaled by his gratitude to Tarzan for bringing her safely to him through the dangers of the night, and his thankfulness that she had been in time to save the man who had once saved her.

No honor that Kadour ben Saden could heap upon the ape-man in acknowledgment of his esteem and friendship was neglected. When the girl had recited the story of the slaying of *el adrea* Tarzan was surrounded by a mob of worshiping Arabs—it was a sure road to their admiration and respect.

The old sheik insisted that Tarzan remain indefinitely as his guest. He even wished to adopt him as a member of the tribe, and there was for some time a half-formed resolution in the ape-man's mind to accept and remain forever with these wild people, whom he understood and who seemed to understand him. His friendship and liking for the girl were potent factors in urging him toward an affirmative decision.

Had she been a man, he argued, he should not have hesitated, for it would have meant a friend after his own heart, with whom he could ride and hunt at will; but as it was they would be hedged by the conventionalities that are even more strictly observed by the wild nomads of the desert than by their more civilized brothers and sisters. And in a little while she would be married to one of these swarthy warriors, and there would be an end to their friendship. So he decided against the sheik's proposal, though he remained a week as his guest.

When he left, Kadour ben Saden and fifty white-robed warriors rode with him to Bou Saada. While they were mounting in the *douar* of Kadour ben Saden the morning of their departure, the girl came to bid farewell to Tarzan.

"I have prayed that you would remain with us," she said simply, as he leaned from his saddle to clasp her hand in farewell, "and now I shall pray that you will return."

There was an expression of wistfulness in her beautiful eyes, and a pathetic droop at the corners of her mouth. Tarzan was touched.

"Who knows?" and then he turned and rode after the departing Arabs.

Outside Bou Saada he bade Kadour ben Saden and his men good-by, for there were reasons which made him wish to make his entry into the town as secret as possible, and when he had explained them to the sheik the latter concurred in his decision. The Arabs were to enter Bou Saada ahead of him, saying nothing as to his presence with them. Later Tarzan would come in alone, and go directly to an obscure native inn.

Thus, making his entrance after dark, as he did, he was not seen by any one who knew him, and reached the inn unobserved. After dining with Kadour ben Saden as his guest, he went to his former hotel by a roundabout way, and, coming in by a rear entrance, sought the proprietor, who seemed much surprised to see him alive.

Yes, there was mail for monsieur; he would fetch it. No, he would mention monsieur's return to no one. Presently he returned with a packet of letters. One was an order from his superior to lay off on his present work, and hasten to Cape Town by the first steamer he could get. His further instructions would be awaiting him there in the hands of another agent whose name and address were given. That was all—brief but explicit. Tarzan arranged to leave Bou Saada early the next morning. Then he started for the garrison to see Captain Gerard, whom the hotel man had told him had returned with his detachment the previous day.

He found the officer in his quarters. He was filled with surprise and pleasure at seeing Tarzan alive and well.

"When Lieutenant Gernois returned and reported that he had not found you at the spot that you had chosen to remain while the detachment was scouting, I was filled with alarm. We searched the mountains for days. Then came word that you had been killed and eaten by a lion. As proof your gun was brought to us. Your horse had returned to camp the second day after your disappearance. We could not doubt. Lieutenant Gernois was grief-stricken—he took all the blame upon himself. It was he who insisted on carrying on the search himself. It was he who found the Arab with your gun. He will be delighted to know that you are safe."

"Doubtless," said Tarzan, with a grim smile.

"He is down in the town now, or I should send for him," continued Captain Gerard. "I shall tell him as soon as he returns."

Tarzan let the officer think that he had been lost, wandering finally into the *douar* of Kadour ben Saden, who had escorted him back to Bou Saada. As soon as possible he bade the good officer adieu, and hastened back into the town. At the native inn he had learned through Kadour ben Saden a piece of interesting information. It told of a black-bearded white man who went always disguised as an Arab. For a time he had nursed a broken wrist. More recently he had been away from Bou Saada, but now he was back, and Tarzan knew his place of concealment. It was for there he headed.

Through narrow, stinking alleys, black as Erebus, he groped, and then up a rickety stairway, at the end of which was a closed door and a tiny, unglazed window. The window was high under the low eaves of the mud building. Tarzan could just reach the sill. He raised himself slowly until his eyes topped it. The room within was lighted, and at a table sat Rokoff and Gernois. Gernois was speaking.

"Rokoff, you are a devil!" he was saying. "You have hounded me until I have lost the last shred of my honor. You have driven me to murder, for the blood of that man Tarzan is on my hands. If it were not that that other devil's spawn, Paulvitch, still knew my secret, I should kill you here tonight with my bare hands."

Rokoff laughed. "You would not do that, my dear lieutenant," he said. "The moment I am reported dead by assassination that dear Alexis will forward to the minister of war full proof of the affair you so ardently long to conceal; and, further, will charge you with my murder. Come, be sensible. I am your best friend. Have I not protected your honor as though it were my own?"

Gernois sneered, and spat out an oath.

"Just one more little payment," continued Rokoff, "and the papers I wish, and you have my word of honor that I shall never ask another cent from you, or further information."

"And a good reason why," growled Gernois. "What you ask will take my last cent, and the only valuable military secret I hold. You ought to be paying me for the information, instead of taking both it and money, too."

"I am paying you by keeping a still tongue in my head," retorted Rokoff. "But let's have done. Will you, or will you not? I give you three minutes to decide. If you are not agreeable I shall send a note to your commandant tonight that will end in the degradation that Dreyfus suffered—the only difference being that he did not deserve it."

For a moment Gernois sat with bowed head. At length he arose. He drew two pieces of paper from his blouse.

"Here," he said hopelessly. "I had them ready, for I knew that there could be but one outcome." He held them toward the Russian.

Rokoff's cruel face lighted in malignant gloating. He seized the bits of paper.

"You have done well, Gernois," he said. "I shall not trouble you again—unless you happen to accumulate some more money or information," and he grinned.

"You never shall again, you dog!" hissed Gernois. "The next time I shall kill you. I came near doing it tonight. For an hour I sat with these two pieces of paper on my table before me ere I came here—beside them lay my loaded revolver. I was trying to decide which I should bring. Next time the choice shall be easier, for I already have decided. You had a close call tonight, Rokoff; do not tempt fate a second time."

Then Gernois rose to leave. Tarzan barely had time to drop to the landing and shrink back into the shadows on the far side of the door. Even then he scarcely hoped to elude detection. The landing was very small, and though he flattened himself against the wall at its far edge he was scarcely more than a foot from the doorway. Almost immediately it opened, and Gernois stepped out. Rokoff was behind him. Neither spoke. Gernois had taken perhaps three steps down the stairway when he halted and half turned, as though to retrace his steps.

Tarzan knew that discovery would be inevitable. Rokoff still stood on the threshold a foot from him, but he was looking in the opposite direction, toward Gernois. Then the officer evidently reconsidered his decision, and resumed his downward course. Tarzan could hear Rokoff's sigh of relief. A moment later the Russian went back into the room and closed the door.

Tarzan waited until Gernois had had time to get well out of hearing, then he pushed open the door and stepped into the room. He was on top of Rokoff before the man could rise from the chair where he sat scanning the paper Gernois had given him. As his eyes turned and fell upon the ape-man's face his own went livid.

"You!" he gasped.

"I," replied Tarzan.

"What do you want?" whispered Rokoff, for the look in the ape-man's eyes frightened him. "Have you come to kill me? You do not dare. They would guillotine you. You do not dare kill me."

"I dare kill you, Rokoff," replied Tarzan, "for no one knows that you are here or that I am here, and Paulvitch would tell them that it was Gernois. I heard you tell Gernois so. But that would not influence me, Rokoff. I would not care who knew that I had killed you; the pleasure of killing you would more than compensate for any punishment they might inflict upon me. You are the most despicable cur of a coward, Rokoff, I have ever heard of. You should be killed. I should love to kill you," and Tarzan approached closer to the man.

Rokoff's nerves were keyed to the breaking point. With a shriek he sprang toward an adjoining room, but the ape-man was upon his back while his leap was yet but half completed. Iron fingers sought his throat—the great coward squealed like a stuck pig, until Tarzan had shut off his wind. Then the ape-man dragged him to his feet, still choking him. The Russian struggled futilely—he was like a babe in the mighty grasp of Tarzan of the Apes.

Tarzan sat him in a chair, and long before there was danger of the man's dying he released his hold upon his throat. When the Russian's coughing spell had abated Tarzan spoke to him again.

"I have given you a taste of the suffering of death," he said. "But I shall not kill—this time. I am sparing you solely for the sake of a very good woman whose great misfortune it was to have been born of the same woman who gave birth to you. But I shall spare you only this once on her account.

Should I ever learn that you have again annoyed her or her husband—should you ever annoy me again—should I hear that you have returned to France or to any French possession, I shall make it my sole business to hunt you down and complete the choking I commenced tonight." Then he turned to the table, on which the two pieces of paper still lay. As he picked them up Rokoff gasped in horror.

Tarzan examined both the check and the other. He was amazed at the information the latter contained. Rokoff had partially read it, but Tarzan knew that no one could remember the salient facts and figures it held which made it of real value to an enemy of France.

"These will interest the chief of staff," he said, as he slipped them into his pocket.

Rokoff groaned. He did not dare curse aloud.

The next morning Tarzan rode north on his way to Bouira and Algiers. As he had ridden past the hotel Lieutenant Gernois was standing on the veranda. As his eyes discovered Tarzan he went white as chalk. The ape-man would have been glad had the meeting not occurred, but he could not avoid it. He saluted the officer as he rode past. Mechanically Gernois returned the salute, but those terrible, wide eyes followed the horseman, expressionless except for horror. It was as though a dead man looked upon a ghost.

At Sidi Aissa Tarzan met a French officer with whom he had become acquainted on the occasion of his recent sojourn in the town.

"You left Bou Saada early?" questioned the officer. "Then you have not heard about poor Gernois."

"He was the last man I saw as I rode away," replied Tarzan. "What about him?"

"He is dead. He shot himself about eight o'clock this morning."

Two days later Tarzan reached Algiers. There he found that he would have a two days' wait before he could catch a ship bound for Cape Town. He occupied his time in writing out a full report of his mission. The secret papers he had taken from Rokoff he did not inclose, for he did not dare trust them out of his own possession until he had been authorized to turn them over to another agent, or himself return to Paris with them.

As Tarzan boarded his ship after what seemed a most tedious wait to him, two men watched him from an upper deck. Both were fashionably dressed and smooth shaven. The taller of the two had sandy hair, but his eyebrows were very black. Later in the day they chanced to meet Tarzan on deck, but as one hurriedly called his companion's attention to something at sea their faces were turned from Tarzan as he passed, so that he did not notice their features. In fact, he had paid no attention to them at all.

Following the instructions of his chief, Tarzan had booked his passage under an assumed name—John Caldwell, London. He did not understand the necessity of this, and it caused him considerable speculation. He wondered what role he was to play in Cape Town.

"Well," he thought, "thank Heaven that I am rid of Rokoff. He was commencing to annoy me. I wonder if I am really becoming so civilized that presently I shall develop a set of nerves. He would give them to me if any one could, for he does not fight fair. One never knows through what new agency he is going to strike. It is as though Numa, the lion, had induced Tantor, the elephant, and Histah, the snake, to join him in attempting to kill me. I would then never have known what minute, or by whom, I was to be attacked next. But the brutes are more chivalrous than man—they do not stoop to cowardly intrigue."

At dinner that night Tarzan sat next to a young woman whose place was at the captain's left. The officer introduced them.

Miss Strong! Where had he heard the name before? It was very familiar. And then the girl's mother gave him the clew, for when she addressed her daughter she called her Hazel.

Hazel Strong! What memories the name inspired. It had been a letter to this girl, penned by the fair hand of Jane Porter, that had carried to him the first message from the woman he loved. How vividly he recalled the night he had stolen it from the desk in the cabin of his long-dead father, where Jane Porter had sat writing it late into the night, while he crouched in the darkness without. How terror-stricken she would have been that night had she known that the wild jungle beast squatted outside her window, watching her every move.

And this was Hazel Strong—Jane Porter's best friend!

12

Ships That Pass

LET us go back a few months to the little, windswept platform of a railway station in northern Wisconsin. The smoke of forest fires hangs low over the surrounding landscape, its acrid fumes smarting the eyes of a little party of six who stand waiting the coming of the train that is to bear them away toward the south.

Professor Archimedes Q. Porter, his hands clasped beneath the tails of his long coat, paces back and forth under the ever-watchful eye of his faithful secretary, Mr. Samuel T. Philander. Twice within the past few minutes he has started absent-mindedly across the tracks in the direction of a near-by swamp, only to be rescued and dragged back by the tireless Mr. Philander.

Jane Porter, the professor's daughter, is in strained and lifeless conversation with William Cecil Clayton and Tarzan of the Apes. Within the little waiting room, but a bare moment before, a confession of love and a renunciation had taken place that had blighted the lives and happiness of two of the party, but William Cecil Clayton, Lord Greystoke, was not one of them.

Behind Miss Porter hovered the motherly Esmeralda. She, too, was happy, for was she not returning to her beloved Maryland? Already she could see dimly through the fog of smoke the murky headlight of the oncoming engine. The men began to gather up the hand baggage. Suddenly Clayton exclaimed.

"By Jove! I've left my ulster in the waiting-room," and hastened off to fetch it.

"Good-bye, Jane," said Tarzan, extending his hand. "God bless you!"

"Good-bye," replied the girl faintly. "Try to forget me—no, not that—I could not bear to think that you had forgotten me."

"There is no danger of that, dear," he answered. "I wish to Heaven that I might forget. It would be so much easier than to go through life always remembering what might have been. You will be happy, though; I am sure you shall—you must be. You may tell the others of my decision to drive my car on to New York—I don't feel equal to bidding Clayton good-bye. I want always to remember him kindly, but I fear that I am too much of a wild beast yet to be trusted too long with the man who stands between me and the one person in all the world I want."

As Clayton stooped to pick up his coat in the waiting room his eyes fell on a telegraph blank lying face down upon the floor. He stooped to pick it up, thinking it might be a message of importance which some one had dropped. He glanced at it hastily, and then suddenly he forgot his coat, the approaching train—everything but that terrible little piece of yellow paper in his hand. He read it twice before he could fully grasp the terrific weight of meaning that it bore to him.

When he had picked it up he had been an English nobleman, the proud and wealthy possessor of vast estates—a moment later he had read it, and he knew that he was an untitled and penniless beggar. It was D'Arnot's cablegram to Tarzan, and it read:

Finger prints prove you Greystoke. Congratulations.
D'ARNOT.

He staggered as though he had received a mortal blow. Just then he heard the others calling to him to hurry—the train was coming to a stop at the little platform. Like a man dazed he gathered up his ulster. He would tell them about the cablegram when they were all on board the train. Then he ran out upon the platform just as the engine whistled twice in the final warning that precedes the first rumbling jerk of coupling pins. The others were on board, leaning out from the platform of a Pullman, crying to him to hurry. Quite five minutes elapsed before they were settled in their seats, nor was it until then that Clayton discovered that Tarzan was not with them.

"Where is Tarzan?" he asked Jane Porter. "In another car?"

"No," she replied; "at the last minute he determined to drive his machine back to New York. He is anxious to see more of America than is possible from a car window. He is returning to France, you know."

Clayton did not reply. He was trying to find the right words to explain to Jane Porter the calamity that had befallen him—and her. He wondered just what the effect of this knowledge would be on her. Would she still wish to marry him—to be plain Mrs. Clayton? Suddenly the awful sacrifice which one of them must make loomed large before his imagination. Then came the question: Will Tarzan claim his own? The ape-man had known the contents of the message before he calmly denied knowledge of his parentage! He had admitted that Kala, the ape, was his mother! Could it have been for love of Jane Porter?

There was no other explanation which seemed reasonable. Then, having ignored the evidence of the message, was it not reasonable to assume that he meant never to claim his birthright? If this were so, what right had he, William Cecil Clayton, to thwart the wishes, to balk the self-sacrifice of this strange man? If Tarzan of the Apes could do this thing to save Jane Porter from unhappiness, why should he, to whose care she was intrusting her whole future, do aught to jeopardize her interests?

And so he reasoned until the first generous impulse to proclaim the truth and relinquish his titles and his estates to their rightful owner was forgotten beneath the mass of sophistries which self-interest had advanced. But during the balance of the trip, and for many days thereafter, he was moody and distraught. Occasionally the thought obtruded itself that possibly at some later day Tarzan would regret his magnanimity, and claim his rights.

Several days after they reached Baltimore Clayton broached the subject of an early marriage to Jane.

"What do you mean by early?" she asked.

"Within the next few days. I must return to England at once—I want you to return with me, dear."

"I can't get ready so soon as that," replied Jane. "It will take a whole month, at least."

She was glad, for she hoped that whatever called him to England might still further delay the wedding. She had made a bad bargain, but she intended carrying her part loyally to the bitter end—if she could manage to secure a temporary reprieve, though, she felt that she was warranted in doing so. His reply disconcerted her.

"Very well, Jane," he said. "I am disappointed, but I shall let my trip to England wait a month; then we can go back together."

But when the month was drawing to a close she found still

another excuse upon which to hang a postponement, until at last, discouraged and doubting, Clayton was forced to go back to England alone.

The several letters that passed between them brought Clayton no nearer to a consummation of his hopes than he had been before, and so it was that he wrote directly to Professor Porter, and enlisted his services. The old man had always favored the match. He liked Clayton, and, being of an old southern family, he put rather an exaggerated value on the advantages of a title, which meant little or nothing to his daughter.

Clayton urged that the professor accept his invitation to be his guest in London, an invitation which included the professor's entire little family—Mr. Philander, Esmeralda, and all. The Englishman argued that once Jane was there, and home ties had been broken, she would not so dread the step which she had so long hesitated to take.

So the evening that he received Clayton's letter Professor Porter announced that they would leave for London the following week.

But once in London Jane Porter was no more tractable than she had been in Baltimore. She found one excuse after another, and when, finally, Lord Tennington invited the party to cruise around Africa in his yacht, she expressed the greatest delight in the idea, but absolutely refused to be married until they had returned to London. As the cruise was to consume a year at least, for they were to stop for indefinite periods at various points of interest, Clayton mentally anathematized Tennington for ever suggesting such a ridiculous trip.

It was Lord Tennington's plan to cruise through the Mediterranean, and the Red Sea to the Indian Ocean, and thus down the East Coast, putting in at every port that was worth the seeing.

And so it happened that on a certain day two vessels passed in the Strait of Gibraltar. The smaller, a trim white yacht, was speeding toward the east, and on her deck sat a young woman who gazed with sad eyes upon a diamond-studded locket which she idly fingered. Her thoughts were far away, in the dim, leafy fastness of a tropical jungle—and her heart was with her thoughts.

She wondered if the man who had given her the beautiful bauble, that had meant so much more to him than the intrinsic value which he had not even known could ever have meant to him, was back in his savage forest.

And upon the deck of the larger vessel, a passenger steamer passing toward the east, the man sat with another young woman, and the two idly speculated upon the identity of the dainty craft gliding so gracefully through the gentle swell of the lazy sea.

When the yacht had passed the man resumed the conversation that her appearance had broken off.

"Yes," he said, "I like America very much, and that means, of course, that I like Americans, for a country is only what its people make it. I met some very delightful people while I was there. I recall one family from your own city, Miss Strong, whom I liked particularly—Professor Porter and his daughter."

"Jane Porter!" exclaimed the girl. "Do you mean to tell me that you know Jane Porter? Why, she is the very best friend I have in the world. We were little children together—we have known each other for ages."

"Indeed!" he answered, smiling. "You would have difficulty in persuading any one of the fact who had seen either of you."

"I'll qualify the statement, then," she answered, with a laugh. "We have known each other for two ages—hers and mine. But seriously we are as dear to each other as sisters, and now that I am going to lose her I am almost heartbroken."

"Going to lose her?" exclaimed Tarzan. "Why, what do you mean? Oh, yes, I understand. You mean that now that she is married and living in England, you will seldom if ever see her."

"Yes," replied she; "and the saddest part of it all is that she is not marrying the man she loves. Oh, it is terrible. Marrying from a sense of duty! I think it is perfectly wicked, and I told her so. I have felt so strongly on the subject that although I was the only person outside of blood relations who was to have been asked to the wedding I would not let her invite me, for I should not have gone to witness the terrible mockery. But Jane Porter is peculiarly positive. She has convinced herself that she is doing the only honorable thing that she can do, and nothing in the world will ever prevent her from marrying Lord Greystoke except Greystoke himself, or death."

"I am sorry for her," said Tarzan.

"And I am sorry for the man she loves," said the girl, "for he loves her. I never met him, but from what Jane tells me he must be a very wonderful person. It seems that he was born in an African jungle, and brought up by fierce, anthropoid apes. He had never seen a white man or woman until Professor Porter and his party were marooned on the coast right at the threshold of his tiny cabin. He saved them from all manner of terrible beasts, and accomplished the most wonderful feats imaginable, and then to cap the climax he fell in love with Jane and she with him, though she never really knew it for sure until she had promised herself to Lord Greystoke."

"Most remarkable," murmured Tarzan, cudgeling his brain for some pretext upon which to turn the subject. He delighted in hearing Hazel Strong talk of Jane, but when he was the subject of the conversation he was bored and embarrassed. But he was soon given a respite, for the girl's mother joined them, and the talk became general.

The next few days passed uneventfully. The sea was quiet. The sky was clear. The steamer plowed steadily on toward the south without pause. Tarzan spent quite a little time with Miss Strong and her mother. They whiled away their hours on deck reading, talking, or taking pictures with Miss Strong's camera. When the sun had set they walked.

One day Tarzan found Miss Strong in conversation with a stranger, a man he had not seen on board before. As he approached the couple the man bowed to the girl and turned to walk away.

"Wait, Monsieur Thuran," said Miss Strong; "you must meet Mr. Caldwell. We are all fellow passengers, and should be acquainted."

The two men shook hands. As Tarzan looked into the eyes of Monsieur Thuran he was struck by the strange familiarity of their expression.

"I have had the honor of monsieur's acquaintance in the past, I am sure," said Tarzan, "though I cannot recall the circumstances."

Monsieur Thuran appeared ill at ease.

"I cannot say, monsieur," he replied. "It may be so. I have had that identical sensation myself when meeting a stranger."

"Monsieur Thuran has been explaining some of the mysteries of navigation to me," explained the girl.

Tarzan paid little heed to the conversation that ensued—he was attempting to recall where he had met Monsieur Thuran before. That it had been under peculiar circumstances he was positive. Presently the sun reached them, and the girl asked Monsieur Thuran to move her chair farther back into the shade. Tarzan happened to be watching the man at the time, and noticed the awkward manner in which he handled the chair—his left wrist was stiff. That clew was sufficient—a sudden train of associated ideas did the rest.

Monsieur Thuran had been trying to find an excuse to make a graceful departure. The lull in the conversation following the moving of their position gave him an opportunity to make his excuses. Bowing low to Miss Strong, and inclining his head to Tarzan, he turned to leave them.

"Just a moment," said Tarzan. "If Miss Strong will pardon me I will accompany you. I shall return in a moment, Miss Strong."

Monsieur Thuran looked uncomfortable. When the two men had passed out of the girl's sight, Tarzan stopped, laying a heavy hand on the other's shoulder.

"What is your game now, Rokoff?" he asked.

"I am leaving France as I promised you," replied the other, in a surly voice.

"I see you are," said Tarzan; "but I know you so well that I can scarcely believe that your being on the same boat with me is purely a coincidence. If I could believe it the fact that you are in disguise would immediately disabuse my mind of any such idea."

"Well," growled Rokoff, with a shrug, "I cannot see what you are going to do about it. This vessel flies the English flag. I have as much right on board her as you, and from the fact that you are booked under an assumed name I imagine that I have more right."

"We will not discuss it, Rokoff. All I wanted to say to you is that you must keep away from Miss Strong—she is a decent woman."

Rokoff turned scarlet.

"If you don't I shall pitch you overboard," continued Tarzan. "Do not forget that I am just waiting for some excuse." Then he turned on his heel, and left Rokoff standing there trembling with suppressed rage.

He did not see the man again for days, but Rokoff was not idle. In his stateroom with Paulvitch he fumed and swore, threatening the most terrible of revenges.

"I would throw him overboard tonight," he cried, "were I sure that those papers were not on his person. I cannot chance pitching them into the ocean with him. If you were not such a stupid coward, Alexis, you would find a way to enter his stateroom and search for the documents."

Paulvitch smiled. "You are supposed to be the brains of this partnership, my dear Nikolas," he replied. "Why do you not find the means to search Monsieur Caldwell's stateroom —eh?"

Two hours later fate was kind to them, for Paulvitch, who was ever on the watch, saw Tarzan leave his room without locking the door. Five minutes later Rokoff was stationed where he could give the alarm in case Tarzan returned, and Paulvitch was deftly searching the contents of the ape-man's luggage.

He was about to give up in despair when he saw a coat which Tarzan had just removed. A moment later he grasped an official envelope in his hand. A quick glance at its contents brought a broad smile to the Russian's face.

When he left the stateroom Tarzan himself could not have told that an article in it had been touched since he left it—Paulvitch was a past master in his chosen field.

When he handed the packet to Rokoff in the seclusion of their stateroom the larger man rang for a steward, and ordered a pint of champagne.

"We must celebrate, my dear Alexis," he said.

"It was luck, Nikolas," explained Paulvitch. "It is evident that he carries these papers always upon his person—just by chance he neglected to transfer them when he changed coats a few minutes since. But there will be the deuce to pay when he discovers his loss. I am afraid that he will immediately connect you with it. Now that he knows that you are on board he will suspect you at once."

"It will make no difference whom he suspects—after to-night," said Rokoff, with a nasty grin.

After Miss Strong had gone below that night Tarzan stood leaning over the rail looking far out to sea. Every night he had done this since he had come on board—sometimes he stood thus for an hour. And the eyes that had been watching his every movement since he had boarded the ship at Algiers knew that this was his habit.

Even as he stood there this night those eyes were on him. Presently the last straggler had left the deck. It was a clear night, but there was no moon—objects on deck were barely discernible.

From the shadows of the cabin two figures crept stealthily upon the ape-man from behind. The lapping of the waves against the ship's sides, the whirring of the propeller, the throbbing of the engines, drowned the almost soundless approach of the two.

They were quite close to him now, and crouching low, like tacklers on a gridiron. One of them raised his hand and lowered it, as though counting off seconds—one—two—three! As one man the two leaped for their victim. Each grasped a leg, and before Tarzan of the Apes, lightning though he was, could turn to save himself he had been pitched over the low rail and was falling into the Atlantic.

Hazel Strong was looking from her darkened port across the dark sea. Suddenly a body shot past her eyes from the deck above. It dropped so quickly into the dark waters below that she could not be sure of what it was—it might have been a man, she could not say. She listened for some outcry from above—for the always-fearsome call, "Man overboard!" but it did not come. All was silence on the ship above—all was silence in the sea below.

The girl decided that she had but seen a bundle of refuse thrown overboard by one of the ship's crew, and a moment later sought her berth.

13

The Wreck of the "Lady Alice"

THE next morning at breakfast Tarzan's place was vacant. Miss Strong was mildly curious, for Mr. Caldwell had always made it a point to wait that he might breakfast with her and her mother. As she was sitting on deck later Monsieur Thuran paused to exchange a half dozen pleasant words with her. He seemed in most excellent spirits—his manner was the extreme of affability. As he passed on Miss Strong thought what a very delightful man was Monsieur Thuran.

The day dragged heavily. She missed the quiet companionship of Mr. Caldwell—there had been something about him that had made the girl like him from the first; he had talked so entertainingly of the places he had seen—the peoples and their customs—the wild beasts; and he had always had a droll way of drawing striking comparisons between savage animals and civilized men that showed a considerable knowledge of the former, and a keen, though somewhat cynical, estimate of the latter.

When Monsieur Thuran stopped again to chat with her in the afternoon she welcomed the break in the day's monotony. But she had begun to become seriously concerned in Mr. Caldwell's continued absence; somehow she constantly associated it with the start she had had the night before, when the dark object fell past her port into the sea. Presently she broached the subject to Monsieur Thuran. Had he seen Mr. Caldwell today? He had not. Why?

"He was not at breakfast as usual, nor have I seen him once since yesterday," explained the girl.

Monsieur Thuran was extremely solicitous.

"I did not have the pleasure of intimate acquaintance with Mr. Caldwell," he said. "He seemed a most estimable gentleman, however. Can it be that he is indisposed, and has remained in his stateroom? It would not be strange."

"No," replied the girl, "it would not be strange, of course; but for some inexplicable reason I have one of those foolish feminine presentiments that all is not right with Mr. Caldwell. It is the strangest feeling—it is as though I knew that he was not on board the ship."

Monsieur Thuran laughed pleasantly. "Mercy, my dear Miss Strong," he said; "where in the world could he be then? We have not been within sight of land for days."

"Of course, it is ridiculous of me," she admitted. And then: "But I am not going to worry about it any longer; I am going to find out where Mr. Caldwell is," and she motioned to a passing steward.

"That may be more difficult than you imagine, my dear girl," thought Monsieur Thuran, but aloud he said: "By all means."

"Find Mr. Caldwell, please," she said to the steward, "and tell him that his friends are much worried by his continued absence."

"You are very fond of Mr. Caldwell?" suggested Monsieur Thuran.

"I think he is splendid," replied the girl. "And mamma is perfectly infatuated with him. He is the sort of man with whom one has a feeling of perfect security—no one could help but have confidence in Mr. Caldwell."

A moment later the steward returned to say that Mr. Caldwell was not in his stateroom. "I cannot find him, Miss Strong, and"—he hesitated—"I have learned that his berth was not occupied last night. I think that I had better report the matter to the captain."

"Most assuredly," exclaimed Miss Strong. "I shall go with you to the captain myself. It is terrible! I know that something awful has happened. My presentiments were not false, after all."

It was a very frightened young woman and an excited steward who presented themselves before the captain a few moments later. He listened to their stories in silence—a look of concern marking his expression as the steward assured him that he had sought for the missing passenger in every part of the ship that a passenger might be expected to frequent.

"And you are sure, Miss Strong, that you saw a body fall overboard last night?" he asked.

"There is not the slightest doubt about that," she answered. "I cannot say that it was a human body—there was no outcry. It might have been only what I thought it was—a bundle of refuse. But if Mr. Caldwell is not found on board I shall always be positive that it was he whom I saw fall past my port."

The captain ordered an immediate and thorough search of the entire ship from stem to stern—no nook or cranny was to be overlooked. Miss Strong remained in his cabin, waiting the outcome of the quest. The captain asked her many questions, but she could tell him nothing about the missing man other than what she had herself seen during their brief acquaintance on shipboard. For the first time she suddenly realized how very little indeed Mr. Caldwell had told her about himself or his past life. That he had been born in Africa and educated in Paris was about all she knew, and this meager information had been the result of her surprise that an Englishman should speak English with such a marked French accent.

"Did he ever speak of any enemies?" asked the captain.

"Never."

"Was he acquainted with any of the other passengers?"

"Only as he had been with me—through the circumstance of casual meeting as fellow shipmates."

"Er—was he, in your opinion, Miss Strong, a man who drank to excess?"

"I do not know that he drank at all—he certainly had not been drinking up to half an hour before I saw that body fall overboard," she answered, "for I was with him on deck up to that time."

"It is very strange," said the captain. "He did not look to me like a man who was subject to fainting spells, or anything of that sort. And even had he been it is scarcely credible that he should have fallen completely over the rail had he been taken with an attack while leaning upon it —he would rather have fallen inside, upon the deck. If he is not on board, Miss Strong, he was thrown overboard—and the fact that you heard no outcry would lead to the assumption that he was dead before he left the ship's deck—murdered."

The girl shuddered.

It was a full hour later that the first officer returned to report the outcome of the search.

"Mr. Caldwell is not on board, sir," he said.

"I fear that there is something more serious than accident here, Mr. Brently," said the captain. "I wish that you would make a personal and very careful examination of Mr. Caldwell's effects, to ascertain if there is any clew to a motive either for suicide or murder—sift the thing to the bottom."

"Aye, aye, sir!" responded Mr. Brently, and left to commence his investigation.

Hazel Strong was prostrated. For two days she did not leave her cabin, and when she finally ventured on deck she was very wan and white, with great, dark circles beneath her eyes. Waking or sleeping, it seemed that she constantly saw that dark body dropping, swift and silent, into the cold, grim sea.

Shortly after her first appearance on deck following the tragedy, Monsieur Thuran joined her with many expressions of kindly solicitude.

"Oh, but it is terrible, Miss Strong," he said. "I cannot rid my mind of it."

"Nor I," said the girl wearily. "I feel that he might have been saved had I but given the alarm."

"You must not reproach yourself, my dear Miss Strong," urged Monsieur Thuran. "It was in no way your fault. Another would have done as you did. Who would think that because something fell into the sea from a ship that it must necessarily be a man? Nor would the outcome have been different had you given an alarm. For a while they would have doubted your story, thinking it but the nervous hallucination of a woman—had you insisted it would have been too late to have rescued him by the time the ship could have been brought to a stop, and the boats lowered and rowed back miles in search of the unknown spot where the tragedy had occurred. No, you must not censure yourself. You have done more than any other of us for poor Mr. Caldwell—you were the only one to miss him. It was you who instituted the search."

The girl could not help but feel grateful to him for his kind and encouraging words. He was with her often—almost constantly for the remainder of the voyage—and she grew to like him very much indeed. Monsieur Thuran had learned that the beautiful Miss Strong, of Baltimore, was an American heiress—a very wealthy girl in her own right, and with future prospects that quite took his breath away when he contemplated them, and since he spent most of his time in that delectable pastime it is a wonder that he breathed at all.

It had been Monsieur Thuran's intention to leave the ship at the first port they touched after the disappearance of Tarzan. Did he not have in his coat pocket the thing he had taken passage upon this very boat to obtain? There was nothing more to detain him here. He could not return to the Continent fast enough, that he might board the first express for St. Petersburg.

But now another idea had obtruded itself, and was rapidly crowding his original intentions into the background. That American fortune was not to be sneezed at, nor was its possessor a whit less attractive.

"*Sapristi!* but she would cause a sensation in St. Petersburg." And he would, too, with the assistance of her inheritance.

After Monsieur Thuran had squandered a few million dollars, he discovered that the vocation was so entirely to his liking that he would continue on down to Cape Town, where he suddenly decided that he had pressing engagements that might detain him there for some time.

Miss Strong had told him that she and her mother were to visit the latter's brother there—they had not decided upon the duration of their stay, and it would probably run into months.

She was delighted when she found that Monsieur Thuran was to be there also.

"I hope that we shall be able to continue our acquaintance," she said. "You must call upon mamma and me as soon as we are settled."

Monsieur Thuran was delighted at the prospect, and lost no time in saying so. Mrs. Strong was not quite so favorably impressed by him as her daughter.

"I do not know why I should distrust him," she said to Hazel one day as they were discussing him. "He seems a perfect gentleman in every respect, but sometimes there is something about his eyes—a fleeting expression which I cannot describe, but which when I see it gives me a very uncanny feeling."

The girl laughed. "You are a silly dear, mamma," she said.

"I suppose so, but I am sorry that we have not poor Mr. Caldwell for company instead."

"And I, too," replied her daughter.

Monsieur Thuran became a frequent visitor at the home of Hazel Strong's uncle in Cape Town. His attentions were very marked, but they were so punctiliously arranged to meet the girl's every wish that she came to depend upon him more and more. Did she or her mother or a cousin require an escort—was there a little friendly service to be rendered, the genial and ubiquitous Monsieur Thuran was always available. Her uncle and his family grew to like him for his unfailing courtesy and willingness to be of service. Monsieur Thuran was becoming indispensable. At length, feeling the moment propitious, he proposed. Miss Strong was startled. She did not know what to say.

"I had never thought that you cared for me in any such way," she told him. "I have looked upon you always as a very dear friend. I shall not give you my answer now. Forget that you have asked me to be your wife. Let us go on as we have been—then I can consider you from an entirely different angle for a time. It may be that I shall discover that my feeling for you is more than friendship. I certainly have not thought for a moment that I loved you."

This arrangement was perfectly satisfactory to Monsieur Thuran. He deeply regretted that he had been hasty, but he had loved her for so long a time, and so devotedly, that he thought that every one must know it.

"From the first time that I saw you, Hazel," he said, "I have loved you. I am willing to wait, for I am certain that so great and pure a love as mine will be rewarded. All that I care to know is that you do not love another. Will you tell me?"

"I have never been in love in my life," she replied, and he was quite satisfied. On the way home that night he purchased a steam yacht, and built a million-dollar villa on the Black Sea.

The next day Hazel Strong enjoyed one of the happiest surprises of her life—she ran face to face upon Jane Porter as she was coming out of a jeweler's shop.

"Why, Jane Porter!" she exclaimed. "Where in the world did you drop from? Why, I can't believe my own eyes."

"Well, of all things!" cried the equally astonished Jane. "And here I have been wasting whole reams of perfectly good imagination picturing you in Baltimore—the very idea!" And she threw her arms about her friend once more, and kissed her a dozen times.

By the time mutual explanations had been made Hazel knew that Lord Tennington's yacht had put in at Cape Town for at least a week's stay, and at the end of that time was to continue on her voyage—this time up the West Coast—and so back to England. "Where," concluded Jane, "I am to be married."

"Then you are not married yet?" asked Hazel.

"Not yet," replied Jane, and then, quite irrelevantly, "I wish England were a million miles from here."

Visits were exchanged between the yacht and Hazel's relatives. Dinners were arranged, and trips into the surrounding country to entertain the visitors. Monsieur Thuran was a welcome guest at every function. He gave a dinner himself to the men of the party, and managed to ingratiate himself in the good will of Lord Tennington by many little acts of hospitality.

Monsieur Thuran had heard dropped a hint of something which might result from this unexpected visit of Lord Tennington's yacht, and he wanted to be counted in on it. Once when he was alone with the Englishman he took occasion to make it quite plain that his engagement to Miss Strong was to be announced immediately upon their return to America. "But not a word of it, my dear Tennington—not a word of it."

"Certainly, I quite understand, my dear fellow," Tennington had replied. "But you are to be congratulated—ripping girl, don't you know—really."

The next day it came. Mrs. Strong, Hazel, and Monsieur Thuran were Lord Tennington's guests aboard his yacht. Mrs. Strong had been telling them how much she had enjoyed her visit at Cape Town, and that she regretted that a letter just received from her attorneys in Baltimore had necessitated her cutting her visit shorter than they had intended.

"When do you sail?" asked Tennington.

"The first of the week, I think," she replied.

"Indeed?" exclaimed Monsieur Thuran. "I am very fortunate. I, too, have found that I must return at once, and now I shall have the honor of accompanying and serving you."

"That is nice of you, Monsieur Thuran," replied Mrs.

Strong. "I am sure that we shall be glad to place ourselves under your protection." But in the bottom of her heart was the wish that they might escape him. Why, she could not have told.

"By Jove!" ejaculated Lord Tennington, a moment later. "Bully idea, by Jove!"

"Yes, Tennington, of course," ventured Clayton; "it must be a bully idea if you had it, but what the deuce is it? Goin' to steam to China via the south pole?"

"Oh, I say now, Clayton," returned Tennington, "you needn't be so rough on a fellow just because you didn't happen to suggest this trip yourself—you've acted a regular bounder ever since we sailed.

"No, sir," he continued, "it's a bully idea, and you'll all say so. It's to take Mrs. Strong and Miss Strong, and Thuran, too, if he'll come, as far as England with us on the yacht. Now, isn't that a corker?"

"Forgive me, Tenny, old boy," cried Clayton. "It certainly *is* a corking idea—I never should have suspected you of it. You're quite sure it's original, are you?"

"And we'll sail the first of the week, or any other time that suits your convenience, Mrs. Strong," concluded the big-hearted Englishman, as though the thing were all arranged except the sailing date.

"Mercy, Lord Tennington, you haven't even given us an opportunity to thank you, much less decide whether we shall be able to accept your generous invitation," said Mrs. Strong.

"Why, of course you'll come," responded Tennington. "We'll make as good time as any passenger boat, and you'll be fully as comfortable; and, anyway, we all want you, and won't take no for an answer."

And so it was settled that they should sail the following Monday.

Two days out the girls were sitting in Hazel's cabin, looking at some prints she had had finished in Cape Town. They represented all the pictures she had taken since she had left America, and the girls were both engrossed in them, Jane asking many questions, and Hazel keeping up a perfect torrent of comment and explanation of the various scenes and people.

"And here," she said suddenly, "here's a man you know. Poor fellow, I have so often intended asking you about him, but I never have been able to think of it when we were together." She was holding the little print so that Jane did not see the face of the man it portrayed.

"His name was John Caldwell," continued Hazel. "Do you recall him? He said that he met you in America. He is an Englishman."

"I do not recollect the name," replied Jane. "Let me see the picture."

"The poor fellow was lost overboard on our trip down the coast," she said, as she handed the print to Jane.

"Lost over— Why, Hazel, Hazel—don't tell me that he is dead—drowned at sea! Hazel! Why don't you say that you are joking!" And before the astonished Miss Strong could catch her Jane Porter had slipped to the floor in a swoon.

After Hazel had restored her chum to consciousness she sat looking at her for a long time before either spoke.

"I did not know, Jane," said Hazel, in a constrained voice, "that you knew Mr. Caldwell so intimately that his death could prove such a shock to you."

"John Caldwell?" questioned Miss Porter. "You do not mean to tell me that you do not know who this man was, Hazel?"

"Why, yes, Jane; I know perfectly well who he was—his name was John Caldwell; he was from London."

"Oh, Hazel, I wish I could believe it," moaned the girl. "I wish I could believe it, but those features are burned so deep into my memory and my heart that I should recognize them anywhere in the world from among a thousand others, who might appear identical to any one but me."

"What do you mean, Jane?" cried Hazel, now thoroughly alarmed. "Who do you think it is?"

"I don't think, Hazel. I know that that is a picture of Tarzan of the Apes."

"Jane!"

"I cannot be mistaken. Oh, Hazel, are you sure that he is dead? Can there be no mistake?"

"I am afraid not, dear," answered Hazel sadly. "I wish I could think that you are mistaken, but now a hundred and one little pieces of corroborative evidence occur to me that meant nothing to me while I thought that he was John Caldwell, of London. He said that he had been born in Africa, and educated in France."

"Yes, that would be true," murmured Jane Porter dully.

"The first officer, who searched his luggage, found nothing to identify John Caldwell, of London. Practically all his belongings had been made, or purchased, in Paris. Everything that bore an initial was marked either with a 'T' alone, or with 'J. C. T.' We thought that he was traveling incognito under his first two names—the J. C. standing for John Caldwell."

"Tarzan of the Apes took the name Jean C. Tarzan," said Jane, in the same lifeless monotone. "And he is dead! Oh, Hazel, it is horrible! He died all alone in this terrible ocean! It is unbelievable that that brave heart should have ceased to beat—that those mighty muscles are quiet and cold forever! That he who was the personification of life and health and manly strength should be the prey of slimy, crawling things, that—" But she could go no further, and with a little moan she buried her head in her arms, and sank sobbing to the floor.

For days Miss Porter was ill, and would see no one except Hazel and the faithful Esmeralda. When at last she came on deck all were struck by the sad change that had taken place in her. She was no longer the alert, vivacious American beauty who had charmed and delighted all who came in contact with her. Instead she was a very quiet and sad little girl—with an expression of hopeless wistfulness that none but Hazel Strong could interpret.

The entire party strove their utmost to cheer and amuse her, but all to no avail. Occasionally the jolly Lord Tennington would wring a wan smile from her, but for the most part she sat with wide eyes looking out across the sea.

With Jane Porter's illness one misfortune after another seemed to attack the yacht. First an engine broke down, and they drifted for two days while temporary repairs were being made. Then a squall struck them unaware, that carried overboard nearly everything above deck that was portable. Later two of the seamen fell to fighting in the forecastle, with the result that one of them was badly wounded with a knife, and the other had to be put in irons. Then, to cap the climax, the mate fell overboard at night, and was drowned before help could reach him. The yacht cruised about the spot for ten hours, but no sign of the man was seen after he disappeared from the deck into the sea.

Every member of the crew and guests was gloomy and depressed after these series of misfortunes. All were apprehensive of worse to come, and this was especially true of the seamen who recalled all sorts of terrible omens and warnings that had occurred during the early part of the voyage, and which they could now clearly translate into the precursors of some grim and terrible tragedy to come.

Nor did the croakers have long to wait. The second night after the drowning of the mate the little yacht was suddenly wracked from stem to stern. About one o'clock in the morning there was a terrific impact that threw the slumbering guests and crew from berth and bunk. A mighty shudder ran through the frail craft; she lay far over to starboard; the engines stopped. For a moment she hung there with her decks at an angle of forty-five degrees—then, with a sullen, rending sound, she slipped back into the sea and righted.

Instantly the men rushed upon deck, followed closely by the women. Though the night was cloudy, there was little wind or sea, nor was it so dark but that just off the port bow a black mass could be discerned floating low in the water.

"A derelict," was the terse explanation of the officer of the watch.

Presently the engineer hurried on deck in search of the captain.

"That patch we put on the cylinder head's blown out, sir," he reported, "and she's makin' water fast for'ard on the port bow."

An instant later a seaman rushed up from below.

"My Gawd!" he cried. "Her whole bleedin' bottom's ripped out. She can't float twenty minutes."

"Shut up!" roared Tennington. "Ladies, go below and get some of your things together. It may not be so bad as that, but we may have to take to the boats. It will be safer to be prepared. Go at once, please. And, Captain Jerrold, send some competent man below, please, to ascertain the exact extent of the damage. In the meantime I might suggest that you have the boats provisioned."

The calm, low voice of the owner did much to reassure the entire party, and a moment later all were occupied with the duties he had suggested. By the time the ladies had returned to the deck the rapid provisioning of the boats had been about completed, and a moment later the officer who had gone below had returned to report. But his opinion was scarcely needed to assure the huddled group of men and women that the end of the *Lady Alice* was at hand.

"Well, sir?" said the captain, as his officer hesitated.

"I dislike to frighten the ladies, sir," he said, "but she can't float a dozen minutes, in my opinion. There's a hole in her you could drive a bally cow through, sir."

For five minutes the *Lady Alice* had been settling rapidly by the bow. Already her stern loomed high in the air, and foothold on the deck was of the most precarious nature. She carried four boats, and these were all filled and lowered away in safety. As they pulled rapidly from the stricken little vessel Jane Porter turned to have one last look at her. Just then there came a loud crash and an ominous rumbling and pounding from the heart of the ship—her machinery had broken loose, and was dashing its way toward the bow, tearing out partitions and bulkheads as it went—the stern rose rapidly high above them; for a moment she seemed to pause there—a vertical shaft protruding from the bosom of the ocean, and then swiftly she dove headforemost beneath the waves.

In one of the boats the brave Lord Tennington wiped a tear from his eye—he had not seen a fortune in money go down forever into the sea, but a dear, beautiful friend whom he had loved.

At last the long night broke, and a tropical sun smote down upon the rolling water. Jane Porter had dropped into a fitful slumber—the fierce light of the sun upon her upturned face awoke her. She looked about her. In the boat with her were three sailors, Clayton, and Monsieur Thuran. Then she looked for the other boats, but as far as the eye could reach there was nothing to break the fearful monotony of that waste of waters—they were alone in a small boat upon the broad Atlantic.

14

Back to the Primitive

AS TARZAN struck the water, his first impulse was to swim clear of the ship and possible danger from her propellers. He knew whom to thank for his present predicament, and as he lay in the sea, just supporting himself by a gentle movement of his hands, his chief emotion was one of chagrin that he had been so easily bested by Rokoff.

He lay thus for some time, watching the receding and rapidly diminishing lights of the steamer without it ever once occurring to him to call for help. He never had called for help in his life, and so it is not strange that he did not think of it now. Always had he depended upon his own prowess and resourcefulness, nor had there ever been since the days of Kala any to answer an appeal for succor. When it did occur to him it was too late.

There was, thought Tarzan, a possible one chance in a hundred thousand that he might be picked up, and an even smaller chance that he would reach land, so he determined that to combine what slight chances there were, he would swim slowly in the direction of the coast—the ship might have been closer in than he had known.

His strokes were long and easy—it would be many hours before those giant muscles would commence to feel fatigue. As he swam, guided toward the east by the stars, he noticed that he felt the weight of his shoes, and so he removed them. His trousers went next, and he would have removed his coat at the same time but for the precious papers in its pocket. To reassure himself that he still had them he slipped his hand in to feel, but to his consternation they were gone.

Now he knew that something more than revenge had prompted Rokoff to pitch him overboard—the Russian had managed to obtain possession of the papers Tarzan had wrested from him at Bou Saada. The ape-man swore softly, and let his coat and shirt sink into the Atlantic. Before many hours he had divested himself of his remaining garments, and was swimming easily and unencumbered toward the east.

The first faint evidence of dawn was paling the stars ahead of him when the dim outlines of a low-lying black mass loomed up directly in his track. A few strong strokes brought him to its side—it was the bottom of a wave-washed derelict. Tarzan clambered upon it—he would rest there until daylight at least. He had no intention to remain there inactive—a prey to hunger and thirst. If he must die he preferred dying in action while making some semblance of an attempt to save himself.

The sea was quiet, so that the wreck had only a gently undulating motion, that was soothing to the swimmer who had had no sleep for twenty hours. Tarzan of the Apes curled up upon the slimy timbers, and was soon asleep.

The heat of the sun awoke him early in the forenoon. His first conscious sensation was of thirst, which grew almost to the proportions of suffering with full returning consciousness; but a moment later it was forgotten in the joy of two almost simultaneous discoveries. The first was a mass of wreckage floating beside the derelict in the midst of which, bottom up, rose and fell an overturned lifeboat; the other was the faint, dim line of a far-distant shore showing on the horizon in the east.

Tarzan dove into the water, and swam around the wreck to the lifeboat. The cool ocean refreshed him almost as much as would a draft of water, so that it was with renewed vigor that he brought the smaller boat alongside the derelict, and, after many herculean efforts, succeeded in dragging it onto the slimy ship's bottom. There he righted and examined it—the boat was quite sound, and a moment later floated upright alongside the wreck. Then Tarzan selected several pieces of wreckage that might answer him as paddles, and presently was making good headway toward the far-off shore.

It was late in the afternoon by the time he came close enough to distinguish objects on land, or to make out the contour of the shore line. Before him lay what appeared to be the entrance to a little, landlocked harbor. The wooded point to the north was strangely familiar. Could it be possible that fate had thrown him up at the very threshold of his own beloved jungle! But as the bow of his boat entered the mouth of the harbor the last shred of doubt was cleared away, for there before him upon the farther shore, under the shadows of his primeval forest, stood his own cabin—built before his birth by the hand of his long-dead father, John Clayton, Lord Greystoke.

With long sweeps of his giant muscles Tarzan sent the little craft speeding toward the beach. Its prow had scarcely touched when the ape-man leaped to shore—his heart beat fast in joy and exultation as each long-familiar object came beneath his roving eyes—the cabin, the beach, the little brook, the dense jungle, the black, impenetrable forest. The myriad birds in their brilliant plumage—the gorgeous tropical blooms upon the festooned creepers falling in great loops from the giant trees.

Tarzan of the Apes had come into his own again, and that all the world might know it he threw back his young head, and gave voice to the fierce, wild challenge of his tribe. For a moment silence reigned upon the jungle, and then, low and weird, came an answering challenge—it was the deep roar of Numa, the lion; and from a great distance, faintly, the fearsome answering bellow of a bull ape.

Tarzan went to the brook first, and slaked his thirst. Then he approached his cabin. The door was still closed and latched as he and D'Arnot had left it. He raised the latch and entered. Nothing had been disturbed; there were the table, the bed, and the little crib built by his father—the shelves and cupboards just as they had stood for over twenty-three years—just as he had left them nearly two years before.

His eyes satisfied, Tarzan's stomach began to call aloud for attention—the pangs of hunger suggested a search for food. There was nothing in the cabin, nor had he any weapons; but upon a wall hung one of his old grass ropes. It had been many times broken and spliced, so that he had discarded it for a better one long before. Tarzan wished that he had a knife. Well, unless he was mistaken he should have that and a spear and bows and arrows before another sun had set—the rope would take care of that, and in the meantime it must be made to procure food for him. He coiled it carefully, and, throwing it about his shoulder, went out, closing the door behind him.

Close to the cabin the jungle commenced, and into it Tarzan of the Apes plunged, wary and noiseless—once more a savage beast hunting its food. For a time he kept to the ground, but finally, discovering no spoor indicative of nearby meat, he took to the trees. With the first dizzy swing from tree to tree all the old joy of living swept over him. Vain regrets and dull heartache were forgotten. Now was he living. Now, indeed, was the true happiness of perfect freedom his. Who would go back to the stifling, wicked cities of civilized man when the mighty reaches of the great jungle offered peace and liberty? Not he.

While it was yet light Tarzan came to a drinking place by the side of a jungle river. There was a ford there, and for countless ages the beasts of the forest had come down to drink at this spot. Here of a night might always be found either Sabor or Numa crouching in the dense foliage of the surrounding jungle awaiting an antelope or a water buck for their meal. Here came Horta, the boar, to water, and here came Tarzan of the Apes to make a kill, for he was very empty.

On a low branch he squatted above the trail. For an hour he waited. It was growing dark. A little to one side of the ford in the densest thicket he heard the faint sound of padded feet, and the brushing of a huge body against tall grasses and tangled creepers. None other than Tarzan might have heard it, but the ape-man heard and translated—it was Numa, the lion, on the same errand as himself. Tarzan smiled.

Presently he heard an animal approaching warily along the trail toward the drinking place. A moment more and it came in view—it was Horta, the boar. Here was delicious meat—and Tarzan's mouth watered. The grasses where Numa lay were very still now—ominously still. Horta passed beneath Tarzan—a few more steps and he would be within the radius of Numa's spring. Tarzan could imagine how old Numa's eyes were shining—how he was already sucking in his breath for the awful roar which would freeze his prey for the brief instant between the moment of the spring and the sinking of terrible fangs into splintering bones.

But as Numa gathered himself, a slender rope flew through the air from the low branches of a near-by tree. A noose settled about Horta's neck. There was a frightened grunt, a squeal, and then Numa saw his quarry dragged backward up the trail, and, as he sprang, Horta, the boar, soared upward beyond his clutches into the tree above, and a mocking face looked down and laughed into his own.

Then indeed did Numa roar. Angry, threatening, hungry, he paced back and forth beneath the taunting ape-man. Now he stopped, and, rising on his hind legs against the stem of the tree that held his enemy, sharpened his huge claws upon the bark, tearing out great pieces that laid bare the white wood beneath.

And in the meantime Tarzan had dragged the struggling Horta to the limb beside him. Sinewy fingers completed the work the choking noose had commenced. The ape-man had no knife, but nature had equipped him with the means of tearing his food from the quivering flank of his prey, and gleaming teeth sank into the succulent flesh while the raging lion looked on from below as another enjoyed the dinner that he had thought already his.

It was quite dark by the time Tarzan had gorged himself. Ah, but it had been delicious! Never had he quite accustomed himself to the ruined flesh that civilized men had served him, and in the bottom of his savage heart there had constantly been the craving for the warm meat of the fresh kill, and the rich, red blood.

He wiped his bloody hands upon a bunch of leaves, slung the remains of his kill across his shoulder, and swung off through the middle terrace of the forest toward his cabin, and at the same instant Jane Porter and William Cecil Clayton arose from a sumptuous dinner upon the *Lady Alice,* thousands of miles to the east, in the Indian Ocean.

Beneath Tarzan walked Numa, the lion, and when the ape-man deigned to glance downward he caught occasional glimpses of the baleful green eyes following through the darkness. Numa did not roar now—instead, he moved stealthily, like the shadow of a great cat; but yet he took no step that did not reach the sensitive ears of the ape-man.

Tarzan wondered if he would stalk him to his cabin door. He hoped not, for that would mean a night's sleep curled in the crotch of a tree, and he much preferred the bed of grasses within his own abode. But he knew just the tree and the most comfortable crotch, if necessity demanded that he sleep out. A hundred times in the past some great jungle cat had followed him home, and compelled him to seek shelter in this same tree, until another mood or the rising sun had sent his enemy away.

But presently Numa gave up the chase and, with a series of blood-curdling moans and roars, turned angrily back in search of another and an easier dinner. So Tarzan came to his cabin unattended, and a few moments later was curled up in the mildewed remnants of what had once been a bed of grasses. Thus easily did Monsieur Jean C. Tarzan slough the thin skin of his artificial civilization, and sink happy and contented into the deep sleep of the wild beast that has fed to repletion. Yet a woman's "yes" would have bound him to that other life forever, and made the thought of this savage existence repulsive.

Tarzan slept late into the following forenoon, for he had been very tired from the labors and exertion of the long night and day upon the ocean, and the jungle jaunt that had brought into play muscles that he had scarce used for nearly two years. When he awoke he ran to the brook first to drink. Then he took a plunge into the sea, swimming about for a quarter of an hour. Afterward he returned to his cabin, and breakfasted off the flesh of Horta. This done, he buried the balance of the carcass in the soft earth outside the cabin, for his evening meal.

Once more he took his rope and vanished into the jungle. This time he hunted nobler quarry—man; although had you asked him his own opinion he could have named a dozen other denizens of the jungle which he considered far the superiors in nobility of the men he hunted. Today Tarzan was in quest of weapons. He wondered if the women and children had remained in Mbonga's village after the punitive expedition from the French cruiser had massacred all the warriors in revenge for D'Arnot's supposed death. He hoped that he should find warriors there, for he knew not how long a quest he should have to make were the village deserted.

The ape-man traveled swiftly through the forest, and about noon came to the site of the village, but to his disappointment found that the jungle had overgrown the plantain fields and that the thatched huts had fallen in decay. There was no sign of man. He clambered about among the ruins for half an hour, hoping that he might discover some forgotten weapon, but his search was without fruit, and so he took up his quest once more, following up the stream, which flowed from a southeasterly direction. He knew that near fresh water he would be most likely to find another settlement.

As he traveled he hunted as he had hunted with his ape people in the past, as Kala had taught him to hunt, turning over rotted logs to find some toothsome vermin, running high into the trees to rob a bird's nest, or pouncing upon a tiny rodent with the quickness of a cat. There were other things that he ate, too, but the less detailed the account of an ape's diet, the better—and Tarzan was again an ape, the same fierce, brutal anthropoid that Kala had taught him to be, and that he had been for the first twenty years of his life.

Occasionally he smiled as he recalled some friend who might even at the moment be sitting placid and immaculate within the precincts of his select Parisian club—just as Tarzan had sat but a few months before; and then he would stop, as though turned suddenly to stone as the gentle breeze carried to his trained nostrils the scent of some new prey or a formidable enemy.

That night he slept far inland from his cabin, securely wedged into the crotch of a giant tree, swaying a hundred feet above the ground. He had eaten heartily again—this time from the flesh of Bara, the deer, who had fallen prey to his quick noose.

Early the next morning he resumed his journey, always following the course of the stream. For three days he continued his quest, until he had come to a part of the jungle in which he never before had been. Occasionally upon the higher ground the forest was much thinner, and in the far distance through the trees he could see ranges of mighty mountains, with wide plains in the foreground. Here, in the open spaces, were new game—countless antelope and vast herds of zebra. Tarzan was entranced—he would make a long visit to this new world.

On the morning of the fourth day his nostrils were suddenly surprised by a faint new scent. It was the scent of man, but yet a long way off. The ape-man thrilled with pleasure. Every sense was on the alert as with crafty stealth he moved quickly through the trees, up-wind, in the direction of his prey. Presently he came upon it—a lone warrior treading softly through the jungle.

Tarzan followed close above his quarry, waiting for a clearer space in which to hurl his rope. As he stalked the unconscious man, new thoughts presented themselves to the ape-man—thoughts born of the refining influences of civilization, and of its cruelties. It came to him that seldom if ever did civilized man kill a fellow being without some pretext, however slight. It was true that Tarzan wished this man's weapons and ornaments, but was it necessary to take his life to obtain them?

The longer he thought about it, the more repugnant became the thought of taking human life needlessly; and thus it happened that while he was trying to decide just what to do, they had come to a little clearing, at the far side of which lay a palisaded village of beehive huts.

As the warrior emerged from the forest, Tarzan caught a fleeting glimpse of a tawny hide worming its way through the matted jungle grasses in his wake—it was Numa, the lion. He, too, was stalking the black man. With the instant that Tarzan realized the native's danger his attitude toward his erstwhile prey altered completely—now he was a fellow man threatened by a common enemy.

Numa was about to charge—there was little time in which to compare various methods or weigh the probable results of any. And then a number of things happened, almost simultaneously—the lion sprang from his ambush toward the retreating black—Tarzan cried out in warning—and the black turned just in time to see Numa halted in mid-flight by a slender strand of grass rope, the noosed end of which had fallen cleanly about his neck.

The ape-man had acted so quickly that he had been unable to prepare himself to withstand the strain and shock of Numa's great weight upon the rope, and so it was that though the rope stopped the beast before his mighty talons could fasten themselves in the flesh of the black, the strain overbalanced Tarzan, who came tumbling to the ground not six paces from the infuriated animal. Like lightning Numa turned upon this new enemy, and, defenseless as he was, Tarzan of the Apes was nearer to death that instant than he ever before had been. It was the black who saved him. The warrior realized in an instant that he owed his life to this strange white man, and he also saw that only a miracle could save his preserver from those fierce yellow fangs that had been so near to his own flesh.

With the quickness of thought his spear arm flew back, and then shot forward with all the force of the sinewy muscles that rolled beneath the shimmering ebon hide. True to its mark the iron-shod weapon flew, transfixing Numa's sleek carcass from the right groin to beneath the left shoulder. With a hideous scream of rage and pain the brute turned again upon the black. A dozen paces he had gone when Tarzan's rope brought him to a stand once more—then he wheeled again upon the ape-man, only to feel the painful prick of a barbed arrow as it sank half its length in his quivering flesh. Again he stopped, and by this time Tarzan had run twice around the stem of a great tree with his rope, and made the end fast.

The black saw the trick, and grinned, but Tarzan knew that Numa must be quickly finished before those mighty teeth had found and parted the slender cord that held him. It was a matter of but an instant to reach the black's side and drag his long knife from its scabbard. Then he signed the warrior to continue to shoot arrows into the great beast while he attempted to close in upon him with the knife; so as one tantalized upon one side, the other sneaked cautiously in upon the other. Numa was furious. He raised his voice in a perfect frenzy of shrieks, growls, and hideous moans, the while he reared upon his hind legs in futile attempt to reach first one and then the other of his tormentors.

But at length the agile ape-man saw his chance, and rushed in upon the beast's left side behind the mighty shoulder. A giant arm encircled the tawny throat, and a long blade sank once, true as a die, into the fierce heart. Then Tarzan arose, and the black man and the white looked into each other's eyes across the body of their kill—and the black made the sign of peace and friendship, and Tarzan of the Apes answered it in kind.

15

From Ape to Savage

The noise of their battle with Numa had drawn an excited horde of savages from the nearby village, and a moment after the lion's death the two men were surrounded by lithe, ebon warriors, gesticulating and jabbering—a thousand questions that drowned each ventured reply.

And then the women came, and the children—eager, curious, and, at sight of Tarzan, more questioning than ever. The ape-man's new friend finally succeeded in making himself heard, and when he had done talking the men and women of the village vied with one another in doing honor to the strange creature who had saved their fellow and battled single-handed with fierce Numa.

At last they led him back to their village, where they brought him gifts of fowl, and goats, and cooked food. When he pointed to their weapons the warriors hastened to fetch spear, shield, arrows, and a bow. His friend of the encounter presented him with the knife with which he had killed Numa. There was nothing in all the village he could not have had for the asking.

How much easier this was, thought Tarzan, than murder and robbery to supply his wants. How close he had been to killing this man whom he never had seen before, and who now was manifesting by every primitive means at his command friendship and affection for his would-be slayer. Tarzan of the Apes was ashamed. Hereafter he would at least wait until he knew men deserved it before he thought of killing them.

The idea recalled Rokoff to his mind. He wished that he might have the Russian to himself in the dark jungle for a few minutes. There was a man who deserved killing if ever any one did. And if he could have seen Rokoff at that moment as he assiduously bent every endeavor to the pleasant task of ingratiating himself into the affections of the beautiful

Miss Strong, he would have longed more than ever to mete out to the man the fate he deserved.

Tarzan's first night with the savages was devoted to a wild orgy in his honor. There was feasting, for the hunters had brought in an antelope and a zebra as trophies of their skill, and gallons of the weak native beer were consumed. As the warriors danced in the firelight, Tarzan was again impressed by the symmetry of their figures and the regularity of their features—the flat noses and thick lips of the typical West Coast savage were entirely missing. In repose the faces of the men were intelligent and dignified, those of the women ofttimes prepossessing.

It was during this dance that the ape-man first noticed that some of the men and many of the women wore ornaments of gold—principally anklets and armlets of great weight, apparently beaten out of the solid metal. When he expressed a wish to examine one of these, the owner removed it from her person and insisted, through the medium of signs, that Tarzan accept it as a gift. A close scrutiny of the bauble convinced the ape-man that the article was of virgin gold, and he was surprised, for it was the first time that he had ever seen golden ornaments among the savages of Africa, other than the trifling baubles those near the coast had purchased or stolen from Europeans. He tried to ask them from whence the metal came, but he could not make them understand.

When the dance was done Tarzan signified his intention to leave them, but they almost implored him to accept the hospitality of a great hut which the chief set apart for his sole use. He tried to explain that he would return in the morning, but they could not understand. When he finally walked away from them toward the side of the village opposite the gate, they were still further mystified as to his intentions.

Tarzan, however, knew just what he was about. In the past he had had experience with the rodents and vermin that infest every native village, and, while he was not overscrupulous about such matters, he much preferred the fresh air of the swaying trees to the fetid atmosphere of a hut.

The natives followed him to where a great tree overhung the palisade, and as Tarzan leaped for a lower branch and disappeared into the foliage above, precisely after the manner of Manu, the monkey, there were loud exclamations of surprise and astonishment. For half an hour they called to him to return, but as he did not answer them they at last desisted, and sought the sleeping-mats within their huts.

Tarzan went back into the forest a short distance until he had found a tree suited to his primitive requirements, and then, curling himself in a great crotch, he fell immediately into a deep sleep.

The following morning he dropped into the village street as suddenly as he had disappeared the preceding night. For a moment the natives were startled and afraid, but when they recognized their guest of the night before they welcomed him with shouts and laughter. That day he accompanied a party of warriors to the nearby plains on a great hunt, and so dexterous did they find this white man with their own crude weapons that another bond of respect and admiration was thereby wrought.

For weeks Tarzan lived with his savage friends, hunting buffalo, antelope, and zebra for meat, and elephant for ivory. Quickly he learned their simple speech, their native customs, and the ethics of their wild, primitive tribal life. He found that they were not cannibals—that they looked with loathing and contempt upon men who ate men.

Busuli, the warrior whom he had stalked to the village, told him many of the tribal legends—how, many years before, his people had come many long marches from the north; how once they had been a great and powerful tribe; and how the slave raiders had wrought such havoc among them with their death-dealing guns that they had been reduced to a mere remnant of their former numbers and power.

"They hunted us down as one hunts a fierce beast," said Busuli. "There was no mercy in them. When it was not slaves they sought it was ivory, but usually it was both. Our men were killed and our women driven away like sheep. We fought against them for many years, but our arrows and spears could not prevail against the sticks which spit fire and lead and death to many times the distance that our mightiest warrior could place an arrow. At last, when my father was a young man, the Arabs came again, but our warriors saw them a long way off, and Chowambi, who was chief then, told his people to gather up their belongings and come away with him—that he would lead them far to the south until they found a spot to which the Arab raiders did not come.

"And they did as he bid, carrying all their belongings, including many tusks of ivory. For months they wandered, suffering untold hardships and privations, for much of the way was through dense jungle, and across mighty mountains, but finally they came to this spot, and although they sent parties farther on to search for an even better location, none has ever been found."

"And the raiders have never found you here?" asked Tarzan.

"About a year ago a small party of Arabs and Manyuema stumbled upon us, but we drove them off, killing many. For days we followed them, stalking them for the wild beasts they are, picking them off one by one, until but a handful remained, but these escaped us."

As Busuli talked he fingered a heavy gold armlet that encircled the glossy hide of his left arm. Tarzan's eyes had been upon the ornament, but his thoughts were elsewhere. Presently he recalled the question he had tried to ask when he first came to the tribe—the question he could not at that time make them understand. For weeks he had forgotten so trivial a thing as gold, for he had been for the time a truly primeval man with no thought beyond today. But of a sudden the sight of gold awakened the sleeping civilization that was in him, and with it came the lust for wealth. That lesson Tarzan had learned well in his brief experience of the ways of civilized man. He knew that gold meant power and pleasure. He pointed to the bauble.

"From whence came the yellow metal, Busuli?" he asked.

The black pointed toward the southeast.

"A moon's march away—maybe more," he replied.

"Have you been there?" asked Tarzan.

"No, but some of our people were there years ago, when my father was yet a young man. One of the parties that searched farther for a location for the tribe when first they settled here came upon a strange people who wore many ornaments of yellow metal. Their spears were tipped with it, as were their arrows, and they cooked in vessels made all of solid metal like my armlet.

"They lived in a great village in huts that were built of stone and surrounded by a great wall. They were very fierce, rushing out and falling upon our warriors before ever they learned that their errand was a peaceful one. Our men were few in number, but they held their own at the top of a little rocky hill, until the fierce people went back at sunset into their wicked city. Then our warriors came down from their hill, and, after taking many ornaments of yellow metal from the bodies of those they had slain, they marched back out of the valley, nor have any of us ever returned.

"They are wicked people—neither white like you nor black

like me, but covered with hair as is Bolgani, the gorilla. Yes, they are very bad people indeed, and Chowambi was glad to get out of their country."

"And are none of those alive who were with Chowambi, and saw these strange people and their wonderful city?" asked Tarzan.

"Waziri, our chief, was there," replied Busuli. "He was a very young man then, but he accompanied Chowambi, who was his father."

So that night Tarzan asked Waziri about it, and Waziri, who was now an old man, said that it was a long march, but that the way was not difficult to follow. He remembered it well.

"For ten days we followed this river which runs beside our village. Up toward its source we traveled until on the tenth day we came to a little spring far up upon the side of a lofty mountain range. In this little spring our river is born. The next day we crossed over the top of the mountain, and upon the other side we came to a tiny rivulet which we followed down into a great forest. For many days we traveled along the winding banks of the rivulet that had now become a river, until we came to a greater river, into which it emptied, and which ran down the center of a mighty valley.

"Then we followed this large river toward its source, hoping to come to more open land. After twenty days of marching from the time we had crossed the mountains and passed out of our own country we came again to another range of mountains. Up their side we followed the great river, that had now dwindled to a tiny rivulet, until we came to a little cave near the mountain-top. In this cave was the mother of the river.

"I remember that we camped there that night, and that it was very cold, for the mountains were high. The next day we decided to ascend to the top of the mountains, and see what the country upon the other side looked like, and if it seemed no better than that which we had so far traversed we would return to our village and tell them that they had already found the best place in all the world to live.

"And so we clambered up the face of the rocky cliffs until we reached the summit, and there from a flat mountain-top we saw, not far beneath us, a shallow valley, very narrow; and upon the far side of it was a great village of stone, much of which had fallen and crumbled into decay."

The balance of Waziri's story was practically the same as that which Busuli had told.

"I should like to go there and see this strange city," said Tarzan, "and get some of their yellow metal from its fierce inhabitants."

"It is a long march," replied Waziri, "and I am an old man, but if you will wait until the rainy season is over and the rivers have gone down I will take some of my warriors and go with you."

And Tarzan had to be contented with that arrangement, though he would have liked it well enough to have set off the next morning—he was as impatient as a child. Really Tarzan of the Apes was but a child, or a primeval man, which is the same thing in a way.

The next day but one a small party of hunters returned to the village from the south to report a large herd of elephant some miles away. By climbing trees they had had a fairly good view of the herd, which they described as numbering several large tuskers, a great many cows and calves, and full-grown bulls whose ivory would be worth having.

The balance of the day and evening was filled with preparation for a great hunt—spears were overhauled, quivers were replenished, bows were restrung; and all the while the village witch doctor passed through the busy throngs disposing of various charms and amulets designed to protect the possessor from hurt, or bring him good fortune in the morrow's hunt.

At dawn the hunters were off. There were fifty sleek, black warriors, and in their midst, lithe and active as a young forest god, strode Tarzan of the Apes, his brown skin contrasting oddly with the ebony of his companions. Except for color he was one of them. His ornaments and weapons were the same as theirs—he spoke their language—he laughed and joked with them, and leaped and shouted in the brief wild dance that preceded their departure from the village, to all intent and purpose a savage among savages. Nor, had he questioned himself, is it to be doubted that he would have admitted that he was far more closely allied to these people and their life than to the Parisian friends whose ways, apelike, he had successfully mimicked for a few short months.

But he did think of D'Arnot, and a grin of amusement showed his strong white teeth as he pictured the immaculate Frenchman's expression could he by some means see Tarzan as he was that minute. Poor Paul, who had prided himself on having eradicated from his friend the last traces of wild savagery. "How quickly have I fallen!" thought Tarzan; but in his heart he did not consider it a fall—rather, he pitied the poor creatures of Paris, penned up like prisoners in their silly clothes, and watched by policemen all their poor lives, that they might do nothing that was not entirely artificial and tiresome.

A two hours' march brought them close to the vicinity in which the elephants had been seen the previous day. From there on they moved very quietly indeed searching for the spoor of the great beasts. At length they found the well-marked trail along which the herd had passed not many hours before. In single file they followed it for about half an hour. It was Tarzan who first raised his hand in signal that the quarry was at hand—his sensitive nose had warned him that the elephants were not far ahead of them.

The blacks were skeptical when he told them how he knew.

"Come with me," said Tarzan, "and we shall see."

With the agility of a squirrel he sprang into a tree and ran nimbly to the top. One of the blacks followed more slowly and carefully. When he had reached a lofty limb beside the ape-man the latter pointed to the south, and there, some few hundred yards away, the black saw a number of huge black backs swaying back and forth above the top of the lofty jungle grasses. He pointed the direction to the watchers below, indicating with his fingers the number of beasts he could count.

Immediately the hunters started toward the elephants. The black in the tree hastened down, but Tarzan stalked, after his own fashion, along the leafy way of the middle terrace.

It is no child's play to hunt wild elephants with the crude weapons of primitive man. Tarzan knew that few native tribes ever attempted it, and the fact that his tribe did so gave him no little pride—already he was commencing to think of himself as a member of the little community.

As Tarzan moved silently through the trees he saw the warriors below creeping in a half circle upon the still unsuspecting elephants. Finally they were within sight of the great beasts. Now they singled out two large tuskers, and at a signal the fifty men rose from the ground where they had lain concealed, and hurled their heavy war spears at the two marked beasts. There was not a single miss; twenty-five spears were embedded in the sides of each of the giant animals. One never moved from the spot where it stood when the avalanche of spears struck it, for two, perfectly aimed, had penetrated its heart, and it lunged forward upon its knees, rolling to the ground without a struggle.

The other, standing nearly head-on toward the hunters, had not proved so good a mark, and though every spear struck not one entered the great heart. For a moment the huge bull stood trumpeting in rage and pain, casting about with its little eyes for the author of its hurt. The blacks had faded into the jungle before the weak eyes of the monster had fallen upon any of them, but now he caught the sound of their retreat, and, amid a terrific crashing of underbrush and branches, he charged in the direction of the noise.

It so happened that chance sent him in the direction of Busuli, whom he was overtaking so rapidly that it was as though the black were standing still instead of racing at full speed to escape the certain death which pursued him. Tarzan had witnessed the entire performance from the branches of a nearby tree, and now that he saw his friend's peril he raced toward the infuriated beast with loud cries, hoping to distract him.

But it had been as well had he saved his breath, for the brute was deaf and blind to all else save the particular object of his rage that raced futilely before him. And now Tarzan saw that only a miracle could save Busuli, and with the same unconcern with which he had once hunted this very man he hurled himself into the path of the elephant to save the black warrior's life.

He still grasped his spear, and while Tantor was yet six or eight paces behind his prey, a sinewy white warrior dropped as from the heavens, almost directly in his path. With a vicious lunge the elephant swerved to the right to dispose of this temerarious foeman who dared intervene between himself and his intended victim; but he had not reckoned on the lightning quickness that could galvanize those steel muscles into action so marvelously swift as to baffle even a keener eyesight than Tantor's.

And so it happened that before the elephant realized that his new enemy had leaped from his path Tarzan had driven his iron-shod spear from behind the massive shoulder straight into the fierce heart, and the colossal pachyderm had toppled to his death at the feet of the ape-man.

Busuli had not beheld the manner of his deliverance, but Waziri, the old chief, had seen, and several of the other warriors, and they hailed Tarzan with delight as they swarmed about him and his great kill. When he leaped upon the mighty carcass, and gave voice to the weird challenge with which he announced a great victory, the blacks shrank back in fear, for to them it marked the brutal Bolgani, whom they feared fully as much as they feared Numa, the lion; but with a fear with which was mixed a certain uncanny awe of the manlike thing to which they attributed supernatural powers.

But when Tarzan lowered his raised head and smiled upon them they were reassured, though they did not understand. Nor did they ever fully understand this strange creature who ran through the trees as quickly as Manu, yet was even more at home upon the ground than themselves; who was except as to color like unto themselves, yet as powerful as ten of them, and singlehanded a match for the fiercest denizens of the fierce jungle.

When the remainder of the warriors had gathered, the hunt was again taken up and the stalking of the retreating herd once more begun; but they had covered a bare hundred yards when from behind them, at a great distance, sounded faintly a strange popping.

For an instant they stood like a group of statuary, intently listening. Then Tarzan spoke.

"Guns!" he said. "The village is being attacked."

"Come!" cried Waziri. "The Arab raiders have returned with their cannibal slaves for our ivory and our women!"

16

The Ivory Raiders

WAZIRI's warriors marched at a rapid trot through the jungle in the direction of the village. For a few minutes the sharp cracking of guns ahead warned them to haste, but finally the reports dwindled to an occasional shot, presently ceasing altogether. Nor was this less ominous than the rattle of musketry, for it suggested but a single solution to the little band of rescuers—that the illy garrisoned village had already succumbed to the onslaught of a superior force.

The returning hunters had covered a little more than three miles of the five that had separated them from the village when they met the first of the fugitives who had escaped the bullets and clutches of the foe. There were a dozen women, youths, and girls in the party, and so excited were they that they could scarce make themselves understood as they tried to relate to Waziri the calamity that had befallen his people.

"They are as many as the leaves of the forest," cried one of the women, in attempting to explain the enemy's force. "There are many Arabs and countless Manyuema, and they all have guns. They crept close to the village before we knew that they were about, and then, with many shouts, they rushed in upon us, shooting down men, and women, and children. Those of us who could fled in all directions into the jungle, but more were killed. I do not know whether they took any prisoners or not—they seemed only bent upon killing us all. The Manyuema called us many names, saying that they would eat us all before they left our country—that this was our punishment for killing their friends last year. I did not hear much, for I ran away quickly."

The march toward the village was now resumed, more slowly and with greater stealth, for Waziri knew that it was too late to rescue—their only mission could be one of revenge. Inside the next mile a hundred more fugitives were met. There were many men among these, and so the fighting strength of the party was augmented.

Now a dozen warriors were sent creeping ahead to reconnoiter. Waziri remained with the main body, which advanced in a thin line that spread in a great crescent through the forest. By the chief's side walked Tarzan.

Presently one of the scouts returned. He had come within sight of the village.

"They are all within the palisade," he whispered.

"Good!" said Waziri. "We shall rush in upon them and slay them all," and he made ready to send word along the line that they were to halt at the edge of the clearing until they saw him rush toward the village—then all were to follow.

"Wait!" cautioned Tarzan. "If there are even fifty guns within the palisade we shall be repulsed and slaughtered. Let me go alone through the trees, so that I may look down upon them from above, and see just how many there be, and what chance we might have were we to charge. It were foolish to lose a single man needlessly if there be no hope of success. I have an idea that we can accomplish more by cunning than by force. Will you wait, Waziri?"

"Yes," said the old chief. "Go!"

So Tarzan sprang into the trees and disappeared in the direction of the village. He moved more cautiously than was his wont, for he knew that men with guns could reach him quite as easily in the treetops as on the ground. And when Tarzan of the Apes elected to adopt stealth, no creature in all the jungle could move so silently or so completely efface himself from the sight of an enemy.

In five minutes he had wormed his way to the great tree that overhung the palisade at one end of the village, and from his point of vantage looked down upon the savage horde beneath. He counted fifty Arabs and estimated that there were five times as many Manyuema. The latter were gorging themselves upon food and, under the very noses of their white masters, preparing the gruesome feast which is the *piece de résistance* that follows a victory in which the bodies of their slain enemies fall into their horrid hands.

The ape-man saw that to charge that wild horde, armed as they were with guns, and barricaded behind the locked gates of the village, would be a futile task, and so he returned to Waziri and advised him to wait; that he, Tarzan, had a better plan.

But a moment before one of the fugitives had related to Waziri the story of the atrocious murder of the old chief's wife, and so crazed with rage was the old man that he cast discretion to the winds. Calling his warriors about him, he commanded them to charge, and, with brandishing spears and savage yells, the little force of scarcely more than a hundred dashed madly toward the village gates. Before the clearing had been half crossed the Arabs opened up a withering fire from behind the palisade.

With the first volley Waziri fell. The speed of the chargers slackened. Another volley brought down a half dozen more. A few reached the barred gates, only to be shot in their tracks, without the ghost of a chance to gain the inside of the palisade, and then the whole attack crumpled, and the remaining warriors scampered back into the forest.

As they ran the raiders opened the gates, rushing after them, to complete the day's work with the utter extermination of the tribe. Tarzan had been among the last to turn back toward the forest, and now, as he ran slowly, he turned from time to time to speed a well-aimed arrow into the body of a pursuer.

Once within the jungle, he found a little knot of determined blacks waiting to give battle to the oncoming horde, but Tarzan cried to them to scatter, keeping out of harm's way until they could gather in force after dark.

"Do as I tell you," he urged, "and I will lead you to victory over these enemies of yours. Scatter through the forest, picking up as many stragglers as you can find, and at night, if you think that you have been followed, come by roundabout ways to the spot where we killed the elephants today. Then I will explain my plan, and you will find that it is good. You cannot hope to pit your puny strength and simple weapons against the numbers and the guns of the Arabs and the Manyuema."

They finally assented. "When you scatter," explained Tarzan, in conclusion, "your foes will have to scatter to follow you, and so it may happen that if you are watchful you can drop many a Manyuema with your arrows from behind some great trees."

They had barely time to hasten away farther into the forest before the first of the raiders had crossed the clearing and entered it in pursuit of them.

Tarzan ran a short distance along the ground before he took to the trees. Then he raced quickly to the upper terrace, there doubling on his tracks and making his way rapidly back toward the village. Here he found that every Arab and Manyuema had joined in the pursuit, leaving the village deserted except for the chained prisoners and a single guard.

The sentry stood at the open gate, looking in the direction of the forest, so that he did not see the agile giant that dropped to the ground at the far end of the village street. With drawn bow the ape-man crept stealthily toward his unsuspecting victim. The prisoners had already discovered him, and with wide eyes filled with wonder and with hope they watched their would-be rescuer. Now he halted not ten paces from the unconscious Manyuema. The shaft was drawn back its full length at the height of the keen gray eye that sighted along its polished surface. There was a sudden twang as the brown fingers released their hold, and without a sound the raider sank forward upon his face, a wooden shaft transfixing his heart and protruding a foot from his black chest.

Then Tarzan turned his attention to the fifty women and youths chained neck to neck on the long slave chain. There was no releasing of the ancient padlocks in the time that was left him, so the ape-man called to them to follow him as they were, and, snatching the gun and cartridge belt from the dead sentry, he led the now happy band out through the village gate and into the forest upon the far side of the clearing.

It was a slow and arduous march, for the slave chain was new to these people, and there were many delays as one of their number would stumble and fall, dragging others down with her. Then, too, Tarzan had been forced to make a wide detour to avoid any possibility of meeting with returning raiders. He was partially guided by occasional shots which indicated that the Arab horde was still in touch with the villagers; but he knew that if they would but follow his advice there would be but few casualties other than on the side of the marauders.

Toward dusk the firing ceased entirely, and Tarzan knew that the Arabs had all returned to the village. He could scarce repress a smile of triumph as he thought of their rage on discovering that their guard had been killed and their prisoners taken away. Tarzan had wished that he might have taken some of the great store of ivory the village contained, solely for the purpose of still further augmenting the wrath of his enemies; but he knew that that was not necessary for its salvation, since he already had a plan mapped out which would effectually prevent the Arabs leaving the country with a single tusk. And it would have been cruel to have needlessly burdened these poor, overwrought women with the extra weight of the heavy ivory.

It was after midnight when Tarzan, with his slow-moving caravan, approached the spot where the elephants lay. Long before they reached it they had been guided by the huge fire the natives had built in the center of a hastily improvised *boma*, partially for warmth and partially to keep off chance lions.

When they had come close to the encampment Tarzan called aloud to let them know that friends were coming. It was a joyous reception the little party received when the blacks within the *boma* saw the long file of fettered friends and relatives enter the firelight. These had all been given up as lost forever, as had Tarzan as well, so that the happy blacks would have remained awake all night to feast on elephant meat and celebrate the return of their fellows, had not Tarzan insisted that they take what sleep they could, against the work of the coming day.

At that, sleep was no easy matter, for the women who had lost their men or their children in the day's massacre and battle made night hideous with their continued wailing and howling. Finally, however, Tarzan succeeded in silencing them, on the plea that their noise would attract the Arabs to their hiding-place, when all would be slaughtered.

When dawn came Tarzan explained his plan of battle to the warriors, and without demur one and all agreed that it was the safest and surest way in which to rid themselves of their unwelcome visitors and be revenged for the murder of their fellows.

First the women and children, with a guard of some twenty old warriors and youths, were started southward, to be entirely out of the zone of danger. They had instructions to erect temporary shelter and construct a protecting *boma* of thorn bush; for the plan of campaign which Tarzan had chosen was one which might stretch out over many days, or even weeks, during which time the warriors would not return to the new camp.

Two hours after daylight a thin circle of black warriors surrounded the village. At intervals one was perched high in the branches of a tree which could overlook the palisade. Presently a Manyuema within the village fell, pierced by a single arrow. There had been no sound of attack—none of the hideous war-cries or vainglorious waving of menacing spears that ordinarily marks the attack of savages—just a silent messenger of death from out of the silent forest.

The Arabs and their followers were thrown into a fine rage at this unprecedented occurrence. They ran for the gates, to wreak dire vengeance upon the foolhardy perpetrator of the outrage; but they suddenly realized that they did not know which way to turn to find the foe. As they stood debating, with many angry shouts and much gesticulating, one of the Arabs sank silently to the ground in their very midst—a thin arrow protruding from his heart.

Tarzan had placed the finest marksmen of the tribe in the surrounding trees, with directions never to reveal themselves while the enemy was faced in their direction. As a black released his messenger of death he would slink behind the sheltering stem of the tree he had selected, nor would he again aim until a watchful eye told him that none was looking toward his tree.

Three times the Arabs started across the clearing in the direction from which they thought the arrows came, but each time another arrow would come from behind to take its toll from among their number. Then they would turn and charge in a new direction. Finally they set out upon a determined search of the forest, but the blacks melted before them, so that they saw no sign of an enemy.

But above them lurked a grim figure in the dense foliage of the mighty trees—it was Tarzan of the Apes, hovering over them as if he had been the shadow of death. Presently a Manyuema forged ahead of his companions; there was none to see from what direction death came, and so it came quickly, and a moment later those behind stumbled over the dead body of their comrade—the inevitable arrow piercing the still heart.

It does not take a great deal of this manner of warfare to get upon the nerves of white men, and so it is little to be wondered at that the Manyuema were soon panic-stricken. Did one forge ahead an arrow found his heart; did one lag behind he never again was seen alive; did one stumble to one side, even for a bare moment from the sight of his fellows, he did not return—and always when they came upon the bodies of their dead they found those terrible arrows driven with the accuracy of superhuman power straight through the victim's heart. But worse than all else was the hideous fact that not once during the morning had they seen or heard the slightest sign of an enemy other than the pitiless arrows.

When finally they returned to the village it was no better. Every now and then, at varying intervals that were maddening in the terrible suspense they caused, a man would plunge forward dead. The blacks besought their masters to leave this terrible place, but the Arabs feared to take up the march through the grim and hostile forest beset by this new and terrible enemy while laden with the great store of ivory they had found within the village; but, worse yet, they hated to leave the ivory behind.

Finally the entire expedition took refuge within the thatched huts—here, at least, they would be free from the arrows. Tarzan, from the tree above the village, had marked the hut into which the chief Arabs had gone, and, balancing himself upon an overhanging limb, he drove his heavy spear with all the force of his giant muscles through the thatched roof. A howl of pain told him that it had found a mark. With this parting salute to convince them that there was no safety for them anywhere within the country, Tarzan returned to the forest, collected his warriors, and withdrew a mile to the south to rest and eat. He kept sentries in several trees that commanded a view of the trail toward the village, but there was no pursuit.

An inspection of his force showed not a single casualty—not even a minor wound; while rough estimates of the enemies' loss convinced the blacks that no fewer than twenty had fallen before their arrows. They were wild with elation, and were for finishing the day in one glorious rush upon the village, during which they would slaughter the last of their foemen. They were even picturing the various tortures they would inflict, and gloating over the suffering of the Manyuema, for whom they entertained a peculiar hatred, when Tarzan put his foot down flatly upon the plan.

"You are crazy!" he cried. "I have shown you the only way to fight these people. Already you have killed twenty of them without the loss of a single warrior, whereas, yesterday, following your own tactics, which you would now renew, you lost at least a dozen, and killed not a single Arab or Manyuema. You will fight just as I tell you to fight, or I shall leave you and go back to my own country."

They were frightened when he threatened this, and promised to obey him scrupulously if he would but promise not to desert them.

"Very well," he said. "We shall return to the elephant *boma* for the night. I have a plan to give the Arabs a little taste of what they may expect if they remain in our country, but I shall need no help. Come! If they suffer no more for the balance of the day they will feel reassured, and the relapse into fear will be even more nerve-racking than as though we continued to frighten them all afternoon."

So they marched back to their camp of the previous night, and, lighting great fires, ate and recounted the adventures of the day until long after dark. Tarzan slept until midnight, then he arose and crept into the Cimmerian blackness of the forest. An hour later he came to the edge of the clearing before the village. There was a camp-fire burning within the palisade. The ape-man crept across the clearing until he stood before the barred gates. Through the interstices he saw a lone sentry sitting before the fire.

Quietly Tarzan went to the tree at the end of the village street. He climbed softly to his place, and fitted an arrow to his bow. For several minutes he tried to sight fairly upon the sentry, but the waving branches and flickering firelight convinced him that the danger of a miss was too great—he must touch the heart full in the center to bring the quiet and sudden death his plan required.

He had brought, besides his bow, arrows, and rope, the gun he had taken the previous day from the other sentry he had killed. Caching all these in a convenient crotch of the tree, he dropped lightly to the ground within the palisade, armed only with his long knife. The sentry's back was toward him. Like a cat Tarzan crept upon the dozing man. He was within two paces of him now—another instant and the knife would slide silently into the fellow's heart.

Tarzan crouched for a spring, for that is ever the quickest and surest attack of the jungle beast—when the man, warned, by some subtle sense, sprang to his feet and faced the ape-man.

17

The White Chief of the Waziri

WHEN the eyes of the black Manyuema savage fell upon the strange apparition that confronted him with menacing knife they went wide in horror. He forgot the gun within his hands; he even forgot to cry out—his one thought was to escape this fearsome-looking white savage, this giant of a man upon whose massive rolling muscles and mighty chest the flickering firelight played.

But before he could turn Tarzan was upon him, and then the sentry thought to scream for aid, but it was too late. A great hand was upon his windpipe, and he was being borne to the earth. He battled furiously but futilely—with the grim tenacity of a bulldog those awful fingers were clinging to his throat. Swiftly and surely life was being choked from him. His eyes bulged, his tongue protruded, his face turned to a ghastly purplish hue—there was a convulsive tremor of the stiffening muscles, and the Manyuema sentry lay quite still.

The ape-man threw the body across one of his broad shoulders and, gathering up the fellow's gun, trotted silently up the sleeping village street toward the tree that gave him such easy ingress to the palisaded village. He bore the dead sentry into the midst of the leafy maze above.

First he stripped the body of cartridge belt and such ornaments as he craved, wedging it into a convenient crotch while his nimble fingers ran over it in search of the loot he could not plainly see in the dark. When he had finished he took the gun that had belonged to the man, and walked far out upon a limb, from the end of which he could obtain a better view of the huts. Drawing a careful bead on the beehive structure in which he knew the chief Arabs to be, he pulled the trigger. Almost instantly there was an answering groan. Tarzan smiled. He had made another lucky hit.

Following the shot there was a moment's silence in the camp, and then Manyuema and Arab came pouring from the huts like a swarm of angry hornets; but if the truth were known they were even more frightened than they were angry. The strain of the preceding day had wrought upon the fears of both black and white, and now this single shot in the night conjured all manner of terrible conjectures in their terrified minds.

When they discovered that their sentry had disappeared, their fears were in no way allayed, and, as though to bolster their courage by warlike actions, they began to fire rapidly at the barred gates of the village, although no enemy was in sight. Tarzan took advantage of the deafening roar of this fusillade to fire into the mob beneath him.

No one heard his shot above the din of rattling musketry in the street, but some who were standing close saw one of their number crumple suddenly to the earth. When they leaned over him he was dead. They were panic-stricken, and it took all the brutal authority of the Arabs to keep the Manyuema from rushing helter-skelter into the jungle—anywhere to escape from this terrible village.

After a time they commenced to quiet down, and as no further mysterious deaths occurred among them they took heart again. But it was a short-lived respite, for just as they had concluded that they would not be disturbed again Tarzan gave voice to a weird moan, and as the raiders looked up in the direction from which the sound seemed to come, the ape-man, who stood swinging the dead body of the sentry gently to and fro, suddenly shot the corpse far out above their heads.

With howls of alarm the throng broke in all directions to escape this new and terrible creature who seemed to be springing upon them. To their fear-distorted imaginations the body of the sentry, falling with wide-sprawled arms and legs, assumed the likeness of a great beast of prey. In their anxiety to escape, many of the blacks scaled the palisade, while others tore down the bars from the gates and rushed madly across the clearing toward the jungle.

For a time no one turned back toward the thing that had frightened them, but Tarzan knew that they would in a moment, and when they discovered that it was but the dead body of their sentry, while they would doubtless be still further terrified, he had a rather definite idea as to what they would do, and so he faded silently away toward the south, taking the moonlit upper terrace back toward the camp of the Waziri.

Presently one of the Arabs turned and saw that the thing that had leaped from the tree upon them lay still and quiet where it had fallen in the center of the village street. Cautiously he crept back toward it until he saw that it was but a man. A moment later he was beside the figure, and in another had recognized it as the corpse of the Manyuema who had stood on guard at the village gate.

His companions rapidly gathered around at his call, and after a moment's excited conversation they did precisely what Tarzan had reasoned they would. Raising their guns to their shoulders, they poured volley after volley into the tree from which the corpse had been thrown—had Tarzan remained there he would have been riddled by a hundred bullets.

When the Arabs and Manyuema discovered that the only marks of violence upon the body of their dead comrade were giant finger prints upon his swollen throat they were again thrown into deeper apprehension and despair. That they were not even safe within a palisaded village at night came as a distinct shock to them. That an enemy could enter into the midst of their camp and kill their sentry with bare hands seemed outside the bounds of reason, and so the superstitious Manyuema commenced to attribute their ill luck to supernatural causes; nor were the Arabs able to offer any better explanation.

With at least fifty of their number flying through the black jungle, and without the slightest knowledge of when their uncanny foemen might resume the cold-blooded slaughter they had commenced, it was a desperate band of cutthroats that waited sleeplessly for the dawn. Only on the promise of the Arabs that they would leave the village at daybreak, and hasten onward toward their own land, would the remaining Manyuema consent to stay at the village a moment longer. Not even fear of their cruel masters was sufficient to overcome this new terror.

And so it was that when Tarzan and his warriors returned to the attack the next morning they found the raiders prepared to march out of the village. The Manyuema were laden with stolen ivory. As Tarzan saw it he grinned, for he knew that they would not carry it far. Then he saw something which caused him anxiety—a number of the Manyuema were lighting torches in the remnant of the camp-fire. They were about to fire the village.

Tarzan was perched in a tall tree some hundred yards from the palisade. Making a trumpet of his hands, he called loudly in the Arab tongue: "Do not fire the huts, or we shall kill you all! Do not fire the huts, or we shall kill you all!"

A dozen times he repeated it. The Manyuema hesitated, then one of them flung his torch into the campfire. The others were about to do the same when an Arab sprung upon them with a stick, beating them toward the huts. Tarzan could see that he was commanding them to fire the little thatched dwellings. Then he stood erect upon the swaying branch a hundred feet above the ground, and, raising one of the Arab guns to his shoulder, took careful aim and fired. With the report the Arab who was urging on his men to burn the village fell in his tracks, and the Manyuema threw away their torches and fled from the village. The last Tarzan saw of them they were racing toward the jungle, while their former masters knelt upon the ground and fired at them.

But however angry the Arabs might have been at the insubordination of their slaves, they were at least convinced that it would be the better part of wisdom to forego the pleasure of firing the village that had given them two such nasty receptions. In their hearts, however, they swore to return again with such force as would enable them to sweep the entire country for miles around, until no vestige of human life remained.

They had looked in vain for the owner of the voice which had frightened off the men who had been detailed to put the torch to the huts, but not even the keenest eye among them had been able to locate him. They had seen the puff of smoke from the tree following the shot that brought down the Arab, but, though a volley had immediately been loosed into its foliage, there had been no indication that it had been effective.

Tarzan was too intelligent to be caught in any such trap, and so the report of his shot had scarcely died away before the ape-man was on the ground and racing for another tree a hundred yards away. Here he again found a suitable perch from which he could watch the preparations of the raiders. It occurred to him that he might have considerable more fun with them, so again he called to them through his improvised trumpet.

"Leave the ivory!" he cried. "Leave the ivory! Dead men have no use for ivory!"

Some of the Manyuema started to lay down their loads, but this was altogether too much for the avaricious Arabs. With loud shouts and curses they aimed their guns full upon the bearers, threatening instant death to any who might lay down his load. They could give up firing the village, but the thought of abandoning this enormous fortune in ivory was quite beyond their conception—better death than that.

And so they marched out of the village of the Waziri, and on the shoulders of their slaves was the ivory ransom of a score of kings. Toward the north they marched, back toward their savage settlement in the wild and unknown country which lies back from the Kongo in the uttermost depths of The Great Forest, and on either side of them traveled an invisible and relentless foe.

Under Tarzan's guidance the black Waziri warriors stationed themselves along the trail on either side in the densest underbrush. They stood at far intervals, and, as the column passed, a single arrow or a heavy spear, well aimed, would pierce a Manyuema or an Arab. Then the Waziri would melt into the distance and run ahead to take his stand farther on. They did not strike unless success were sure and the danger of detection almost nothing, and so the arrows and the spears were few and far between, but so persistent and inevitable that the slow-moving column of heavy-laden raiders was in a constant state of panic—panic at the pierced body of the comrade who had just fallen—panic at the uncertainty of who the next would be to fall, and when.

It was with the greatest difficulty that the Arabs prevented their men a dozen times from throwing away their burdens and fleeing like frightened rabbits up the trail toward the north. And so the day wore on—a frightful nightmare of a day for the raiders—a day of weary but well-repaid work for the Waziri. At night the Arabs constructed a rude *boma* in a little clearing by a river, and went into camp.

At intervals during the night a rifle would bark close above their heads, and one of the dozen sentries which they now had posted would tumble to the ground. Such a condition was insupportable, for they saw that by means of these hideous tactics they would be completely wiped out, one by one, without inflicting a single death upon their enemy. But yet, with the persistent avariciousness of the white man, the Arabs clung to their loot, and when morning came forced the demoralized Manyuema to take up their burdens of death and stagger on into the jungle.

For three days the withering column kept up its frightful march. Each hour was marked by its deadly arrow or cruel spear. The nights were made hideous by the barking of the invisible gun that made sentry duty equivalent to a death sentence.

On the morning of the fourth day the Arabs were compelled to shoot two of their blacks before they could compel the balance to take up the hated ivory, and as they did so a voice rang out, clear and strong, from the jungle: "Today you die, oh, Manyuema, unless you lay down the ivory. Fall upon your cruel masters and kill them! You have guns, why do you not use them? Kill the Arabs, and we will not harm you. We will take you back to our village and feed you, and lead you out of our country in safety and in peace. Lay down the ivory, and fall upon your masters—we will help you. Else you die!"

As the voice died down the raiders stood as though turned to stone. The Arabs eyed their Manyuema slaves; the slaves looked first at one of their fellows, and then at another—they were but waiting for some one to take the initiative. There were some thirty Arabs left, and about one hundred and fifty blacks. All were armed—even those who were acting as porters had their rifles slung across their backs.

The Arabs drew together. The sheik ordered the Manyuema to take up the march, and as he spoke he cocked his rifle and raised it. But at the same instant one of the blacks threw down his load, and, snatching his rifle from his back, fired point-blank at the group of Arabs. In an instant the camp was a cursing, howling mass of demons, fighting with guns and knives and pistols. The Arabs stood together, and defended their lives valiantly, but with the rain of lead that poured upon them from their own slaves, and the shower of arrows and spears which now leaped from the surrounding jungle aimed solely at them, there was little question from the first what the outcome would be. In ten minutes from the time the first porter had thrown down his load the last of the Arabs lay dead.

When the firing had ceased Tarzan spoke again to the Manyuema:

"Take up our ivory, and return it to our village, from whence you stole it. We shall not harm you."

For a moment the Manyuema hesitated. They had no stomach to retrace that difficult three days' trail. They talked together in low whispers, and one turned toward the jungle, calling aloud to the voice that had spoken to them from out of the foliage.

"How do we know that when you have us in your village you will not kill us all?" he asked.

"You do not know," replied Tarzan, "other than that we have promised not to harm you if you will return our ivory to us. But this you do know, that it lies within our power to kill you all if you do not return as we direct, and are we not more likely to do so if you anger us than if you do as we bid?"

"Who are you that speaks the tongue of our Arab masters?" cried the Manyuema spokesman. "Let us see you, and then we shall give you our answer."

Tarzan stepped out of the jungle a dozen paces from them.

"Look!" he said. When they saw that he was white they were filled with awe, for never had they seen a white savage before, and at his great muscles and giant frame they were struck with wonder and admiration.

"You may trust me," said Tarzan. "So long as you do as I tell you, and harm none of my people, we shall do you no hurt. Will you take up our ivory and return in peace to our village, or shall we follow along your trail toward the north as we have followed for the past three days?"

The recollection of the horrid days that had just passed was the thing that finally decided the Manyuema, and so, after a short conference, they took up their burdens and set off to retrace their steps toward the village of the Waziri.

At the end of the third day they marched into the village gate, and were greeted by the survivors of the recent massacre, to whom Tarzan had sent a messenger in their temporary camp to the south on the day that the raiders had quitted the village, telling them that they might return in safety.

It took all the mastery and persuasion that Tarzan possessed to prevent the Waziri falling on the Manyuema tooth and nail, and tearing them to pieces, but when he had explained that he had given his word that they would not be molested if they carried the ivory back to the spot from which they had stolen it, and had further impressed upon his people that they owed their entire victory to him, they finally acceded to his demands, and allowed the cannibals to rest in peace within their palisade.

That night the village warriors held a big palaver to celebrate their victories, and to choose a new chief. Since old Waziri's death Tarzan had been directing the warriors in battle, and the temporary command had been tacitly conceded to him. There had been no time to choose a new chief from among their own number, and, in fact, so remarkably successful had they been under the ape-man's generalship that they had had no wish to delegate the supreme authority to another for fear that what they already had gained might be lost. They had so recently seen the results of running counter to this savage white man's advice in the disastrous charge ordered by Waziri, in which he himself had died, that it had not been difficult for them to accept Tarzan's authority as final.

The principal warriors sat in a circle about a small fire to discuss the relative merits of whomever might be suggested as old Waziri's successor. It was Busuli who spoke first:

"Since Waziri is dead, leaving no son, there is but one among us whom we know from experience is fitted to make us a good king. There is only one who has proved that he can successfully lead us against the guns of the white man, and bring us easy victory without the loss of a single life. There is only one, and that is the white man who has led us for the past few days," and Busuli sprang to his feet, and with uplifted spear and half-bent, crouching body commenced to dance slowly about Tarzan, chanting in time to his steps: "Waziri, king of the Waziri; Waziri, killer of Arabs; Waziri, king of the Waziri."

One by one the other warriors signified their acceptance of Tarzan as their king by joining in the solemn dance. The women came and squatted about the rim of the circle, beating upon tom-toms, clapping their hands in time to the steps of the dancers, and joining in the chant of the warriors. In the center of the circle sat Tarzan of the Apes—Waziri, king of the Waziri, for, like his predecessor, he was to take the name of his tribe as his own.

Faster and faster grew the pace of the dancers, louder and louder their wild and savage shouts. The women rose and fell in unison, shrieking now at the tops of their voices. The spears were brandishing fiercely, and as the dancers stooped down and beat their shields upon the hard-tramped earth of the village street the whole sight was as terribly primeval and savage as though it were being staged in the dim dawn of humanity, countless ages in the past.

As the excitement waxed the ape-man sprang to his feet and joined in the wild ceremony. In the center of the circle of glittering black bodies he leaped and roared and shook his heavy spear in the same mad abandon that enthralled his fellow savages. The last remnant of his civilization was forgotten—he was a primitive man to the fullest now; reveling in the freedom of the fierce, wild life he loved, gloating in his kingship among these wild blacks.

Ah, if Olga de Coude had but seen him then—could she have recognized the well-dressed, quiet young man whose well-bred face and irreproachable manners had so captivated her but a few short months ago? And Jane Porter! Would she have still loved this savage warrior chieftain, dancing naked among his naked savage subjects? And D'Arnot! Could D'Arnot have believed that this was the same man he had introduced into half a dozen of the most select clubs of Paris? What would his fellow peers in the House of Lords have said had one pointed to this dancing giant, with his barbaric headdress and his metal ornaments, and said: "There, my lords, is John Clayton, Lord Greystoke."

And so Tarzan of the Apes came into a real kingship among men—slowly but surely was he following the evolution of his ancestors, for had he not started at the very bottom?

18

The Lottery of Death

JANE PORTER had been the first of those in the lifeboat to awaken the morning after the wreck of the *Lady Alice*. The other members of the party were asleep upon the thwarts or huddled in cramped positions in the bottom of the boat.

When the girl realized that they had become separated from the other boats she was filled with alarm. The sense of utter loneliness and helplessness which the vast expanse of deserted ocean aroused in her was so depressing that, from the first, contemplation of the future held not the slightest ray of promise for her. She was confident that they were lost—lost beyond possibility of succor.

Presently Clayton awoke. It was several minutes before he could gather his senses sufficiently to realize where he was, or recall the disaster of the previous night. Finally his bewildered eyes fell upon the girl.

"Jane!" he cried. "Thank God that we are together!"

"Look," said the girl dully, indicating the horizon with an apathetic gesture. "We are all alone."

Clayton scanned the water in every direction.

"Where can they be?" he cried. "They cannot have gone down, for there has been no sea, and they were afloat after the yacht sank—I saw them all."

He awoke the other members of the party, and explained their plight.

"It is just as well that the boats are scattered, sir," said one of the sailors. "They are all provisioned, so that they do not need each other on that score, and should a storm blow up they could be of no service to one another even if they were together, but scattered about the ocean there is a much better chance that one at least will be picked up, and then a search will be at once started for the others. Were we together there would be but one chance of rescue, where now there may be four."

They saw the wisdom of his philosophy, and were cheered by it, but their joy was short-lived, for when it was decided that they should row steadily toward the east and the continent, it was discovered that the sailors who had been at the only two oars with which the boat had been provided had fallen asleep at their work, and allowed both to slip into the sea, nor were they in sight anywhere upon the water.

During the angry words and recriminations which followed the sailors nearly came to blows, but Clayton succeeded in quieting them; though a moment later Monsieur Thuran almost precipitated another row by making a nasty remark about the stupidity of all Englishmen, and especially English sailors.

"Come, come, mates," spoke up one of the men, Tompkins, who had taken no part in the altercation, "shootin' off our bloomin' mugs won't get us nothin'. As Spider 'ere said afore, we'll all bloody well be picked up, anyway, sez 'e, so wot's the use o' squabblin'? Let's eat, sez I."

"That's not a bad idea," said Monsieur Thuran, and then, turning to the third sailor, Wilson, he said: "Pass one of those tins aft, my good man."

"Fetch it yerself," retorted Wilson sullenly. "I ain't a-takin' no orders from no—— furriner—you ain't captain o' this ship yet."

The result was that Clayton himself had to get the tin, and then another angry altercation ensued when one of the sailors accused Clayton and Monsieur Thuran of conspiring to control the provisions so that they could have the lion's share.

"Some one should take command of this boat," spoke up Jane Porter, thoroughly disgusted with the disgraceful wrangling that had marked the very opening of a forced companionship that might last for many days. "It is terrible enough to be alone in a frail boat on the Atlantic, without having the added misery and danger of constant bickering and brawling among the members of our party. You men should elect a leader, and then abide by his decisions in all matters. There is greater need for strict discipline here than there is upon a well-ordered ship."

She had hoped before she voiced her sentiments that it would not be necessary for her to enter into the transaction at all, for she believed that Clayton was amply able to cope with every emergency, but she had to admit that so far at least he had shown no greater promise of successfully handling the situation than any of the others, though he had at least refrained from adding in any way to the unpleasantness, even going so far as to give up the tin to the sailors when they objected to its being opened by him.

The girl's words temporarily quieted the men, and finally it was decided that the two kegs of water and the four tins of food should be divided into two parts, one-half going forward to the three sailors to do with as they saw best, and the balance aft to the three passengers.

Thus was the little company divided into two camps, and when the provisions had been apportioned each immediately set to work to open and distribute food and water. The sailors were the first to get one of the tins of "food" open, and their curses of rage and disappointment caused Clayton to ask what the trouble might be.

"Trouble!" shrieked Spider. "Trouble! It's worse than trouble—it's death! This —— tin is full of coal oil!"

Hastily now Clayton and Monsieur Thuran tore open one of theirs, only to learn the hideous truth that it also contained, not food, but coal oil. One after another the four tins on board were opened. And as the contents of each became known howls of anger announced the grim truth—there was not an ounce of food upon the boat.

"Well, thank Gawd it wasn't the water," cried Tompkins. "It's easier to get along without food than it is without water. We can eat our shoes if worse comes to worst, but we couldn't drink 'em."

As he spoke Wilson had been boring a hole in one of the water kegs, and as Spider held a tin cup he tilted the keg to pour a draft of the precious fluid. A thin stream of blackish, dry particles filtered slowly through the tiny aperture into the bottom of the cup. With a groan Wilson dropped the keg, and sat staring at the dry stuff in the cup, speechless with horror.

"The kegs are filled with gunpowder," said Spider, in a low tone, turning to those aft. And so it proved when the last had been opened.

"Coal oil and gunpowder!" cried Monsieur Thuran. "*Sapristi!* What a diet for shipwrecked mariners!"

With the full knowledge that there was neither food nor water on board, the pangs of hunger and thirst became immediately aggravated, and so on the first day of their tragic adventure real suffering commenced in grim earnest, and the full horrors of shipwreck were upon them.

As the days passed conditions became horrible. Aching

eyes scanned the horizon day and night until the weak and weary watchers would sink exhausted to the bottom of the boat, and there wrest in dream-disturbed slumber a moment's respite from the horrors of the waking reality.

The sailors, goaded by the remorseless pangs of hunger, had eaten their leather belts, their shoes, the sweatbands from their caps, although both Clayton and Monsieur Thuran had done their best to convince them that these would only add to the suffering they were enduring.

Weak and hopeless, the entire party lay beneath the pitiless tropic sun, with parched lips and swollen tongues, waiting for the death they were beginning to crave. The intense suffering of the first few days had become deadened for the three passengers who had eaten nothing, but the agony of the sailors was pitiful, as their weak and impoverished stomachs attempted to cope with the bits of leather with which they had filled them. Tompkins was the first to succumb. Just a week from the day the *Lady Alice* went down the sailor died horribly in frightful convulsions.

For hours his contorted and hideous features lay grinning back at those in the stern of the little boat, until Jane Porter could endure the sight no longer.

"Can you not drop his body overboard, William?" she asked.

Clayton rose and staggered toward the corpse. The two remaining sailors eyed him with a strange, baleful light in their sunken orbs. Futilely the Englishman tried to lift the corpse over the side of the boat, but his strength was not equal to the task.

"Lend me a hand here, please," he said to Wilson, who lay nearest him.

"Wot do you want to throw 'im over for?" questioned the sailor, in a querulous voice.

"We've got to before we're too weak to do it," replied Clayton. "He'd be awful by tomorrow, after a day under that broiling sun."

"Better leave well enough alone," grumbled Wilson. "We may need him before tomorrow."

Slowly the meaning of the man's words percolated into Clayton's understanding. At last he realized the fellow's reason for objecting to the disposal of the dead man.

"God!" whispered Clayton, in a horrified tone. "You don't mean—"

"W'y not?" growled Wilson. "Ain't we gotta live? He's

dead," he added, jerking his thumb in the direction of the corpse. "He won't care."

"Come here, Thuran," said Clayton, turning toward the Russian. "We'll have something worse than death aboard us if we don't get rid of this body before dark."

Wilson staggered up menacingly to prevent the contemplated act, but when his comrade, Spider, took sides with Clayton and Monsieur Thuran he gave up, and sat eying the corpse hungrily as the three men, by combining their efforts, succeeded in rolling it overboard.

All the balance of the day Wilson sat glaring at Clayton, in his eyes the gleam of insanity. Toward evening, as the sun was sinking into the sea, he commenced to chuckle and mumble to himself, but his eyes never left Clayton.

After it became quite dark Clayton could still feel those terrible eyes upon him. He dared not sleep, and yet so exhausted was he that it was a constant fight to retain consciousness. After what seemed an eternity of suffering his head dropped upon a thwart, and he slept. How long he was unconscious he did not know—he was awakened by a shuffling noise quite close to him. The moon had risen, and as he opened his startled eyes he saw Wilson creeping stealthily toward him, his mouth open and his swollen tongue hanging out.

The slight noise had awakened Jane Porter at the same time, and as she saw the hideous tableau she gave a shrill cry of alarm, and at the same instant the sailor lurched forward and fell upon Clayton. Like a wild beast his teeth sought the throat of his intended prey, but Clayton, weak though he was, still found sufficient strength to hold the maniac's mouth from him.

At Jane Porter's scream Monsieur Thuran and Spider awoke. On seeing the cause of her alarm, both men crawled to Clayton's rescue, and between the three of them were able to subdue Wilson and hurl him to the bottom of the boat. For a few minutes he lay there chattering and laughing, and then, with an awful scream, and before any of his companions could prevent, he staggered to his feet and leaped overboard.

The reaction from the terrific strain of excitement left the weak survivors trembling and prostrated. Spider broke down and wept; Jane Porter prayed; Clayton swore softly to himself; Monsieur Thuran sat with his head in his hands, thinking. The result of his cogitation developed the following morning in a proposition he made to Spider and Clayton.

"Gentlemen," said Monsieur Thuran, "you see the fate that awaits us all unless we are picked up within a day or two. That there is little hope of that is evidenced by the fact that during all the days we have drifted we have seen no sail, nor the faintest smudge of smoke upon the horizon.

"There might be a chance if we had food, but without food there is none. There remains for us, then, but one of two alternatives, and we must choose at once. Either we must all die together within a few days, or one must be sacrificed that the others may live. Do you quite clearly grasp my meaning?"

Jane Porter, who had overheard, was horrified. If the proposition had come from the poor, ignorant sailor, she might possibly have not been so surprised; but that it should come from one who posed as a man of culture and refinement, from a gentleman, she could scarcely credit.

"It is better that we die together, then," said Clayton.

"That is for the majority to decide," replied Monsieur Thuran. "As only one of us three will be the object of sacrifice, we shall decide. Miss Porter is not interested, since she will be in no danger."

"How shall we know who is to be first?" asked Spider.

"It may be fairly fixed by lot," replied Monsieur Thuran. "I have a number of franc pieces in my pocket. We can choose a certain date from among them—the one to draw this date first from beneath a piece of cloth will be the first."

"I shall have nothing to do with any such diabolical plan," muttered Clayton; "even yet land may be sighted or a ship appear—in time."

"You will do as the majority decide, or you will be 'the first' without the formality of drawing lots," said Monsieur Thuran threateningly. "Come, let us vote on the plan; I for one am in favor of it. How about you, Spider?"

"And I," replied the sailor.

"It is the will of the majority," announced Monsieur Thuran, "and now let us lose no time in drawing lots. It is as fair for one as for another. That three may live, one of us must die perhaps a few hours sooner than otherwise."

Then he began his preparations for the lottery of death, while Jane Porter sat wide-eyed and horrified at thought of the thing that she was about to witness. Monsieur Thuran spread his coat upon the bottom of the boat, and then from a handful of money he selected six franc pieces. The other two men bent close above him as he inspected them. Finally he handed them all to Clayton.

"Look at them carefully," he said. "The oldest date is eighteen-seventy-five, and there is only one of that year."

Clayton and the sailor inspected each coin. To them there seemed not the slightest difference that could be detected other than the dates. They were quite satisfied. Had they known that Monsieur Thuran's past experience as a card sharp had trained his sense of touch to so fine a point that he could almost differentiate between cards by the mere feel of them, they would scarcely have felt that the plan was so entirely fair. The 1875 piece was a hair thinner than the other coins, but neither Clayton nor Spider could have detected it without the aid of a micrometer.

"In what order shall we draw?" asked Monsieur Thuran, knowing from past experience that the majority of men always prefer last chance in a lottery where the single prize is some distasteful thing—there is always the chance and the hope that another will draw it first. Monsieur Thuran, for reasons of his own, preferred to draw first if the drawing should happen to require a second adventure beneath the coat.

And so when Spider elected to draw last he graciously offered to take the first chance himself. His hand was under the coat for but a moment, yet those quick, deft fingers had felt of each coin, and found and discarded the fatal piece. When he brought forth his hand it contained an 1888 franc piece. Then Clayton drew. Jane Porter leaned forward with a tense and horrified expression on her face as the hand of the man she was to marry groped about beneath the coat. Presently he withdrew it, a franc piece lying in the palm. For an instant he dared not look, but Monsieur Thuran, who had leaned nearer to see the date, exclaimed that he was safe.

Jane Porter sank weak and trembling against the side of the boat. She felt sick and dizzy. And now, if Spider should not draw the 1875 piece she must endure the whole horrid thing again.

The sailor already had his hand beneath the coat. Great beads of sweat were standing upon his brow. He trembled as though with a fit of ague. Aloud he cursed himself for having taken the last draw, for now his chances for escape were but three to one, whereas Monsieur Thuran's had been five to one, and Clayton's four to one.

The Russian was very patient, and did not hurry the man, for he knew that he himself was quite safe whether the 1875 piece came out this time or not. When the sailor withdrew his hand and looked at the piece of money within, he dropped fainting to the bottom of the boat. Both Clayton and Monsieur Thuran hastened weakly to examine the coin, which had rolled from the man's hand and lay beside him. It was not dated 1875. The reaction from the state of fear he had been in had overcome Spider quite as effectually as though he had drawn the fated piece.

But now the whole proceeding must be gone through again. Once more the Russian drew forth a harmless coin. Jane Porter closed her eyes as Clayton reached beneath the coat. Spider bent, wide-eyed, toward the hand that was to decide his fate, for whatever luck was Clayton's on this last draw, the opposite would be Spider's.

Then William Cecil Clayton, Lord Greystoke, removed his hand from beneath the coat, and with a coin tight pressed within his palm where none might see it, he looked at Jane Porter. He did not dare open his hand.

"Quick!" hissed Spider. "My Gawd, let's see it."

Clayton opened his fingers. Spider was the first to see the date, and ere any knew what his intention was he raised himself to his feet, and lunged over the side of the boat, to disappear forever into the green depths beneath—the coin had not been the 1875 piece.

The strain had exhausted those who remained to such an extent that they lay half unconscious for the balance of the day, nor was the subject referred to again for several days. Horrible days of increasing weakness and hopelessness. At length Monsieur Thuran crawled to where Clayton lay.

"We must draw once more before we are too weak even to eat," he whispered.

Clayton was in such a state that he was scarcely master of his own will. Jane Porter had not spoken for three days. He knew that she was dying. Horrible as the thought was, he hoped that the sacrifice of either Thuran or himself might be the means of giving her renewed strength, and so he immediately agreed to the Russian's proposal.

They drew under the same plan as before, but there could be but one result—Clayton drew the 1875 piece.

"When shall it be?" he asked Thuran.

The Russian had already drawn a pocketknife from his trousers, and was weakly attempting to open it.

"Now," he muttered, and his greedy eyes gloated upon the Englishman.

"Can't you wait until dark?" asked Clayton. "Miss Porter

must not see this thing done. We were to have been married, you know."

A look of disappointment came over Monsieur Thuran's face.

"Very well," he replied hesitatingly. "It will not be long until night. I have waited for many days—I can wait a few hours longer."

"Thank you, my friend," murmured Clayton. "Now I shall go to her side and remain with her until it is time. I would like to have an hour or two with her before I die."

When Clayton reached the girl's side she was unconscious—he knew that she was dying, and he was glad that she should not have to see or know the awful tragedy that was shortly to be enacted. He took her hand and raised it to his cracked and swollen lips. For a long time he lay caressing the emaciated, clawlike thing that had once been the beautiful, shapely white hand of the young Baltimore belle.

It was quite dark before he knew it, but he was recalled to himself by a voice out of the night. It was the Russian calling him to his doom.

"I am coming, Monsieur Thuran," he hastened to reply.

Thrice he attempted to turn himself upon his hands and knees, that he might crawl back to his death, but in the few hours that he had lain there he had become too weak to return to Thuran's side.

"You will have to come to me, monsieur," he called weakly. "I have not sufficient strength to gain my hands and knees."

"*Sapristi!*" muttered Monsieur Thuran. "You are attempting to cheat me out of my winnings."

Clayton heard the man shuffling about in the bottom of the boat. Finally there was a despairing groan. "I cannot crawl," he heard the Russian wail. "It is too late. You have tricked me, you dirty English dog."

"I have not tricked you, monsieur," replied Clayton. "I have done my best to rise, but I shall try again, and if you will try possibly each of us can crawl halfway, and then you shall have your 'winnings.' "

Again Clayton exerted his remaining strength to the utmost, and he heard Thuran apparently doing the same. Nearly an hour later the Englishman succeeded in raising himself to his hands and knees, but at the first forward movement he pitched upon his face.

A moment later he heard an exclamation of relief from Monsieur Thuran.

"I am coming," whispered the Russian.

Again Clayton essayed to stagger on to meet his fate, but once more he pitched headlong to the boat's bottom, nor, try as he would, could he again rise. His last effort caused him to roll over on his back, and there he lay looking up at the stars, while behind him, coming ever nearer and nearer, he could hear the laborious shuffling, and the stertorous breathing of the Russian.

It seemed that he must have lain thus an hour waiting for the thing to crawl out of the dark and end his misery. It was quite close now, but there were longer and longer pauses between its efforts to advance, and each forward movement seemed to the waiting Englishman to be almost imperceptible.

Finally he knew that Thuran was quite close beside him. He heard a cackling laugh, something touched his face, and he lost consciousness.

19

The City of Gold

THE very night that Tarzan of the Apes became chief of the Waziri the woman he loved lay dying in a tiny boat two hundred miles west of him upon the Atlantic. As he danced among his naked fellow savages, the firelight gleaming against his great, rolling muscles, the personification of physical perfection and strength, the woman who loved him lay thin and emaciated in the last coma that precedes death by thirst and starvation.

The week following the induction of Tarzan into the kingship of the Waziri was occupied in escorting the Manyuema of the Arab raiders to the northern boundary of Waziri in accordance with the promise which Tarzan had made them. Before he left them he exacted a pledge from them that they would not lead any expeditions against the Waziri in the future, nor was it a difficult promise to obtain. They had had sufficient experience with the fighting tactics of the new Waziri chief not to have the slightest desire to accompany another predatory force within the boundaries of his domain.

Almost immediately upon his return to the village Tarzan commenced making preparations for leading an expedition in search of the ruined city of gold which old Waziri had described to him. He selected fifty of the sturdiest warriors of his tribe, choosing only men who seemed anxious to accompany him on the arduous march, and share the dangers of a new and hostile country.

The fabulous wealth of the fabled city had been almost constantly in his mind since Waziri had recounted the strange adventures of the former expedition which had stumbled upon the vast ruins by chance. The lure of adventure may have been quite as powerful a factor in urging Tarzan of the Apes to undertake the journey as the lure of gold, but the lure of gold was there, too, for he had learned among civilized men something of the miracles that may be wrought by the possessor of the magic yellow metal. What he would do with a golden fortune in the heart of savage Africa it had not occurred to him to consider—it would be enough to possess the power to work wonders, even though he never had an opportunity to employ it.

So one glorious tropical morning Waziri, chief of the Waziri, set out at the head of fifty clean-limbed ebon warriors in quest of adventure and of riches. They followed the course which old Waziri had described to Tarzan. For days they marched—up one river, across a low divide; down another river; up a third, until at the end of the twenty-fifth day they camped upon a mountainside, from the summit of which they hoped to catch their first view of the marvelous city of treasure.

Early the next morning they were climbing the almost perpendicular crags which formed the last, but greatest, natural barrier between them and their destination. It was nearly noon before Tarzan, who headed the thin line of climbing warriors, scrambled over the top of the last cliff and stood upon the little flat table-land of the mountaintop.

On either hand towered mighty peaks thousands of feet higher than the pass through which they were entering the forbidden valley. Behind him stretched the wooded valley across which they had marched for many days, and at the opposite side the low range which marked the boundary of their own country.

But before him was the view that centered his attention. Here lay a desolate valley—a shallow, narrow valley dotted with stunted trees and covered with many great bowlders.

And on the far side of the valley lay what appeared to be a mighty city, its great walls, its lofty spires, its turrets, minarets, and domes showing red and yellow in the sunlight. Tarzan was yet too far away to note the marks of ruin—to him it appeared a wonderful city of magnificent beauty, and in imagination he peopled its broad avenues and its huge temples with a throng of happy, active people.

For an hour the little expedition rested upon the mountaintop, and then Tarzan led them down into the valley below. There was no trail, but the way was less arduous than the ascent of the opposite face of the mountain had been. Once in the valley their progress was rapid, so that it was still light when they halted before the towering walls of the ancient city.

The outer wall was fifty feet in height where it had not fallen into ruin, but nowhere as far as they could see had more than ten or twenty feet of the upper courses fallen away. It was still a formidable defense. On several occasions Tarzan had thought that he discerned things moving behind the ruined portions of the wall near to them, as though creatures were watching them from behind the bulwarks of the ancient pile. And often he felt the sensation of unseen eyes upon him, but not once could he be sure that it was more than imagination.

That night they camped outside the city. Once, at midnight, they were awakened by a shrill scream from beyond the great wall. It was very high at first, descending gradually until it ended in a series of dismal moans. It had a strange effect upon the blacks, almost paralyzing them with terror while it lasted, and it was an hour before the camp settled down to sleep once more. In the morning the effects of it were still visible in the fearful, sidelong glances that the Waziri continually cast at the massive and forbidding structure which loomed above them.

It required considerable encouragement and urging on Tarzan's part to prevent the blacks from abandoning the venture on the spot and hastening back across the valley toward the cliffs they had scaled the day before. But at length, by dint of commands, and threats that he would enter the city alone, they agreed to accompany him.

For fifteen minutes they marched along the face of the wall before they discovered a means of ingress. Then they came to a narrow cleft about twenty inches wide. Within, a flight of concrete steps, worn hollow by centuries of use, rose before them, to disappear at a sharp turning of the passage a few yards ahead.

Into this narrow alley Tarzan made his way, turning his giant shoulders sideways that they might enter at all. Behind him trailed his black warriors. At the turn in the cleft the stairs ended, and the path was level; but it wound and twisted in a serpentine fashion, until suddenly at a sharp angle it debouched upon a narrow court, across which loomed an inner wall equally as high as the outer. This inner wall was set with little round towers alternating along its entire summit with pointed monoliths. In places these had fallen, and the wall was ruined, but it was in a much better state of preservation than the outer wall.

Another narrow passage led through this wall, and at its end Tarzan and his warriors found themselves in a broad avenue, on the opposite side of which crumbling edifices of hewn granite loomed dark and forbidding. Upon the crumbled débris along the face of the buildings trees had grown, and vines wound in and out of the hollow, staring windows; but the building directly opposite them seemed less overgrown than the others, and in a much better state of preservation. It was a massive pile, surmounted by an enormous dome. At either side of its great entrance stood rows of tall pillars, each capped by a huge, grotesque bird carved from the solid rock of the monoliths.

As the ape-man and his companions stood gazing in varying degrees of wonderment at this ancient city in the midst of savage Africa, several of them became aware of movement within the structure at which they were looking. Dim, shadowy shapes appeared to be moving about in the semi-darkness of the interior. There was nothing tangible that the eye could grasp—only an uncanny suggestion of life where it seemed that there should be no life, for living things seemed out of place in this weird, dead city of the long-dead past.

Tarzan recalled something that he had read in the library at Paris of a lost race of white men that native legend described as living in the heart of Africa. He wondered if he were not looking upon the ruins of the civilization that this strange people had wrought amid the savage surroundings of their strange and savage home. Could it be possible that even now a remnant of that lost race inhabited the ruined grandeur that had once been their progenitors? Again he became conscious of a stealthy movement within the great temple before him.

"Come!" he said, to his Waziri. "Let us have a look at what lies behind those ruined walls."

His men were loath to follow him, but when they saw that he was bravely entering the frowning portal they trailed a few paces behind in a huddled group that seemed the personification of nervous terror. A single shriek such as they had heard the night before would have been sufficient to have sent them all racing madly for the narrow cleft that led through the great walls to the outer world.

As Tarzan entered the building he was distinctly aware of many eyes upon him. There was a rustling in the shadows of a near-by corridor, and he could have sworn that he saw a human hand withdrawn from an embrasure that opened above him into the domelike rotunda in which he found himself.

The floor of the chamber was of concrete, the walls of smooth granite, upon which strange figures of men and beasts were carved. In places tablets of yellow metal had been set in the solid masonry of the walls.

When he approached closer to one of these tablets he saw that it was of gold, and bore many hieroglyphics. Beyond this first chamber there were others, and back of them the building branched out into enormous wings. Tarzan passed through several of these chambers, finding many evidences of the fabulous wealth of the original builders. In one room were seven pillars of solid gold, and in another the floor itself was of the precious metal. And all the while that he explored, his blacks huddled close together at his back, and strange shapes hovered upon either hand and before them and behind, yet never close enough that any might say that they were not alone.

The strain, however, was telling upon the nerves of the Waziri. They begged Tarzan to return to the sunlight. They said that no good could come of such an expedition, for the ruins were haunted by the spirits of the dead who had once inhabited them.

"They are watching us, O king," whispered Busuli. "They are waiting until they have led us into the innermost recesses of their stronghold, and then they will fall upon us and tear us to pieces with their teeth. That is the way with spirits. My mother's uncle, who is a great witch doctor, has told me all about it many times."

Tarzan laughed. "Run back into the sunlight, my children," he said. "I will join you when I have searched this old ruin from top to bottom, and found the gold, or found that there is none. At least we may take the tablets from the walls, though the pillars are too heavy for us to handle; but there should be great storerooms filled with gold—gold that we can carry away upon our backs with ease. Run on now, out into the fresh air where you may breathe easier."

Some of the warriors started to obey their chief with alacrity, but Busuli and several others hesitated to leave him —hesitated between love and loyalty for their king, and superstitious fear of the unknown. And then, quite unexpectedly, that occurred which decided the question without the necessity for further discussion. Out of the silence of the ruined temple there rang, close to their ears, the same hideous shriek they had heard the previous night, and with horrified cries the black warriors turned and fled through the empty halls of the age-old edifice.

Behind them stood Tarzan of the Apes where they had left him, a grim smile upon his lips—waiting for the enemy he fully expected was about to pounce upon him. But again silence reigned, except for the faint suggestion of the sound of naked feet moving stealthily in near-by places.

Then Tarzan wheeled and passed on into the depths of the temple. From room to room he went, until he came to one at which a rude, barred door still stood, and as he put his shoulder against it to push it in, again the shriek of warning rang out almost beside him. It was evident that he was being warned to refrain from desecrating this particular room. Or could it be that within lay the secret to the treasure stores?

At any rate, the very fact that the strange, invisible guardians of this weird place had some reason for wishing him not to enter this particular chamber was sufficient to treble Tarzan's desire to do so, and though the shrieking was repeated continuously, he kept his shoulder to the door until it gave before his giant strength to swing open upon creaking wooden hinges.

Within all was black as the tomb. There was no window to let in the faintest ray of light, and as the corridor upon which it opened was itself in semi-darkness, even the open door shed no relieving rays within. Feeling before him upon the floor with the butt of his spear, Tarzan entered the Stygian gloom. Suddenly the door behind him closed, and at the same time hands clutched him from every direction out of the darkness.

The ape-man fought with all the savage fury of self-preservation backed by the herculean strength that was his.

But though he felt his blows land, and his teeth sink into soft flesh, there seemed always two new hands to take the place of those that he fought off. At last they dragged him down, and slowly, very slowly, they overcame him by the mere weight of their numbers. And then they bound him—his hands behind his back and his feet trussed up to meet them.

He had heard no sound except the heavy breathing of his antagonists, and the noise of the battle. He knew not what manner of creatures had captured him, but that they were human seemed evident from the fact that they had bound him.

Presently they lifted him from the floor, and half dragging, half pushing him, they brought him out of the black chamber through another doorway into an inner courtyard of the temple. Here he saw his captors. There must have been a hundred of them—short, stocky men, with great beards that covered their faces and fell upon their hairy breasts.

The thick, matted hair upon their heads grew low over their receding brows, and hung about their shoulders and their backs. Their crooked legs were short and heavy, their arms long and muscular. About their loins they wore the skins of leopards and lions, and great necklaces of the claws of these same animals depended upon their breasts. Massive circlets of virgin gold adorned their arms and legs. For weapons they carried heavy, knotted bludgeons, and in the belts that confined their single garments each had a long, wicked-looking knife.

But the feature of them that made the most startling impression upon their prisoner was their white skins—neither in color nor feature was there a trace of the negroid about them. Yet, with their receding foreheads, wicked little close-set eyes, and yellow fangs, they were far from prepossessing in appearance.

During the fight within the dark chamber, and while they had been dragging Tarzan to the inner court, no word had been spoken, but now several of them exchanged grunting, monosyllabic conversation in a language unfamiliar to the ape-man, and presently they left him lying upon the concrete floor while they trooped off on their short legs into another part of the temple beyond the court.

As Tarzan lay there upon his back he saw that the temple entirely surrounded the little inclosure, and that on all sides its lofty walls rose high above him. At the top a little patch of blue sky was visible, and, in one direction, through an embrasure, he could see foliage, but whether it was beyond or within the temple he did not know.

About the court, from the ground to the top of the temple, were series of open galleries, and now and then the captive caught glimpses of bright eyes gleaming from beneath masses of tumbling hair, peering down upon him from above.

The ape-man gently tested the strength of the bonds that held him, and while he could not be sure it seemed that they were of insufficient strength to withstand the strain of his mighty muscles when the time came to make a break for freedom; but he did not dare to put them to the crucial test until darkness had fallen, or he felt that no spying eyes were upon him.

He had lain within the court for several hours before the first rays of sunlight penetrated the vertical shaft; almost simultaneously he heard the pattering of bare feet in the corridors about him, and a moment later saw the galleries above fill with crafty faces as a score or more entered the courtyard.

For a moment every eye was bent upon the noonday sun, and then in unison the people in the galleries and those in the court below took up the refrain of a low, weird chant. Presently those about Tarzan began to dance to the cadence of their solemn song. They circled him slowly, resembling in their manner of dancing a number of clumsy, shuffling bears; but as yet they did not look at him, keeping their little eyes fixed upon the sun.

For ten minutes or more they kept up their monotonous chant and steps, and then suddenly, and in perfect unison, they turned toward their victim with upraised bludgeons and emitting fearful howls, the while they contorted their features into the most diabolical expressions, they rushed upon him.

At the same instant a female figure dashed into the midst of the bloodthirsty horde, and, with a bludgeon similar to their own, except that it was wrought from gold, beat back the advancing men.

20

La

FOR a moment Tarzan thought that by some strange freak of fate a miracle had saved him, but when he realized the ease with which the girl had, single-handed, beaten off twenty gorilla-like males, and an instant later, as he saw them again take up their dance about him while she addressed them in a singsong monotone, which bore every evidence of rote, he came to the conclusion that it was all but a part of the ceremony of which he was the central figure.

After a moment or two the girl drew a knife from her girdle, and, leaning over Tarzan, cut the bonds from his legs. Then, as the men stopped their dance, and approached, she motioned to him to rise. Placing the rope that had been about his legs around his neck, she led him across the courtyard, the men following in twos.

Through winding corridors she led, farther and farther into the remoter precincts of the temple, until they came to a great chamber in the center of which stood an altar. Then it was that Tarzan translated the strange ceremony that had preceded his introduction into this holy of holies.

He had fallen into the hands of descendants of the ancient sun worshippers. His seeming rescue by a votaress of the high priestess of the sun had been but a part of the mimicry of their heathen ceremony—the sun looking down upon him through the opening at the top of the court had claimed him as his own, and the priestess had come from the inner temple to save him from the polluting hands of worldings—to save him as a human offering to their flaming deity.

And had he needed further assurance as to the correctness of his theory he had only to cast his eyes upon the brownish-red stains that caked the stone altar and covered the floor in its immediate vicinity, or to the human skulls which grinned from countless niches in the towering walls.

The priestess led the victim to the altar steps. Again the galleries above filled with watchers, while from an arched doorway at the east end of the chamber a procession of females filed slowly into the room. They wore, like the men, only skins of wild animals caught about their waists with rawhide belts or chains of gold; but the black masses of their hair were incrusted with golden headgear composed of many circular and oval pieces of gold ingeniously held together to form a metal cap from which depended, at each side of the head, long strings of oval pieces falling to the waist.

The females were more symmetrically proportioned than the males, their features were much more perfect, the shapes of their heads and their large, soft, black eyes denoting far greater intelligence and humanity than was possessed by their lords and masters.

Each priestess bore two golden cups, and as they formed in line along one side of the altar the men formed opposite them, advancing and taking each a cup from the female opposite. Then the chant began once more, and presently from a dark passageway beyond the altar another female emerged from the cavernous depths beneath the chamber.

The high priestess, thought Tarzan. She was a young woman with a rather intelligent and shapely face. Her ornaments were similar to those worn by her votaries, but much more elaborate, many being set with diamonds. Her bare arms and legs were almost concealed by the massive, bejeweled ornaments which covered them, while her single leopard skin was supported by a close-fitting girdle of golden rings set in strange designs with innumerable small diamonds. In the girdle she carried a long, jeweled knife, and in her hand a slender wand in lieu of a bludgeon.

As she advanced to the opposite side of the altar she halted, and the chanting ceased. The priests and priestesses knelt before her, while with wand extended above them she recited a long and tiresome prayer. Her voice was soft and musical—Tarzan could scarce realize that its possessor in a moment more would be transformed by the fanatical ecstasy of religious zeal into a wild-eyed and bloodthirsty executioner, who, with dripping knife, would be the first to drink her victim's red, warm blood from the little golden cup that stood upon the altar.

As she finished her prayer she let her eyes rest for the first time upon Tarzan. With every indication of considerable curiosity she examined him from head to foot. Then she addressed him, and when she had finished stood waiting, as though she expected a reply.

"I do not understand your language," said Tarzan. "Possibly we may speak together in another tongue?" But she could not understand him, though he tried French, English, Arab, Waziri, and, as a last resort, the mongrel tongue of the West Coast.

She shook her head, and it seemed that there was a note of weariness in her voice as she motioned to the priests to continue with the rites. These now circled in a repetition of their idiotic dance, which was terminated finally at a command from the priestess, who had stood throughout, still looking intently upon Tarzan.

At her signal the priests rushed upon the ape-man, and, lifting him bodily, laid him upon his back across the altar, his head hanging over one edge, his legs over the opposite. Then they and the priestesses formed in two lines, with their little golden cups in readiness to capture a share of the victim's lifeblood after the sacrificial knife had accomplished its work.

In the line of priests an altercation arose as to who should have first place. A burly brute with all the refined intelligence of a gorilla stamped upon his bestial face was attempting to push a smaller man to second place, but the smaller one appealed to the high priestess, who in a cold peremptory voice sent the larger to the extreme end of the line. Tarzan could hear him growling and rumbling as he went slowly to the inferior station.

Then the priestess, standing above him, began reciting what Tarzan took to be an invocation, the while she slowly raised her thin, sharp knife aloft. It seemed ages to the ape-man before her arm ceased its upward progress and the knife halted high above his unprotected breast.

Then it started downward, slowly at first, but as the incantation increased in rapidity, with greater speed. At the end of the line Tarzan could still hear the grumbling of the disgruntled priest. The man's voice rose louder and louder. A priestess near him spoke in sharp tones of rebuke. The knife was quite near to Tarzan's breast now, but it halted for an instant as the high priestess raised her eyes to shoot her swift displeasure at the instigator of this sacrilegious interruption.

There was a sudden commotion in the direction of the disputants, and Tarzan rolled his head in their direction in time to see the burly brute of a priest leap upon the woman opposite him, dashing out her brains with a single blow of his heavy cudgel. Then that happened which Tarzan had witnessed a hundred times before among the wild denizens of his own savage jungle. He had seen the thing fall upon Kerchak, and Tublat, and Terkoz; upon a dozen of the other mighty bull apes of his tribe; and upon Tantor, the elephant; there was scarce any of the males of the forest that did not at times fall prey to it. The priest went mad, and with his heavy bludgeon ran amuck among his fellows.

His screams of rage were frightful as he dashed hither and thither, dealing terrific blows with his giant weapon, or sinking his yellow fangs into the flesh of some luckless victim. And during it the priestess stood with poised knife above Tarzan, her eyes fixed in horror upon the maniacal thing that was dealing out death and destruction to her votaries.

Presently the room was emptied except for the dead and dying on the floor, the victim upon the altar, the high priestess, and the madman. As the cunning eyes of the latter fell upon the woman they lighted with a new and sudden lust. Slowly he crept toward her, and now he spoke; but this time there fell upon Tarzan's surprised ears a language he could understand; the last one that he would ever have thought of employing in attempting to converse with human beings—the low guttural barking of the tribe of great anthropoids—his own mother tongue. And the woman answered the man in the same language.

He was threatening—she attempting to reason with him, for it was quite evident that she saw that he was past her authority. The brute was quite close now—creeping with clawlike hands extended toward her around the end of the altar.

Tarzan strained at the bonds which held his arms pinioned behind him. The woman did not see—she had forgotten her prey in the horror of the danger that threatened herself. As the brute leaped past Tarzan to clutch his victim, the ape-man gave one superhuman wrench at the thongs that held him. The effort sent him rolling from the altar to the stone floor on the opposite side from that on which the priestess stood; but as he sprang to his feet the thongs dropped from his freed arms, and at the same time he realized that he was alone in the inner temple—the high priestess and the mad priest had disappeared.

And then a muffled scream came from the cavernous mouth of the dark hole beyond the sacrificial altar through which the priestess had entered the temple. Without even a thought for his own safety, or the possibility for escape which this rapid series of fortuitous circumstances had thrust upon him, Tarzan of the Apes answered the call of the woman in danger. With a lithe bound he was at the gaping entrance to the subterranean chamber, and a moment later was running down a flight of age-old concrete steps that led he knew not where.

The faint light that filtered in from above showed him a large, low-ceiled vault from which several doorways led off into inky darkness, but there was no need to thread an unknown way, for there before him lay the objects of his search—the mad brute had the girl upon the floor, and gorilla-like fingers were clutching frantically at her throat as she struggled to escape the fury of the awful thing upon her.

As Tarzan's heavy hand fell upon his shoulder the priest dropped his victim, and turned upon her would-be rescuer. With foam-flecked lips and bared fangs the mad sun-worshiper battled with the tenfold power of the maniac. In the blood lust of his fury the creature had undergone a sudden reversion to type, which left him a wild beast, forgetful of the dagger that projected from his belt—thinking only of nature's weapons with which his brute prototype had battled.

But if he could use his teeth and hands to advantage, he found one even better versed in the school of savage warfare to which he had reverted, for Tarzan of the Apes closed with him, and they fell to the floor tearing and rending at one another like two bull apes; while the primitive priestess stood flattened against the wall, watching with wide, fear-fascinated eyes the growling, snapping beasts at her feet.

At last she saw the stranger close one mighty hand upon the throat of his antagonist, and as he forced the bruteman's head far back rain blow after blow upon the upturned face. A moment later he threw the still thing from him, and, arising, shook himself like a lion. He placed a foot upon the carcass before him, and raised his head to give the victory cry of his kind, but as his eyes fell upon the opening above him leading into the temple of human sacrifice he thought better of his intended act.

The girl, who had been half paralyzed by fear as the two men fought, had just commenced to give thought to her probable fate now that, though released from the clutches of a madman, she had fallen into the hands of one whom but a moment before she had been upon the point of killing. She looked about for some means of escape. The black mouth of a diverging corridor was near at hand, but as she turned to dart into it the ape-man's eyes fell upon her, and with a quick leap he was at her side, and a restraining hand was laid upon her arm.

"Wait!" said Tarzan of the Apes, in the language of the tribe of Kerchak.

The girl looked at him in astonishment.

"Who are you," she whispered, "who speaks the language of the first man?"

"I am Tarzan of the Apes," he answered in the vernacular of the anthropoids.

"What do you want of me?" she continued. "For what purpose did you save me from Tha?"

"I could not see a woman murdered?" It was a half question that answered her.

"But what do you intend to do with me now?" she continued.

"Nothing," he replied, "but you can do something for me—you can lead me out of this place to freedom." He made the suggestion without the slightest thought that she would accede. He felt quite sure that the sacrifice would go on from the point where it had been interrupted if the high priestess had her way, though he was equally positive that they would find Tarzan of the Apes unbound and with a long dagger in his hand a much less tractable victim than Tarzan disarmed and bound.

The girl stood looking at him for a long moment before she spoke.

"You are a very wonderful man," she said. "You are such a man as I have seen in my daydreams ever since I was a little girl. You are such a man as I imagine the forbears of my people must have been—the great race of people who built this mighty city in the heart of a savage world that they might wrest from the bowels of the earth the fabulous wealth for which they had sacrificed their far-distant civilization.

"I cannot understand why you came to my rescue in the first place, and now I cannot understand why, having me within your power, you do not wish to be revenged upon me for having sentenced you to death—for having almost put you to death with my own hand."

"I presume," replied the ape-man, "that you but followed the teachings of your religion. I cannot blame *you* for that, no matter what I may think of your creed. But who are you—what people have I fallen among?"

"I am La, high priestess of the Temple of the Sun, in the city of Opar. We are descendants of a people who came to this savage world more than ten thousand years ago in search of gold. Their cities stretched from a great sea under the rising sun to a great sea into which the sun descends at night to cool his flaming brow. They were very rich and very powerful, but they lived only a few months of the year in their magnificent palaces here; the rest of the time they spent in their native land, far, far to the north.

"Many ships went back and forth between this new world and the old. During the rainy season there were but few of the inhabitants remained here, only those who superintended the working of the mines by the black slaves, and the merchants who had to stay to supply their wants, and the soldiers who guarded the cities and the mines.

"It was at one of these times that the great calamity occurred. When the time came for the teeming thousands to return none came. For weeks the people waited. Then they sent out a great galley to learn why no one came from the mother country, but though they sailed about for many months, they were unable to find any trace of the mighty land that had for countless ages borne their ancient civilization —it had sunk into the sea.

"From that day dated the downfall of my people. Disheartened and unhappy, they soon became a prey to the black hordes of the north and the black hordes of the south. One by one the cities were deserted or overcome. The last remnant was finally forced to take shelter within this mighty mountain fortress. Slowly we have dwindled in power, in civilization, in intellect, in numbers, until now we are no more than a small tribe of savage apes.

"In fact, the apes live with us, and have for many ages. We call them the first men—we speak their language quite as much as we do our own; only in the rituals of the temple do we make any attempt to retain our mother tongue. In time it will be forgotten, and we will speak only the language of the apes; in time we will no longer banish those of our people who mate with apes, and so in time we shall descend to the very beasts from which ages ago our progenitors may have sprung."

"But why are you more human than the others?" asked the man.

"For some reason the women have not reverted to savagery so rapidly as the men. It may be because only the lower types of men remained here at the time of the great catastrophe, while the temples were filled with the noblest daughters of the race. My strain has remained clearer than the rest because for countless ages my foremothers were high priestesses—the sacred office descends from mother to daughter. Our husbands are chosen for us from the noblest in the land. The most perfect man, mentally and physically, is selected to be the husband of the high priestess."

"From what I saw of the gentlemen above," said Tarzan, with a grin, "there should be little trouble in choosing from among them."

The girl looked at him quizzically for a moment.

"Do not be sacrilegious," she said. "They are very holy men—they are priests."

"Then there are others who are better to look upon?" he asked.

"The others are all more ugly than the priests," she replied.

Tarzan shuddered at her fate, for even in the dim light of the vault he was impressed by her beauty.

"But how about myself?" he asked suddenly. "Are you going to lead me to liberty?"

"You have been chosen by The Flaming God as his own," she answered solemnly. "Not even I have the power to save you—should they find you again. But I do not intend that they shall find you. You risked your life to save mine. I may do no less for you. It will be no easy matter—it may require days; but in the end I think that I can lead you beyond the walls. Come, they will look here for me presently, and if they find us together we shall both be lost—they would kill me did they think that I had proved false to my god."

"You must not take the risk, then," he said quickly. "I will return to the temple, and if I can fight my way to freedom there will be no suspicion thrown upon you."

But she would not have it so, and finally persuaded him to follow her, saying that they had already remained in the vault too long to prevent suspicion from falling upon her even if they returned to the temple.

"I will hide you, and then return alone," she said, "telling them that I was long unconscious after you killed Tha, and that I do not know whither you escaped."

And so she led him through winding corridors of gloom, until finally they came to a small chamber into which a little light filtered through a stone grating in the ceiling.

"This is the Chamber of the Dead," she said. "None will think of searching here for you—they would not dare. I will return after it is dark. By that time I may have found a plan to effect your escape."

She was gone, and Tarzan of the Apes was left alone in the Chamber of the Dead, beneath the long-dead city of Opar.

21

The Castaways

CLAYTON dreamed that he was drinking his fill of water, pure, delightful drafts of fresh water. With a start he gained consciousness to find himself wet through by torrents of rain that were falling upon his body and his upturned face. A heavy tropical shower was beating down upon them. He opened his mouth and drank. Presently he was so revived and strengthened that he was enabled to raise himself upon his hands. Across his legs lay Monsieur Thuran. A few feet aft Jane Porter was huddled in a pitiful little heap in the bottom of the boat—she was quite still. Clayton knew that she was dead.

After infinite labor he released himself from Thuran's pinioning body, and with renewed strength crawled toward the girl. He raised her head from the rough boards of the boat's bottom. There might be life in that poor, starved frame even yet. He could not quite abandon all hope, and so he seized a water-soaked rag and squeezed the precious drops between the swollen lips of the hideous thing that had but a few short days before glowed with the resplendent life of happy youth and glorious beauty.

For some time there was no sign of returning animation, but at last his efforts were rewarded by a slight tremor of the half-closed lids. He chafed the thin hands, and forced a few more drops of water into the parched throat. The girl opened her eyes, looking up at him for a long time before she could recall her surroundings.

"Water?" she whispered. "Are we saved?"

"It is raining," he explained. "We may at least drink. Already it has revived us both."

"Monsieur Thuran?" she asked. "He did not kill you. Is he dead?"

"I do not know," replied Clayton. "If he lives and this rain revives him—" But he stopped there, remembering too late that he must not add further to the horrors which the girl already had endured.

But she guessed what he would have said.

"Where is he?" she asked.

Clayton nodded his head toward the prostrate form of the Russian. For a time neither spoke.

"I will see if I can revive him," said Clayton at length.

"No," she whispered, extending a detaining hand toward him. "Do not do that—he will kill you when the water has given him strength. If he is dying, let him die. Do not leave me alone in this boat with that beast."

Clayton hesitated. His honor demanded that he attempt to revive Thuran, and there was the possibility, too, that the Russian was beyond human aid. It was not dishonorable to hope so. As he sat fighting out his battle he presently raised his eyes from the body of the man, and as they passed above the gunwale of the boat he staggered weakly to his feet with a little cry of joy.

"Land, Jane!" he almost shouted through his cracked lips. "Thank God, land!"

The girl looked, too, and there, not a hundred yards away, she saw a yellow beach, and, beyond, the luxurious foliage of a tropical jungle.

"Now you may revive him," said Jane Porter, for she, too, had been haunted with the pangs of conscience which had resulted from her decision to prevent Clayton from offering succor to their companion.

It required the better part of half an hour before the Russian evinced sufficient symptoms of returning consciousness to open his eyes, and it was some time later before they could bring him to a realization of their good fortune. By this time the boat was scraping gently upon the sandy bottom.

Between the refreshing water that he had drunk and the stimulus of renewed hope, Clayton found strength to stagger through the shallow water to the shore with a line made fast to the boat's bow. This he fastened to a small tree which grew at the top of a low bank, for the tide was at flood, and he feared that the boat might carry them all out to sea again with the ebb, since it was quite likely that it would be beyond his strength to get Jane Porter to the shore for several hours.

Next he managed to stagger and crawl toward the near-by jungle, where he had seen evidences of profusion of tropical fruit. His former experience in the jungle of Tarzan of the Apes had taught him which of the many growing things were edible, and after nearly an hour of absence he returned to the beach with a little armful of food.

The rain had ceased, and the hot sun was beating down so mercilessly upon her that Jane Porter insisted on making an immediate attempt to gain the land. Still further invigorated by the food Clayton had brought, the three were able to reach the half shade of the small tree to which their boat was moored. Here, thoroughly exhausted, they threw themselves down to rest, sleeping until dark.

For a month they lived upon the beach in comparative safety. As their strength returned the two men constructed a rude shelter in the branches of a tree, high enough from the ground to insure safety from the larger beasts of prey. By day they gathered fruits and trapped small rodents; at night they lay cowering within their frail shelter while savage denizens of the jungle made hideous the hours of darkness.

They slept upon litters of jungle grasses, and for covering at night Jane Porter had only an old ulster that belonged to Clayton, the same garment that he had worn upon that memorable trip to the Wisconsin woods. Clayton had erected a frail partition of boughs to divide their arboreal shelter into two rooms—one for the girl and the other for Monsieur Thuran and himself.

From the first the Russian had exhibited every trait of his true character—selfishness, boorishness, arrogance, cowardice, and lust. Twice had he and Clayton come to blows because of Thuran's attitude toward the girl. Clayton dared not leave her alone with him for an instant. The existence of the Englishman and his fiancée was one continual nightmare of horror, and yet they lived on in hope of ultimate rescue.

Jane Porter's thoughts often reverted to her other experience on this savage shore. Ah, if the invincible forest god of that dead past were but with them now. No longer would there be aught to fear from prowling beasts, or from the bestial Russian. She could not well refrain from comparing the scant protection afforded her by Clayton with what she might have expected had Tarzan of the Apes been for a single instant confronted by the sinister and menacing attitude of Monsieur Thuran. Once, when Clayton had gone to the little stream for water, and Thuran had spoken coarsely to her, she voiced her thoughts.

"It is well for you, Monsieur Thuran," she said, "that the poor Monsieur Tarzan who was lost from the ship that brought you and Miss Strong to Cape Town is not here now."

"You knew the pig?" asked Thuran, with a sneer.

"I knew the man," she replied. "The only real man, I think, that I have ever known."

There was something in her tone of voice that led the Russian to attribute to her a deeper feeling for his enemy than friendship, and he grasped at the suggestion to be further revenged upon the man whom he supposed dead by besmirching his memory to the girl.

"He was worse than a pig," he cried. "He was a poltroon and a coward. To save himself from the righteous wrath of the husband of a woman he had wronged, he perjured his soul in an attempt to place the blame entirely upon her. Not succeeding in this, he ran away from France to escape meeting the husband upon the field of honor. That is why he was on board the ship that bore Miss Strong and myself to Cape Town. I know whereof I speak, for the woman in the case is my sister. Something more I know that I have never told another—your brave Monsieur Tarzan leaped overboard in an agony of fear because I recognized him, and insisted that he make reparation to me the following morning—we could have fought with knives in my stateroom."

Jane Porter laughed. "You do not for a moment imagine that one who has known both Monsieur Tarzan and you could ever believe such an impossible tale?"

"Then why did he travel under an assumed name?" asked Monsieur Thuran.

"I do not believe you," she cried, but nevertheless the seed of suspicion was sown, for she knew that Hazel Strong had known her forest god only as John Caldwell, of London.

A scant five miles north of their rude shelter, all unknown to them, and practically as remote as though separated by thousands of miles of impenetrable jungle, lay the snug little cabin of Tarzan of the Apes. While farther up the coast, a few miles beyond the cabin, in crude but well-built shelters, lived a little party of eighteen souls—the occupants of the three boats from the *Lady Alice* from which Clayton's boat had become separated.

Over a smooth sea they had rowed to the mainland in less than three days. None of the horrors of shipwreck had been theirs, and though depressed by sorrow, and suffering from the shock of the catastrophe and the unaccustomed hardships of their new existence there was none much the worse for the experience.

All were buoyed by the hope that the fourth boat had been picked up, and that a thorough search of the coast would be quickly made. As all the firearms and ammunition on the yacht had been placed in Lord Tennington's boat, the party was well equipped for defense, and for hunting the larger game for food.

Professor Archimedes Q. Porter was their only immediate anxiety. Fully assured in his own mind that his daughter had been picked up by a passing steamer, he gave over the last vestige of apprehension concerning her welfare, and devoted his giant intellect solely to the consideration of those momentous and abstruse scientific problems which he considered the only proper food for thought in one of his erudition. His mind appeared blank to the influence of all extraneous matters.

"Never," said the exhausted Mr. Samuel T. Philander, to Lord Tennington, "never has Professor Porter been more difficult—er—I might say, impossible. Why, only this morning, after I had been forced to relinquish my surveillance for a brief half hour he was entirely missing upon my return. And, bless me, sir, where do you imagine I discovered him? A half mile out in the ocean, sir, in one of the lifeboats, rowing away for dear life. I do not know how he attained even that magnificent distance from shore, for he had but a single oar, with which he was blissfully rowing about in circles.

"When one of the sailors had taken me out to him in another boat the professor became quite indignant at my suggestion that we return at once to land. 'Why, Mr. Philander,' he said, 'I am surprised that you, sir, a man of letters yourself, should have the temerity so to interrupt the progress of science. I had about deduced from certain astronomic phenomena I have had under minute observation during the past several tropic nights an entirely new nebular hypothesis which will unquestionably startle the scientific world. I wish to consult a very excellent monograph on Laplace's hypothesis, which I understand is in a certain private collection in New York City. Your interference, Mr. Philander, will result in an irreparable delay, for I was just rowing over to obtain this pamphlet.' And it was with the greatest difficulty that I persuaded him to return to shore, without resorting to force," concluded Mr. Philander.

Miss Strong and her mother were very brave under the strain of almost constant apprehension of the attacks of savage beasts. Nor were they quite able to accept so readily as the others the theory that Jane, Clayton, and Monsieur Thuran had been picked up safely.

Jane Porter's Esmeralda was in a constant state of tears at the cruel fate which had separated her from her "po, li'le honey."

Lord Tennington's great-hearted good nature never deserted him for a moment. He was still the jovial host, seeking always for the comfort and pleasure of his guests. With the men of his yacht he remained the just but firm commander—there was never any more question in the jungle than there had been on board the *Lady Alice* as to who was the final authority in all questions of importance, and in all emergencies requiring cool and intelligent leadership.

Could this well-organized and comparatively secure party of castaways have seen the ragged, fear-haunted trio a few miles south of them they would scarcely have recognized in them the formerly immaculate members of the little company that had laughed and played upon the *Lady Alice*.

Clayton and Monsieur Thuran were almost naked, so torn had their clothes been by the thorn bushes and tangled vegetation of the matted jungle through which they had been compelled to force their way in search of their ever more difficult food supply.

Jane Porter had of course not been subjected to these strenuous expeditions, but her apparel was, nevertheless, in a sad state of disrepair.

Clayton, for lack of any better occupation, had carefully saved the skin of every animal they had killed. By stretching them upon the stems of trees, and diligently scraping them, he had managed to save them in a fair condition, and now that his clothes were threatening to cover his nakedness no longer, he commenced to fashion a rude garment of them, using a sharp thorn for a needle, and bits of tough grass and animal tendons in lieu of thread.

The result when completed was a sleeveless garment which fell nearly to his knees. As it was made up of numerous small pelts of different species of rodents, it presented a rather strange and wonderful appearance, which, together with the vile stench which permeated it, rendered it anything other than a desirable addition to a wardrobe. But the time came when for the sake of decency he was compelled to don it, and even the misery of their condition could not prevent Jane Porter from laughing heartily at sight of him.

Later, Thuran also found it necessary to construct a similar primitive garment, so that, with their bare legs and heavily bearded faces, they looked not unlike reincarnations of two prehistoric progenitors of the human race. Thuran acted like one.

Nearly two months of this existence had passed when the first great calamity befell them. It was prefaced by an adventure which came near terminating abruptly the sufferings of two of them—terminating them in the grim and horrible manner of the jungle, forever.

Thuran, down with an attack of jungle fever, lay in the shelter among the branches of their tree of refuge. Clayton had been into the jungle a few hundred yards in search of food. As he returned Jane Porter walked to meet him. Behind the man, cunning and crafty, crept an old and mangy lion. For three days his ancient thews and sinews had proved insufficient for the task of providing his cavernous belly with meat. For months he had eaten less and less frequently, and farther and farther had he roamed from his accustomed haunts in search of easier prey. At last he had found nature's weakest and most defenseless creature—in a moment more Numa would dine.

Clayton, all unconscious of the lurking death behind him, strode out into the open toward Jane. He had reached her side, a hundred feet from the tangled edge of jungle when past his shoulder the girl saw the tawny head and the wicked yellow eyes as the grasses parted, and the huge beast, nose to ground, stepped softly into view.

So frozen with horror was she that she could utter no sound, but the fixed and terrified gaze of her fear-widened eyes spoke as plainly to Clayton as words. A quick glance behind him revealed the hopelessness of their situation. The lion was scarce thirty paces from them, and they were equally as far from the shelter. The man was armed with a stout stick—as efficacious against a hungry lion, he realized, as a toy pop-gun charged with a tethered cork.

Numa, ravenous with hunger, had long since learned the futility of roaring and moaning as he searched for prey, but now that it was as surely his as though already he had felt the soft flesh beneath his still mighty paw, he opened his huge jaws, and gave vent to his long-pent rage in a series of deafening roars that made the air tremble.

"Run, Jane!" cried Clayton. "Quick! Run for the shelter!" But her paralyzed muscles refused to respond, and she stood mute and rigid, staring with ghastly countenance at the living death creeping toward them.

Thuran, at the sound of that awful roar, had come to the opening of the shelter, and as he saw the tableau below him he hopped up and down, shrieking to them in Russian.

"Run! Run!" he cried. "Run, or I shall be left all alone in this horrible place," and then he broke down and commenced to weep.

For a moment this new voice distracted the attention of the lion, who halted to cast an inquiring glance in the direction of the tree. Clayton could endure the strain no longer. Turning his back upon the beast, he buried his head in his arms and waited.

The girl looked at him in horror. Why did he not do something? If he must die, why not die like a man—bravely; beating at that terrible face with his puny stick, no matter how futile it might be. Would Tarzan of the Apes have done thus? Would he not at least have gone down to his death fighting heroically to the last?

Now the lion was crouching for the spring that would end their young lives beneath cruel, rending, yellow fangs. Jane Porter sank to her knees in prayer, closing her eyes to shut out the last hideous instant. Thuran, weak from fever, fainted.

Seconds dragged into minutes, long minutes into an eternity, and yet the beast did not spring. Clayton was almost unconscious from the prolonged agony of fright—his knees trembled—a moment more and he would collapse.

Jane Porter could endure it no longer. She opened her eyes. Could she be dreaming?

"William," she whispered; "look!"

Clayton mastered himself sufficiently to raise his head and turn toward the lion. An ejaculation of surprise burst from his lips. At their very feet the beast lay crumpled in death. A heavy war spear protruded from the tawny hide. It had entered the great back above the right shoulder, and, passing entirely through the body, had pierced the savage heart.

Jane Porter had risen to her feet; as Clayton turned back to her she staggered in weakness. He put out his arms to save her from falling, and then drew her close to him—pressing her head against his shoulder, he stooped to kiss her in thanksgiving.

Gently the girl pushed him away.

"Please do not do that, William," she said. "I have lived a thousand years in the past brief moments. I have learned in the face of death how to live. I do not wish to hurt you more than is necessary; but I can no longer bear to live out the impossible position I have attempted because of a false sense of loyalty to an impulsive promise I made you.

"The last few seconds of my life have taught me that it would be hideous to attempt further to deceive myself and you, or to entertain for an instant longer the possibility of ever becoming your wife, should we regain civilization."

"Why, Jane," he cried, "what do you mean? What has our providential rescue to do with altering your feelings toward me? You are but unstrung—tomorrow you will be yourself again."

"I am more nearly myself this minute than I have been for over a year," she replied. "The thing that has just happened has again forced to my memory the fact that the bravest man that ever lived honored me with his love. Until it was too late I did not realize that I returned it, and so I sent him away. He is dead now, and I shall never marry. I certainly could not wed another less brave than he without harboring constantly a feeling of contempt for the relative cowardice of my husband. Do you understand me?"

"Yes," he answered, with bowed head, his face mantling with the flush of shame.

And it was the next day that the great calamity befell.

22

The Treasure Vaults of Opar

IT WAS quite dark before La, the high priestess, returned to the Chamber of the Dead with food and drink for Tarzan. She bore no light, feeling with her hands along the crumbling walls until she gained the chamber. Through the stone grating above, a tropic moon served dimly to illuminate the interior.

Tarzan, crouching in the shadows at the far side of the room as the first sound of approaching footsteps reached him, came forth to meet the girl as he recognized that it was she.

"They are furious," were her first words. "Never before has a human sacrifice escaped the altar. Already fifty have gone forth to track you down. They have searched the temple—all save this single room."

"Why do they fear to come here?" he asked.

"It is the Chamber of the Dead. Here the dead return to worship. See this ancient altar? It is here that the dead sacrifice the living—if they find a victim here. That is the reason our people shun this chamber. Were one to enter he knows that the waiting dead would seize him for their sacrifice."

"But you?" he asked.

"I am high priestess—I alone am safe from the dead. It is I who at rare intervals bring them a human sacrifice from the world above. I alone may enter here in safety."

"Why have they not seized me?" he asked, humoring her grotesque belief.

She looked at him quizzically for a moment. Then she replied:

"It is the duty of a high priestess to instruct, to interpret—according to the creed that others, wiser than herself, have laid down; but there is nothing in the creed which says that she must believe. The more one knows of one's religion the less one believes—no one living knows more of mine than I."

"Then your only fear in aiding me to escape is that your fellow mortals may discover your duplicity?"

"That is all—the dead are dead; they cannot harm—or help. We must therefore depend entirely upon ourselves, and the sooner we act the better it will be. I had difficulty in eluding their vigilance but now in bringing you this morsel of food. To attempt to repeat the thing daily would be the height of folly. Come, let us see how far we may go toward liberty before I must return."

She led him back to the chamber beneath the altar room. Here she turned into one of the several corridors leading from it. In the darkness Tarzan could not see which one. For ten minutes they groped slowly along a winding passage, until at length they came to a closed door. Here he heard her fumbling with a key, and presently came the sound of a metal bolt grating against metal. The door swung in on scraping hinges, and they entered.

"You will be safe here until tomorrow night," she said.

Then she went out, and, closing the door, locked it behind her.

Where Tarzan stood it was dark as Erebus. Not even his trained eyes could penetrate the utter blackness. Cautiously he moved forward until his out-stretched hand touched a wall, then very slowly he traveled around the four walls of the chamber.

Apparently it was about twenty feet square. The floor was of concrete, the walls of the dry masonry that marked the method of construction above ground. Small pieces of granite of various sizes were ingeniously laid together without mortar to construct these ancient foundations.

The first time around the walls Tarzan thought he detected a strange phenomenon for a room with no windows and but a single door. Again he crept carefully around close to the wall. No, he could not be mistaken! He paused before the center of the wall opposite the door. For a moment he stood quite motionless, then he moved a few feet to one side. Again he returned, only to move a few feet to the other side.

Once more he made the entire circuit of the room, feeling carefully every foot of the walls. Finally he stopped again before the particular section that had aroused his curiosity. There was no doubt of it! A distinct draft of fresh air was blowing into the chamber through the interstices of the masonry at that particular point—and nowhere else.

Tarzan tested several pieces of the granite which made up the wall at this spot, and finally was rewarded by finding one which lifted out readily. It was about ten inches wide, with a face some three by six inches showing within the chamber. One by one the ape-man lifted out similarly shaped stones. The wall at this point was constructed entirely, it seemed, of these almost perfect slabs. In a short time he had removed some dozen, when he reached in to test the next layer of masonry. To his surprise, he felt nothing behind the masonry he had removed as far as his long arm could reach.

It was a matter of but a few minutes to remove enough of the wall to permit his body to pass through the aperture. Directly ahead of him he thought he discerned a faint glow—scarcely more than a less impenetrable darkness. Cautiously he moved forward on hands and knees, until at about fifteen feet, or the average thickness of the foundation walls, the floor ended abruptly in a sudden drop. As far out as he could reach he felt nothing, nor could he find the bottom of the black abyss that yawned before him, though, clinging to the edge of the floor, he lowered his body into the darkness to its full length.

Finally it occurred to him to look up, and there above him he saw through a round opening a tiny circular patch of starry sky. Feeling up along the sides of the shaft as far as he could reach, the ape-man discovered that so much of the wall as he could feel converged toward the center of the shaft as it rose. This fact precluded possibility of escape in that direction.

As he sat speculating on the nature and uses of this strange passage and its terminal shaft, the moon topped the opening above, letting a flood of soft, silvery light into the shadowy place. Instantly the nature of the shaft became apparent to Tarzan, for far below him he saw the shimmering surface of water. He had come upon an ancient well—but what was the purpose of the connection between the well and the dungeon in which he had been hidden?

As the moon crossed the opening of the shaft its light flooded the whole interior, and then Tarzan saw directly across from him another opening in the opposite wall. He wondered if this might not be the mouth of a passage leading to possible escape. It would be worth investigating, at least, and this he determined to do.

Quickly returning to the wall he had demolished to explore what lay beyond it, he carried the stones into the passageway and replaced them from that side. The deep deposits of dust which he had noticed upon the blocks as he had first removed them from the wall had convinced him that even if the present occupants of the ancient pile had knowledge of this hidden passage they had made no use of it for perhaps generations.

The wall replaced, Tarzan turned to the shaft, which was some fifteen feet wide at this point. To leap across the intervening space was a small matter to the ape-man, and a moment later he was proceeding along a narrow tunnel, moving cautiously for fear of being precipitated into another shaft such as he had just crossed.

He had advanced some hundred feet when he came to a flight of steps leading downward into Stygian gloom. Some twenty feet below, the level floor of the tunnel recommenced, and shortly afterward his progress was stopped by a heavy wooden door which was secured by massive wooden bars upon the side of Tarzan's approach. This fact suggested to the ape-man that he might surely be in a passageway leading to the outer world, for the bolts, barring progress from the opposite side, tended to substantiate this hypothesis, unless it were merely a prison to which it led.

Along the tops of the bars were deep layers of dust—a further indication that the passage had lain long unused. As he pushed the massive obstacle aside, its great hinges shrieked out in weird protest against this unaccustomed disturbance. For a moment Tarzan paused to listen for any responsive note which might indicate that the unusual night noise had alarmed the inmates of the temple; but as he heard nothing he advanced beyond the doorway.

Carefully feeling about, he found himself within a large chamber, along the walls of which, and down the length of the floor, were piled many tiers of metal ingots of an odd though uniform shape. To his groping hands they felt not unlike double-headed bootjacks. The ingots were quite heavy, and but for the enormous number of them he would have been positive that they were gold; but the thought of the fabulous wealth these thousands of pounds of metal would have represented were they in reality gold, almost convinced him that they must be of some baser metal.

At the far end of the chamber he discovered another barred door, and again the bars upon the inside renewed the hope that he was traversing an ancient and forgotten passageway to liberty. Beyond the door the passage ran straight as a war spear, and it soon became evident to the ape-man that it had already led him beyond the outer walls of the temple. If he but knew the direction it was leading him! If toward the west, then he must also be beyond the city's outer walls.

With increasing hopes he forged ahead as rapidly as he dared, until at the end of half an hour he came to another flight of steps leading upward. At the bottom this flight was of concrete, but as he ascended his naked feet felt a sudden change in the substance they were treading. The steps of concrete had given place to steps of granite. Feeling with his hands, the ape-man discovered that these latter were evidently hewed from rock, for there was no crack to indicate a joint.

For a hundred feet the steps wound spirally up, until at a sudden turning Tarzan came into a narrow cleft between two rocky walls. Above him shone the starry sky, and before him a steep incline replaced the steps that had terminated at its foot. Up this pathway Tarzan hastened, and at its upper end came out upon the rough top of a huge granite bowlder.

A mile away lay the ruined city of Opar, its domes and turrets bathed in the soft light of the equatorial moon. Tarzan dropped his eyes to the ingot he had brought away with him. For a moment he examined it by the moon's bright rays, then he raised his head to look out upon the ancient piles of crumbling grandeur in the distance.

"Opar," he mused, "Opar, the enchanted city of a dead and forgotten past. The city of the beauties and the beasts. City of horrors and death; but—city of fabulous riches." The ingot was of virgin gold.

The bowlder on which Tarzan found himself lay well out in the plain between the city and the distant cliffs he and his black warriors had scaled the morning previous. To descend its rough and precipitous face was a task of infinite labor and considerable peril even to the ape-man; but at last he felt the soft soil of the valley beneath his feet, and without a backward glance at Opar he turned his face toward the guardian cliffs, and at a rapid trot set off across the valley.

The sun was just rising as he gained the summit of the flat mountain at the valley's western boundary. Far beneath him he saw smoke arising above the tree-tops of the forest at the base of the foothills.

"Man," he murmured. "And there were fifty who went forth to track me down. Can it be they?"

Swiftly he descended the face of the cliff, and, dropping into a narrow ravine which led down to the far forest, he hastened onward in the direction of the smoke. Striking the forest's edge about a quarter of a mile from the point at which the slender column arose into the still air, he took to the trees. Cautiously he approached until there suddenly burst upon his view a rude *boma,* in the center of which, squatted about their tiny fires, sat his fifty black Waziri. He called to them in their own tongue:

"Arise, my children, and greet thy king!"

With exclamations of surprise and fear the warriors leaped to their feet, scarcely knowing whether to flee or not. Then Tarzan dropped lightly from an overhanging branch into their midst. When they realized that it was indeed their chief in the flesh, and no materialized spirit, they went mad with joy.

"We were cowards, oh, Waziri," cried Busuli. "We ran away and left you to your fate; but when our panic was over we swore to return and save you, or at least take revenge upon your murderers. We were but now preparing to scale the heights once more and cross the desolate valley to the terrible city."

"Have you seen fifty frightful men pass down from the cliffs into this forest, my children?" asked Tarzan.

"Yes, Waziri," replied Busuli. "They passed us late yesterday, as we were about to turn back after you. They had no woodcraft. We heard them coming for a mile before we saw them, and as we had other business in hand we withdrew into the forest and let them pass. They were waddling rapidly along upon short legs, and now and then one would go upon all fours like Bolgani, the gorilla. They were indeed fifty frightful men, Waziri."

When Tarzan had related his adventures and told them of the yellow metal he had found, not one demurred when he outlined a plan to return by night and bring away what they could carry of the vast treasure; and so it was that as dusk fell across the desolate valley of Opar fifty ebon warriors trailed at a smart trot over the dry and dusty ground toward the giant bowlder that loomed before the city.

If it had seemed a difficult task to descend the face of the bowlder, Tarzan soon found that it would be next to impossible to get his fifty warriors to the summit. Finally the feat was accomplished by dint of herculean efforts upon the part of the ape-man. Ten spears were fastened end to end, and with one end of this remarkable chain attached to his waist, Tarzan at last succeeded in reaching the summit.

Once there, he drew up one of his blacks, and in this way the entire party was finally landed in safety upon the bowlder's top. Immediately Tarzan led them to the treasure chamber, where to each was allotted a load of two ingots, for each about eighty pounds.

By midnight the entire party stood once more at the foot of the bowlder, but with their heavy loads it was midforenoon ere they reached the summit of the cliffs. From there on the homeward journey was slow, as these proud fighting men were unaccustomed to the duties of porters. But they bore their burdens uncomplainingly, and at the end of thirty days entered their own country.

Here, instead of continuing on toward the northwest and their village, Tarzan guided them almost directly west, until on the morning of the thirty-third day he bade them break camp and return to their own village, leaving the gold where they had stacked it the previous night.

"And you, Waziri?" they asked.

"I shall remain here for a few days, my children," he replied. "Now hasten back to thy wives and children."

When they had gone Tarzan gathered up two of the ingots and, springing into a tree, ran lightly above the tangled and impenetrable mass of undergrowth for a couple of hundred yards, to emerge suddenly upon a circular clearing about which the giants of the jungle forest towered like a guardian host. In the center of this natural amphitheater, was a little flat-topped mound of hard earth.

Hundreds of times before had Tarzan been to this secluded spot, which was so densely surrounded by thorn bushes and tangled vines and creepers of huge girth that not even Sheeta, the leopard, could worm his sinuous way within, nor Tantor, with his giant strength, force the barriers which protected the council chamber of the great apes from all but the harmless denizens of the savage jungle.

Fifty trips Tarzan made before he had deposited all the ingots within the precincts of the amphitheater. Then from the hollow of an ancient, lightning-blasted tree he produced the very spade with which he had uncovered the chest of Professor Archimedes Q. Porter which he had once, apelike, buried in this selfsame spot. With this he dug a long trench, into which he laid the fortune that his blacks had carried from the forgotten treasure vaults of the city of Opar.

That night he slept within the amphitheater, and early the next morning set out to revisit his cabin before returning to his Waziri. Finding things as he had left them, he went forth into the jungle to hunt, intending to bring his prey to the cabin where he might feast in comfort, spending the night upon a comfortable couch.

For five miles toward the south he roamed, toward the banks of a fair-sized river that flowed into the sea about six miles from his cabin. He had gone inland about half a mile when there came suddenly to his trained nostrils the one scent that sets the whole savage jungle aquiver—Tarzan smelled man.

The wind was blowing off the ocean, so Tarzan knew that the authors of the scent were west of him. Mixed with the man scent was the scent of Numa. Man and lion. "I had better hasten," thought the ape-man, for he had recognized the scent of whites. "Numa may be a-hunting."

When he came through the trees to the edge of the jungle he saw a woman kneeling in prayer, and before her stood a wild, primitive-looking white man, his face buried in his arms. Behind the man a mangy lion was advancing slowly toward this easy prey. The man's face was averted; the woman's bowed in prayer. He could not see the features of either.

Already Numa was about to spring. There was not a second to spare. Tarzan could not even unsling his bow and fit an arrow in time to send one of his deadly poisoned shafts into the yellow hide. He was too far away to reach the beast in time with his knife. There was but a single hope—a lone alternative. And with the quickness of thought the ape-man acted.

A brawny arm flew back—for the briefest fraction of an instant a huge spear poised above the giant's shoulder—and then the mighty arm shot out, and swift death tore through the intervening leaves to bury itself in the heart of the leaping lion. Without a sound he rolled over at the very feet of his intended victims—dead.

For a moment neither the man nor the woman moved. Then the latter opened her eyes to look with wonder upon the dead beast behind her companion. As that beautiful head went up Tarzan of the Apes gave a gasp of incredulous astonishment. Was he mad? It could not be the woman he loved! But, indeed, it was none other.

And the woman rose, and the man took her in his arms to kiss her, and of a sudden the ape-man saw red through a bloody mist of murder, and the old scar upon his forehead burned scarlet against his brown hide.

There was a terrible expression upon his savage face as he fitted a poisoned shaft to his bow. An ugly light gleamed in those gray eyes as he sighted full at the back of the unsuspecting man beneath him.

For an instant he glanced along the polished shaft, drawing the bowstring far back, that the arrow might pierce through the heart for which it was aimed.

But he did not release the fatal messenger. Slowly the point of the arrow drooped; the scar upon the brown forehead faded; the bowstring relaxed; and Tarzan of the Apes, with bowed head, turned sadly into the jungle toward the village of the Waziri.

23

The Fifty Frightful Men

FOR several long minutes Jane Porter and William Cecil Clayton stood silently looking at the dead body of the beast whose prey they had so narrowly escaped becoming.

The girl was the first to speak again after her outbreak of impulsive avowal.

"Who could it have been?" she whispered.

"God knows!" was the man's only reply.

"If it is a friend, why does he not show himself?" continued Jane. "Wouldn't it be well to call out to him, and at least thank him?"

Mechanically Clayton did her bidding, but there was no response.

Jane Porter shuddered. "The mysterious jungle," she murmured. "The terrible jungle. It renders even the manifestations of friendship terrifying."

"We had best return to the shelter," said Clayton. "You will be at least a little safer there. I am no protection whatever," he added bitterly.

"Do not say that, William," she hastened to urge, acutely sorry for the wound her words had caused. "You have done the best you could. You have been noble, and self-sacrificing, and brave. It is no fault of yours that you are not a superman. There is only one other man I have ever known who could have done more than you. My words were ill chosen in the excitement of the reaction—I did not wish to wound you. All that I wish is that we may both understand once and for all that I can never marry you—that such a marriage would be wicked."

"I think I understand," he replied. "Let us not speak of it again—at least until we are back in civilization."

The next day Thuran was worse. Almost constantly he was in a state of delirium. They could do nothing to relieve him, nor was Clayton over-anxious to attempt anything. On the girl's account he feared the Russian—in the bottom of his heart he hoped the man would die. The thought that something might befall him that would leave her entirely at the mercy of this beast caused him greater anxiety than the probability that almost certain death awaited her should she be left entirely alone upon the outskirts of the cruel forest.

The Englishman had extracted the heavy spear from the body of the lion, so that when he went into the forest to hunt that morning he had a feeling of much greater security than at any time since they had been cast upon the savage shore. The result was that he penetrated farther from the shelter than ever before.

To escape as far as possible from the mad ravings of the fever-stricken Russian, Jane Porter had descended from the shelter to the foot of the tree—she dared not venture farther. Here, beside the crude ladder Clayton had constructed for her, she sat looking out to sea, in the always surviving hope that a vessel might be sighted.

Her back was toward the jungle, and so she did not see the grasses part, or the savage face that peered from between. Little, bloodshot, close-set eyes scanned her intently, roving from time to time about the open beach for indications of the presence of others than herself.

Presently another head appeared, and then another and another. The man in the shelter commenced to rave again, and the heads disappeared as silently and as suddenly as they had come. But soon they were thrust forth once more, as the girl gave no sign of perturbation at the continued wailing of the man above.

One by one grotesque forms emerged from the jungle to creep stealthily upon the unsuspecting woman. A faint rustling of the grasses attracted her attention. She turned, and at the sight that confronted her staggered to her feet with a little shriek of fear. Then they closed upon her with a rush. Lifting her bodily in his long, gorilla-like arms, one of the creatures turned and bore her into the jungle. A filthy paw covered her mouth to stifle her screams. Added to the weeks of torture she had already undergone, the shock was more than she could withstand. Shattered nerves collapsed, and she lost consciousness.

When she regained her senses she found herself in the thick of the primeval forest. It was night. A huge fire burned brightly in the little clearing in which she lay. About it squatted fifty frightful men. Their heads and faces were covered with matted hair. Their long arms rested upon the bent knees of their short, crooked legs. They were gnawing, like beasts, upon unclean food. A pot boiled upon the edge of the fire, and out of it one of the creatures would occasionally drag a hunk of meat with a sharpened stick.

When they discovered that their captive had regained consciousness, a piece of this repulsive stew was tossed to her from the foul hand of a nearby feaster. It rolled close to her side, but she only closed her eyes as a qualm of nausea surged through her.

For many days they traveled through the dense forest. The girl, footsore and exhausted, was half dragged, half pushed through the long, hot, tedious days. Occasionally, when she would stumble and fall, she was cuffed and kicked by the nearest of the frightful men. Long before they reached their journey's end her shoes had been discarded —the soles entirely gone. Her clothes were torn to mere shreds and tatters, and through the pitiful rags her once white and tender skin showed raw and bleeding from contact with the thousand pitiless thorns and brambles through which she had been dragged.

The last two days of the journey found her in such utter exhaustion that no amount of kicking and abuse could force her to her poor, bleeding feet. Outraged nature had reached the limit of endurance, and the girl was physically powerless to raise herself even to her knees.

As the beasts surrounded her, chattering threateningly the while they goaded her with their cudgels and beat and kicked her with their fists and feet, she lay with closed eyes, praying for the merciful death that she knew alone could give her surcease from suffering; but it did not come, and presently the fifty frightful men realized that their victim was no longer able to walk, and so they picked her up and carried her the balance of the journey.

Late one afternoon she saw the ruined walls of a mighty city looming before them, but so weak and sick was she that it inspired not the faintest shadow of interest. Wherever they were bearing her, there could be but one end to her captivity among these fierce half brutes.

At last they passed through two great walls and came to the ruined city within. Into a crumbling pile they bore her, and here she was surrounded by hundreds more of the same creatures that had brought her; but among them were females who looked less horrible. At sight of them the first faint hope that she had entertained came to mitigate her misery. But it was short-lived, for the women offered her no sympathy, though, on the other hand, neither did they abuse her.

After she had been inspected to the entire satisfaction of the inmates of the building she was borne to a dark chamber in the vaults beneath, and here upon the bare floor she was left, with a metal bowl of water and another of food.

For a week she saw only some of the women whose duty it was to bring her food and water. Slowly her strength was returning—soon she would be in fit condition to offer as a sacrifice to The Flaming God. Fortunate indeed it was that she could not know the fate for which she was destined.

As Tarzan of the Apes moved slowly through the jungle after casting the spear that saved Clayton and Jane Porter from the fangs of Numa, his mind was filled with all the sorrow that belongs to a freshly opened heart wound.

He was glad that he had stayed his hand in time to prevent the consummation of the thing that in the first mad wave of jealous wrath he had contemplated. Only the fraction of a second had stood between Clayton and death at the hands of the ape-man. In the short moment that had elapsed after he had recognized the girl and her companion and the relaxing of the taut muscles that held the poisoned shaft directed at the Englishman's heart, Tarzan had been swayed by the swift and savage impulses of brute life.

He had seen the woman he craved—his woman—his mate—in the arms of another. There had been but one course open to him, according to the fierce jungle code that guided him in this other existence; but just before it had become too late the softer sentiments of his inherent chivalry had risen above the flaming fires of his passion and saved him. A thousand times he gave thanks that they had triumphed before his fingers had released that polished arrow.

As he contemplated his return to the Waziri the idea became repugnant. He did not wish to see a human being again. At least he would range alone through the jungle for a time, until the sharp edge of his sorrow had become blunted. Like his fellow beasts, he preferred to suffer in silence and alone.

That night he slept again in the amphitheater of the apes, and for several days he hunted from there, returning at night. On the afternoon of the third day he returned early. He had lain stretched upon the soft grass of the circular clearing for but a few moments when he heard far to the south a familiar sound. It was the passing through the jungle of a band of great apes—he could not mistake that. For several minutes he lay listening. They were coming in the direction of the amphitheater.

Tarzan arose lazily and stretched himself. His keen ears followed every movement of the advancing tribe. They were upwind, and presently he caught their scent, though he had not needed this added evidence to assure him that he was right.

As they came closer to the amphitheater Tarzan of the Apes melted into the branches upon the other side of the arena. There he waited to inspect the newcomers. Nor had he long to wait.

Presently a fierce, hairy face appeared among the lower branches opposite him. The cruel little eyes took in the clearing at a glance, then there was a chattered report returned to those behind. Tarzan could hear the words. The scout was telling the other members of the tribe that the coast was clear and that they might enter the amphitheater in safety.

First the leader dropped lightly upon the soft carpet of the grassy floor, and then, one by one, nearly a hundred anthropoids followed him. There were the huge adults and several young. A few nursing babes clung close to the shaggy necks of their savage mothers.

Tarzan recognized many members of the tribe. It was the same into which he had come as a tiny babe. Many of the adults had been little apes during his boyhood. He had frolicked and played about this very jungle with them during their brief childhood. He wondered if they would remember him—the memory of some apes is not overlong, and two years may be an eternity to them.

From the talk which he overheard he learned that they had come to choose a new king—their late chief had fallen a hundred feet beneath a broken limb to an untimely end.

Tarzan walked to the end of an overhanging limb in plain view of them. The quick eyes of a female caught sight of him first. With a barking guttural she called the attention of the others. Several huge bulls stood erect to get a better view of the intruder. With bared fangs and bristling necks they advanced slowly toward him, with deep-throated, ominous growls.

"Karnath, I am Tarzan of the Apes," said the ape-man in the vernacular of the tribe. "You remember me. Together we teased Numa when we were still little apes, throwing sticks and nuts at him from the safety of high branches."

The brute he had addressed stopped with a look of half-comprehending, dull wonderment upon his savage face.

"And Magor," continued Tarzan, addressing another, "do you not recall your former king—he who slew the mighty Kerchak? Look at me! Am I not the same Tarzan—mighty hunter—invincible fighter—that you all knew for many seasons?"

The apes all crowded forward now, but more in curiosity than threatening. They muttered among themselves for a few moments.

"What do you want among us now?" asked Karnath.

"Only peace," answered the ape-man.

Again the apes conferred. At length Karnath spoke again.

"Come in peace, then, Tarzan of the Apes," he said.

And so Tarzan of the Apes dropped lightly to the turf into the midst of the fierce and hideous horde—he had completed the cycle of evolution, and had returned to be once again a brute among brutes.

There were no greetings such as would have taken place among men after a separation of two years. The majority of the apes went on about the little activities that the advent of the ape-man had interrupted, paying no further attention to him than as though he had not been gone from the tribe at all.

One or two young bulls who had not been old enough to remember him sidled up on all fours to sniff at him, and one bared his fangs and growled threateningly—he wished to put Tarzan immediately into his proper place. Had Tarzan backed off, growling, the young bull would quite probably have been satisfied, but always after Tarzan's station among his fellow apes would have been beneath that of the bull which had made him step aside.

But Tarzan of the Apes did not back off. Instead, he swung his giant palm with all the force of his mighty muscles, and, catching the young bull alongside the head, sent him sprawling across the turf. The ape was up and at him again in a second, and this time they closed with tearing fingers and rending fangs—or at least that had been the intention of the young bull; but scarcely had they gone down, growling and snapping, than the ape-man's fingers found the throat of his antagonist.

Presently the young bull ceased to struggle, and lay quite still. Then Tarzan released his hold and arose—he did not wish to kill, only to teach the young ape, and others who might be watching, that Tarzan of the Apes was still master.

The lesson served its purpose—the young apes kept out of his way, as young apes should when their betters were about, and the old bulls made no attempt to encroach upon his prerogatives. For several days the she-apes with young remained suspicious of him, and when he ventured too near rushed upon him with wide mouths and hideous roars. Then Tarzan discreetly skipped out of harm's way, for that also is a custom among the apes—only mad bulls will attack a mother. But after a while even they became accustomed to him.

He hunted with them as in days gone by, and when they found that his superior reason guided him to the best food sources, and that his cunning rope ensnared toothsome game that they seldom if ever tasted, they came again to look up to him as they had in the past after he had become their king. And so it was that before they left the amphitheater to return to their wanderings they had once more chosen him as their leader.

The ape-man felt quite contented with his new lot. He was not happy—that he never could be again, but he was at least as far from everything that might remind him of his past misery as he could be. Long since he had given up every intention of returning to civilization, and now he had decided to see no more his black friends of the Waziri. He had forsworn humanity forever. He had started life an ape—as an ape he would die.

He could not, however, erase from his memory the fact that the woman he loved was within a short journey of the stamping-ground of his tribe; nor could he banish the haunting fear that she might be constantly in danger. That she was illy protected he had seen in the brief instant that had witnessed Clayton's inefficiency. The more Tarzan thought of it, the more keenly his conscience pricked him.

Finally he came to loathe himself for permitting his own selfish sorrow and jealousy to stand between Jane Porter and safety. As the days passed the thing preyed more and more upon his mind, and he had about determined to return to the coast and place himself on guard over Jane Porter and Clayton, when news reached him that altered all his plans and sent him dashing madly toward the east in reckless disregard of accident and death.

Before Tarzan had returned to the tribe, a certain young bull, not being able to secure a mate from among his own people, had, according to custom, fared forth through the wild jungle, like some knight-errant of old, to win a fair lady from some neighboring community.

He had but just returned with his bride, and was narrating his adventures quickly before he should forget them. Among other things he told of seeing a great tribe of strange-looking apes.

"They were all hairy-faced bulls but one," he said, "and that one was a she, lighter in color even than this stranger," and he chucked a thumb at Tarzan.

The ape-man was all attention in an instant. He asked questions as rapidly as the slow-witted anthropoid could answer them.

"Were the bulls short, with crooked legs?"

"They were."

"Did they wear the skins of Numa and Sheeta about their loins, and carry sticks and knives?"

"They did."

"And were there many yellow rings about their arms and legs?"

"Yes."

"And the she one—was she small and slender, and very white?"

"Yes."

"Did she seem to be one of the tribe, or was she a prisoner?"

"They dragged her along—sometimes by an arm—sometimes by the long hair that grew upon her head; and always they kicked and beat her. Oh, but it was great fun to watch them."

"God!" muttered Tarzan.

"Where were they when you saw them, and which way were they going?" continued the ape-man.

"They were beside the second water back there," and he pointed to the south. "When they passed me they were going toward the morning, upward along the edge of the water."

"When was this?" asked Tarzan.

"Half a moon since."

Without another word the ape-man sprang into the trees and fled like a disembodied spirit eastward in the direction of the forgotten city of Opar.

24

How Tarzan Came Again to Opar

When Clayton returned to the shelter and found Jane Porter was missing, he became frantic with fear and grief. He found Monsieur Thuran quite rational, the fever having left him with the surprising suddenness which is one of its peculiarities. The Russian, weak and exhausted, still lay upon his bed of grasses within the shelter.

When Clayton asked him about the girl he seemed surprised to know that she was not there.

"I have heard nothing unusual," he said. "But then I have been unconscious much of the time."

Had it not been for the man's very evident weakness, Clayton should have suspected him of having sinister knowledge of the girl's whereabouts; but he could see that Thuran lacked sufficient vitality even to descend, unaided, from the shelter. He could not, in his present physical condition, have harmed the girl, nor could he have climbed the rude ladder back to the shelter.

Until dark the Englishman searched the nearby jungle for a trace of the missing one or a sign of the trail of her abductor. But though the spoor left by the fifty frightful men, unversed in woodcraft as they were, would have been as plain to the densest denizen of the jungle as a city street to the Englishman, yet he crossed and recrossed it twenty times without observing the slightest indication that many men had passed that way but a few short hours since.

As he searched, Clayton continued to call the girl's name aloud, but the only result of this was to attract Numa, the lion. Fortunately the man saw the shadowy form worming its way toward him in time to climb into the branches of a tree before the beast was close enough to reach him. This put an end to his search for the balance of the afternoon, as the lion paced back and forth beneath him until dark.

Even after the beast had left, Clayton dared not descend

into the awful blackness beneath him, and so he spent a terrifying and hideous night in the tree. The next morning he returned to the beach, relinquishing the last hope of succoring Jane Porter.

During the week that followed, Monsieur Thuran rapidly regained his strength, lying in the shelter while Clayton hunted food for both. The men never spoke except as necessity demanded. Clayton now occupied the section of the shelter which had been reserved for Jane Porter, and only saw the Russian when he took food or water to him, or performed the other kindly offices which common humanity required.

When Thuran was again able to descend in search of food, Clayton was stricken with fever. For days he lay tossing in delirium and suffering, but not once did the Russian come near him. Food the Englishman could not have eaten, but his craving for water amounted practically to torture. Between the recurrent attacks of delirium, weak though he was, he managed to reach the brook once a day and fill a tiny can that had been among the few appointments of the lifeboat.

Thuran watched him on these occasions with an expression of malignant pleasure—he seemed really to enjoy the suffering of the man who, despite the just contempt in which he held him, had ministered to him to the best of his ability while he lay suffering the same agonies.

At last Clayton became so weak that he was no longer able to descend from the shelter. For a day he suffered for water without appealing to the Russian, but finally, unable to endure it longer, he asked Thuran to fetch him a drink.

The Russian came to the entrance to Clayton's room, a dish of water in his hand. A nasty grin contorted his features.

"Here is water," he said. "But first let me remind you that you maligned me before the girl—that you kept her to yourself, and would not share her with me—"

Clayton interrupted him. "Stop!" he cried. "Stop! What manner of cur are you that you traduce the character of a good woman whom we believe dead! God! I was a fool ever to let you live—you are not fit to live even in this vile land."

"Here is your water," said the Russian. "All you will get," and he raised the basin to his lips and drank; what was left he threw out upon the ground below. Then he turned and left the sick man.

Clayton rolled over, and, burying his face in his arms, gave up the battle.

The next day Thuran determined to set out toward the north along the coast, for he knew that eventually he must come to the habitations of civilized men—at least he could be no worse off than he was here, and, furthermore, the ravings of the dying Englishman were getting on his nerves.

So he stole Clayton's spear and set off upon his journey. He would have killed the sick man before he left had it not occurred to him that it would really have been a kindness to do so.

That same day he came to a little cabin by the beach, and his heart filled with renewed hope as he saw this evidence of the proximity of civilization, for he thought it but the outpost of a nearby settlement. Had he known to whom it belonged, and that its owner was at that very moment but a few miles inland, Nikolas Rokoff would have fled the place as he would a pestilence. But he did not know, and so he remained for a few days to enjoy the security and comparative comforts of the cabin. Then he took up his northward journey once more.

In Lord Tennington's camp preparations were going forward to build permanent quarters, and then to send out an expedition of a few men to the north in search of relief.

As the days had passed without bringing the longed-for succor, hope that Jane Porter, Clayton, and Monsieur Thuran had been rescued began to die. No one spoke of the matter longer to Professor Porter, and he was so immersed in his scientific dreaming that he was not aware of the elapse of time.

Occasionally he would remark that within a few days they should certainly see a steamer drop anchor off their shore, and that then they should all be reunited happily. Sometimes he spoke of it as a train, and wondered if it were being delayed by snowstorms.

"If I didn't know the dear old fellow so well by now," Tennington remarked to Miss Strong, "I should be quite certain that he was—er—not quite right, don't you know."

"If it were not so pathetic it would be ridiculous," said the girl, sadly. "I, who have known him all my life, know how he worships Jane; but to others it must seem that he is perfectly callous to her fate. It is only that he is so absolutely impractical that he cannot conceive of so real a thing as death unless nearly certain proof of it is thrust upon him."

"You'd never guess what he was about yesterday," continued Tennington. "I was coming in alone from a little hunt when I met him walking rapidly along the game trail that I was following back to camp. His hands were clasped beneath the tails of his long black coat, and his top hat was set firmly down upon his head, as with eyes bent upon the ground he hastened on, probably to some sudden death had I not intercepted him.

" 'Why, where in the world are you bound, professor?' I asked him. 'I am going into town, Lord Tennington,' he said, as seriously as possible, 'to complain to the postmaster about the rural free delivery service we are suffering from here. Why, sir, I haven't had a piece of mail in weeks. There should be several letters for me from Jane. The matter must be reported to Washington at once.'

"And would you believe it, Miss Strong," continued Tennington, "I had the very deuce of a job to convince the old fellow that there was not only no rural free delivery, but no town, and that he was not even on the same continent as Washington, nor in the same hemisphere.

"When he did realize he commenced to worry about his daughter—I think it is the first time that he really has appreciated our position here, or the fact that Miss Porter may not have been rescued."

"I hate to think about it," said the girl, "and yet I can think of nothing else than the absent members of our party."

"Let us hope for the best," replied Tennington. "You yourself have set us each a splendid example of bravery, for in a way your loss has been the greatest."

"Yes," she replied; "I could have loved Jane Porter no more had she been my own sister."

Tennington did not show the surprise he felt. That was not at all what he meant. He had been much with this fair daughter of Maryland since the wreck of the *Lady Alice*, and it had recently come to him that he had grown much more fond of her than would prove good for the peace of his mind, for he recalled almost constantly now the confidence which Monsieur Thuran had imparted to him that he and Miss Strong were engaged. He wondered if, after all, Thuran had been quite accurate in his statement. He had never seen the slightest indication on the girl's part of more than ordinary friendship.

"And then in Monsieur Thuran's loss, if they are lost, you would suffer a severe bereavement," he ventured.

She looked up at him quickly. "Monsieur Thuran had become a very dear friend," she said. "I liked him very much, though I have known him but a short time."

"Then you were not engaged to marry him?" he blurted out.

"Heavens, no!" she cried. "I did not care for him at all in that way."

There was something that Lord Tennington wanted to say to Hazel Strong—he wanted very badly to say it, and to say it at once; but somehow the words stuck in his throat. He started lamely a couple of times, cleared his throat, became red in the face, and finally ended by remarking that he hoped the cabins would be finished before the rainy season commenced.

But, though he did not know it, he had conveyed to the girl the very message he intended, and it left her happy—happier than she had ever before been in all her life.

Just then further conversation was interrupted by the sight of a strange and terrible-looking figure which emerged from the jungle just south of the camp. Tennington and the girl saw it at the same time. The Englishman reached for his revolver, but when the half-naked, bearded creature called his name aloud and came running toward them he dropped his hand and advanced to meet it.

None would have recognized in the filthy, emaciated creature, covered by a single garment of small skins, the immaculate Monsieur Thuran the party had last seen upon the deck of the *Lady Alice.*

Before the other members of the little community were apprised of his presence Tennington and Miss Strong questioned him regarding the other occupants of the missing boat.

"They are all dead," replied Thuran. "The three sailors died before we made land. Miss Porter was carried off into the jungle by some wild animal while I was lying delirious with fever. Clayton died of the same fever but a few days since. And to think that all this time we have been separated by but a few miles—scarcely a day's march. It is terrible!"

How long Jane Porter lay in the darkness of the vault beneath the temple in the ancient city of Opar she did not know. For a time she was delirious with fever, but after this passed she commenced slowly to regain her strength. Every day the woman who brought her food beckoned to her to arise, but for many days the girl could only shake her head to indicate that she was too weak.

But eventually she was able to gain her feet, and then to stagger a few steps by supporting herself with one hand upon the wall. Her captors now watched her with increasing interest. The day was approaching, and the victim was gaining in strength.

Presently the day came, and a young woman whom Jane Porter had not seen before came with several others to her dungeon. Here some sort of ceremony was performed—that it was of a religious nature the girl was sure, and so she took new heart, and rejoiced that she had fallen among people upon whom the refining and softening influences of religion evidently had fallen. They would treat her humanely—of that she was now quite sure.

And so when they led her from her dungeon, through long, dark corridors, and up a flight of concrete steps to a brilliant courtyard, she went willingly, even gladly—for was she not among the servants of God? It might be, of course, that their interpretation of the supreme being differed from her own, but that they owned a god was sufficient evidence to her that they were kind and good.

But when she saw a stone altar in the center of the courtyard, and dark-brown stains upon it and the nearby concrete of the floor, she began to wonder and to doubt. And as they stooped and bound her ankles, and secured her wrists behind her, her doubts were turned to fear. A moment later, as she was lifted and placed supine across the altar's top, hope left her entirely, and she trembled in an agony of fright.

During the grotesque dance of the votaries which followed, she lay frozen in horror, nor did she require the sight of the thin blade in the hands of the high priestess as it rose slowly above her to enlighten her further as to her doom.

As the hand began its descent, Jane Porter closed her eyes and sent up a silent prayer to the Maker she was so soon to face—then she succumbed to the strain upon her tired nerves, and swooned.

Day and night Tarzan of the Apes raced through the primeval forest toward the ruined city in which he was positive the woman he loved lay either a prisoner or dead.

In a day and a night he covered the same distance that the fifty frightful men had taken the better part of a week to traverse, for Tarzan of the Apes traveled along the middle terrace high above the tangled obstacles that impede progress upon the ground.

The story the young bull ape had told made it clear to him that the girl captive had been Jane Porter, for there was not another small white "she" in all the jungle. The "bulls" he had recognized from the ape's crude description as the grotesque parodies upon humanity who inhabit the ruins of Opar. And the girl's fate he could picture as plainly as though he were an eyewitness to it. When they would lay her across that grim altar he could not guess, but that her dear, frail body would eventually find its way there he was confident.

But finally, after what seemed long ages to the impatient ape-man, he topped the barrier cliffs that hemmed the desolate valley, and below him lay the grim and awful ruins of the now hideous city of Opar. At a rapid trot he started across the dry and dusty, bowlder-strewn ground toward the goal of his desires.

Would he be in time to rescue? He hoped against hope. At least he could be revenged, and in his wrath it seemed to him that he was equal to the task of wiping out the entire population of that terrible city. It was nearly noon when he reached the great bowlder at the top of which terminated the secret passage to the pits beneath the city. Like a cat he scaled the precipitous sides of the frowning granite *kopje*. A moment later he was running through the darkness of the long, straight tunnel that led to the treasure vault. Through this he passed, then on and on until at last he came to the well-like shaft upon the opposite side of which lay the dungeon with the false wall.

As he paused a moment upon the brink of the well a faint sound came to him through the opening above. His quick ears caught and translated it—it was the dance of death that preceded a sacrifice, and the singsong ritual of the high priestess. He could even recognize the woman's voice.

Could it be that the ceremony marked the very thing he had so hastened to prevent? A wave of horror swept over him. Was he, after all, to be just a moment too late? Like a frightened deer he leaped across the narrow chasm to the continuation of the passage beyond. At the false wall he tore like one possessed to demolish the barrier that confronted him—with giant muscles he forced the opening, thrusting his head and shoulders through the first small hole he made, and carrying the balance of the wall with him, to clatter resoundingly upon the cement floor of the dungeon.

With a single leap he cleared the length of the chamber and threw himself against the ancient door. But here he stopped. The mighty bars upon the other side were proof even against such muscles as his. It needed but a moment's effort to convince him of the futility of endeavoring to force that impregnable barrier. There was but one other way, and that led back through the long tunnels to the bowlder a mile beyond the city's walls, and then back across the open as he had come to the city first with his Waziri.

He realized that to retrace his steps and enter the city from above ground would mean that he would be too late to save the girl, if it were indeed she who lay upon the sacrificial altar above him. But there seemed no other way, and so he turned and ran swiftly back into the passageway beyond the broken wall. At the well he heard again the monotonous voice of the high priestess, and, as he glanced aloft, the opening, twenty feet above, seemed so near that he was tempted to leap for it in a mad endeavor to reach the inner courtyard that lay so near.

If he could but get one end of his grass rope caught upon some projection at the top of that tantalizing aperture! In the instant's pause and thought an idea occurred to him. He would attempt it. Turning back to the tumbled wall, he seized one of the large, flat slabs that had composed it. Hastily making one end of his rope fast to the piece of granite, he returned to the shaft, and, coiling the balance of the rope on the floor beside him, the ape-man took the heavy slab in both hands, and, swinging it several times to get the distance and the direction fixed, he let the weight fly up at a slight angle, so that, instead of falling straight back into the shaft again, it grazed the far edge, tumbling over into the court beyond.

Tarzan dragged for a moment upon the slack end of the rope until he felt that the stone was lodged with fair security at the shaft's top, then he swung out over the black depths beneath. The moment his full weight came upon the rope he felt it slip from above. He waited there in awful suspense as it dropped in little jerks, inch by inch. The stone was being dragged up the outside of the masonry surrounding the top of the shaft—would it catch at the very edge, or would his weight drag it over to fall upon him as he hurtled into the unknown depths below?

25

Through the Forest Primeval

FOR a brief, sickening moment Tarzan felt the slipping of the rope to which he clung, and heard the scraping of the block of stone against the masonry above.

Then of a sudden the rope was still—the stone had caught at the very edge. Gingerly the ape-man clambered up the frail rope. In a moment his head was above the edge of the shaft. The court was empty. The inhabitants of Opar were viewing the sacrifice. Tarzan could hear the voice of La from the nearby sacrificial court. The dance had ceased. It must be almost time for the knife to fall; but even as he thought these things he was running rapidly toward the sound of the high priestess' voice.

Fate guided him to the very doorway of the great roofless chamber. Between him and the altar was the long row of priests and priestesses, awaiting with their golden cups the spilling of the warm blood of their victim.

La's hand was descending slowly toward the bosom of the frail, quiet figure that lay stretched upon the hard stone. Tarzan gave a gasp that was almost a sob as he recognized the features of the girl he loved. And then the scar upon his forehead turned to a flaming band of scarlet, a red mist floated before his eyes, and, with the awful roar of the bull ape gone mad, he sprang like a huge lion into the midst of the votaries.

Seizing a cudgel from the nearest priest, he laid about him like a veritable demon as he forged his rapid way toward the altar. The hand of La had paused at the first noise of interruption. When she saw who the author of it was she went white. She had never been able to fathom the secret of the strange white man's escape from the dungeon in which she had locked him. She had not intended that he should ever leave Opar, for she had looked upon his giant frame and handsome face with the eyes of a woman and not those of a priestess.

In her clever mind she had concocted a story of wonderful revelation from the lips of the flaming god himself, in which she had been ordered to receive this white stranger as a messenger from him to his people on earth. That would satisfy the people of Opar, she knew. The man would be satisfied, she felt quite sure, to remain and be her husband rather than to return to the sacrificial altar.

But when she had gone to explain her plan to him he had disappeared, though the door had been tightly locked as she had left it. And now he had returned—materialized from thin air—and was killing her priests as though they had been sheep. For the moment she forgot her victim, and before she could gather her wits together again the huge white man was standing before her, the woman who had lain upon the altar in his arms.

"One side, La," he cried. "You saved me once, and so I would not harm you; but do not interfere or attempt to follow, or I shall have to kill you also."

As he spoke he stepped past her toward the entrance to the subterranean vaults.

"Who is she?" asked the high priestess, pointing at the unconscious woman.

"She is mine," said Tarzan of the Apes.

For a moment the girl of Opar stood wide-eyed and staring. Then a look of hopeless misery suffused her eyes—tears welled into them, and with a little cry she sank to the cold floor, just as a swarm of frightful men dashed past her to leap upon the ape-man.

But Tarzan of the Apes was not there when they reached out to seize him. With a light bound he had disappeared into the passage leading to the pits below, and when his pursuers came more cautiously after they found the chamber empty, they but laughed and jabbered to one another, for they knew that there was no exit from the pits other than the one through which he had entered. If he came out at all he must come this way, and they would wait and watch for him above.

And so Tarzan of the Apes, carrying the unconscious Jane Porter, came through the pits of Opar beneath the temple of The Flaming God without pursuit. But when the men of Opar had talked further about the matter, they recalled to mind that this very man had escaped once before into the pits, and, though they had watched the entrance he had not come forth; and yet today he had come upon them from the outside. They would again send fifty men out into the valley to find and capture this desecrater of their temple.

After Tarzan reached the shaft beyond the broken wall, he felt so positive of the successful issue of his flight that he stopped to replace the tumbled stones, for he was not anxious that any of the inmates should discover this forgotten passage, and through it come upon the treasure chamber. It was in his mind to return again to Opar and bear away a still greater fortune than he had already buried in the amphitheater of the apes.

On through the passageways he trotted, past the first door and through the treasure vault; past the second door and into the long, straight tunnel that led to the lofty hidden exit beyond the city. Jane Porter was still unconscious.

At the crest of the great bowlder he halted to cast a backward glance toward the city. Coming across the plain he saw a band of the hideous men of Opar. For a moment he hesitated. Should he descend and make a race for the distant cliffs, or should he hide here until night? And then a glance at the girl's white face determined him. He could not keep her here and permit her enemies to get between them and liberty. For aught he knew they might have been followed through the tunnels, and to have foes before and behind would result in almost certain capture, since he could not fight his way through the enemy burdened as he was with the unconscious girl.

To descend the steep face of the bowlder with Jane Porter was no easy task, but by binding her across his shoulders with the grass rope he succeeded in reaching the ground in safety before the Oparians arrived at the great rock. As the descent had been made upon the side away from the city, the searching party saw nothing of it, nor did they dream that their prey was so close before them.

By keeping the *kopje* between them and their pursuers, Tarzan of the Apes managed to cover nearly a mile before the men of Opar rounded the granite sentinel and saw the fugitive before them. With loud cries of savage delight, they broke into a mad run, thinking doubtless that they would soon overhaul the burdened runner; but they both underestimated the powers of the ape-man and overestimated the possibilities of their own short, crooked legs.

By maintaining an easy trot, Tarzan kept the distance between them always the same. Occasionally he would glance at the face so near his own. Had it not been for the faint beating of the heart pressed so close against his own, he would not have known that she was alive, so white and drawn was the poor, tired face.

And thus they came to the flat-topped mountain and the barrier cliffs. During the last mile Tarzan had let himself out, running like a deer that he might have ample time to descend the face of the cliffs before the Oparians could reach the summit and hurl rocks down upon them. And so it was that he was half a mile down the mountainside ere the fierce little men came panting to the edge.

With cries of rage and disappointment they ranged along the cliff top shaking their cudgels, and dancing up and down in a perfect passion of anger. But this time they did not pursue beyond the boundary of their own country. Whether it was because they recalled the futility of their former long and irksome search, or after witnessing the ease with which the ape-man swung along before them, and the last burst of speed, they realized the utter hopelessness of further pursuit, it is difficult to say; but as Tarzan reached the woods that began at the base of the foothills which skirted the barrier cliffs they turned their faces once more toward Opar.

Just within the forest's edge, where he could yet watch the cliff tops, Tarzan laid his burden upon the grass, and going to the near-by rivulet brought water with which he bathed her face and hands; but even this did not revive her, and, greatly worried, he gathered the girl into his strong arms once more and hurried on toward the west.

Late in the afternoon Jane Porter regained consciousness. She did not open her eyes at once—she was trying to recall the scenes that she had last witnessed. Ah, she remembered now. The altar, the terrible priestess, the descending knife. She gave a little shudder, for she thought that either this was death or that the knife had buried itself in her heart and she was experiencing the brief delirium preceding death.

And when finally she mustered courage to open her eyes, the sight that met them confirmed her fears, for she saw that she was being borne through a leafy paradise in the arms of her dead love. "If this be death," she murmured, "thank God that I am dead."

"You spoke, Jane!" cried Tarzan. "You are regaining consciousness!"

"Yes, Tarzan of the Apes," she replied, and for the first time in months a smile of peace and happiness lighted her face.

"Thank God!" cried the ape-man, coming to the ground in a little grassy clearing beside the stream. "I was in time, after all."

"In time? What do you mean?" she questioned.

"In time to save you from death upon the altar, dear," he replied. "Do you not remember?"

"Save me from death?" she asked, in a puzzled tone. "Are we not both dead, my Tarzan?"

He had placed her upon the grass by now, her back resting against the stem of a huge tree. At her question he stepped back where he could the better see her face.

"Dead!" he repeated, and then he laughed. "You are not, Jane; and if you will return to the city of Opar and ask them who dwell there they will tell you that I was not dead a few short hours ago. No, dear, we are both very much alive."

"But both Hazel and Monsieur Thuran told me that you had fallen into the ocean many miles from land," she urged, as though trying to convince him that he must indeed be dead. "They said that there was no question but that it must have been you, and less that you could have survived or been picked up."

"How can I convince you that I am no spirit?" he asked, with a laugh. "It was I whom the delightful Monsieur Thuran pushed overboard, but I did not drown—I will tell you all about it after a while—and here I am very much the same wild man you first knew, Jane Porter."

The girl rose slowly to her feet and came toward him.

"I cannot even yet believe it," she murmured. "It cannot be that such happiness can be true after all the hideous things that I have passed through these awful months since the *Lady Alice* went down."

She came close to him and laid a hand, soft and trembling, upon his arm.

"It must be that I am dreaming, and that I shall awaken in a moment to see that awful knife descending toward my heart—kiss me, dear, just once before I lose my dream forever."

Tarzan of the Apes needed no second invitation. He took the girl he loved in his strong arms, and kissed her not once, but a hundred times, until she lay there panting for breath; yet when he stopped she put her arms about his neck and drew his lips down to hers once more.

"Am I alive and a reality, or am I but a dream?" he asked.

"If you are not alive, my man," she answered, "I pray

that I may die thus before I awaken to the terrible realities of my last waking moments."

For a while both were silent—gazing into each others' eyes as though each still questioned the reality of the wonderful happiness that had come to them. The past, with all its hideous disappointments and horrors, was forgotten—the future did not belong to them; but the present—ah, it was theirs; none could take it from them. It was the girl who first broke the sweet silence.

"Where are we going, dear?" she asked. "What are we going to do?"

"Where would you like best to go?" he asked. "What would you like best to do?"

"To go where you go, my man; to do whatever seems best to you," she answered.

"But Clayton?" he asked. For a moment he had forgotten that there existed upon the earth other than they two. "We have forgotten your husband."

"I am not married, Tarzan of the Apes," she cried. "Nor am I longer promised in marriage. The day before those awful creatures captured me I spoke to Mr. Clayton of my love for you, and he understood then that I could not keep the wicked promise that I had made. It was after we had been miraculously saved from an attacking lion." She paused suddenly and looked up at him, a questioning light in her eyes. "Tarzan of the Apes," she cried, "it was you who did that thing? It could have been no other."

He dropped his eyes, for he was ashamed.

"How could you have gone away and left me?" she cried reproachfully.

"Don't, Jane!" he pleaded. "Please don't! You cannot know how I have suffered since for the cruelty of that act, or how I suffered then, first in jealous rage, and then in bitter resentment against the fate that I had not deserved. I went back to the apes after that, Jane, intending never again to see a human being." He told her then of his life since he had returned to the jungle—of how he had dropped like a plummet from a civilized Parisian to a savage Waziri warrior, and from there back to the brute that he had been raised.

She asked him many questions, and at last fearfully of the things that Monsieur Thuran had told her—of the woman in Paris. He narrated every detail of his civilized life to her, omitting nothing, for he felt no shame, since his heart always had been true to her. When he had finished he sat looking at her, as though waiting for her judgment, and his sentence.

"I knew that he was not speaking the truth," she said. "Oh, what a horrible creature he is!"

"You are not angry with me, then?" he asked.

And her reply, though apparently most irrelevant, was truly feminine.

"Is Olga de Coude very beautiful?" she asked.

And Tarzan laughed and kissed her again. "Not one-tenth so beautiful as you, dear," he said.

She gave a contented little sigh, and let her head rest against his shoulder. He knew that he was forgiven.

That night Tarzan built a snug little bower high among the swaying branches of a giant tree, and there the tired girl slept, while in a crotch beneath her the ape-man curled, ready, even in sleep, to protect her.

It took them many days to make the long journey to the coast. Where the way was easy they walked hand in hand beneath the arching boughs of the mighty forest, as might in a far-gone past have walked their primeval forbears. When the underbrush was tangled he took her in his great arms, and bore her lightly through the trees, and the days were all too short, for they were very happy. Had it not been for their anxiety to reach and succor Clayton they would have drawn out the sweet pleasure of that wonderful journey indefinitely.

On the last day before they reached the coast Tarzan caught the scent of men ahead of them—the scent of black men. He told the girl, and cautioned her to maintain silence. "There are few friends in the jungle," he remarked dryly.

In half an hour they came stealthily upon a small party of black warriors filing toward the west. As Tarzan saw them he gave a cry of delight—it was a band of his own Waziri. Busuli was there, and others who had accompanied him to Opar. At sight of him they danced and cried out in exuberant joy. For weeks they had been searching for him, they told him.

The blacks exhibited considerable wonderment at the presence of the white girl with him, and when they found that she was to be his woman they vied with one another to do her honor. With the happy Waziri laughing and dancing about them they came to the rude shelter by the shore.

There was no sign of life, and no response to their calls. Tarzan clambered quickly to the interior of the little tree hut, only to emerge a moment later with an empty tin.

Throwing it down to Busuli, he told him to fetch water, and then he beckoned Jane Porter to come up.

Together they leaned over the emaciated thing that once had been an English nobleman. Tears came to the girl's eyes as she saw the poor, sunken cheeks and hollow eyes, and the lines of suffering upon the once young and handsome face.

"He still lives," said Tarzan. "We will do all that can be done for him, but I fear that we are too late."

When Busuli had brought the water Tarzan forced a few drops between the cracked and swollen lips. He wetted the hot forehead and bathed the pitiful limbs.

Presently Clayton opened his eyes. A faint, shadowy smile lighted his countenance as he saw the girl leaning over him. At sight of Tarzan the expression changed to one of wonderment.

"It's all right, old fellow," said the ape-man. "We've found you in time. Everything will be all right now, and we'll have you on your feet again before you know it."

The Englishman shook his head weakly. "It's too late," he whispered. "But it's just as well. I'd rather die."

"Where is Monsieur Thuran?" asked the girl.

"He left me after the fever got bad. He is a devil. When I begged for the water that I was too weak to get he drank before me, threw the rest out, and laughed in my face." At the thought of it the man was suddenly animated by a spark of vitality. He raised himself upon one elbow. "Yes," he almost shouted; "I will live. I will live long enough to find and kill that beast!" But the brief effort left him weaker than before, and he sank back again upon the rotting grasses that, with his old ulster, had been the bed of Jane Porter.

"Don't worry about Thuran," said Tarzan of the Apes, laying a reassuring hand on Clayton's forehead. "He belongs to me, and I shall get him in the end, never fear."

For a long time Clayton lay very still. Several times Tarzan had to put his ear quite close to the sunken chest to catch the faint beating of the wornout heart. Toward evening he aroused again for a brief moment.

"Jane," he whispered. The girl bent her head closer to catch the faint message. "I have wronged you—and him," he nodded weakly toward the ape-man. "I loved you so—it is a poor excuse to offer for injuring you; but I could not bear to think of giving you up. I do not ask your forgiveness. I only wish to do now the thing I should have done over a year ago." He fumbled in the pocket of the ulster beneath him for something that he had discovered there while he lay between the paroxysms of fever. Presently he found it—a crumpled bit of yellow paper. He handed it to the girl, and as she took it his arm fell limply across his chest, his head dropped back, and with a little gasp he stiffened and was still. Then Tarzan of the Apes drew a fold of the ulster across the upturned face.

For a moment they remained kneeling there, the girl's lips moving in silent prayer, and as they rose and stood on either side of the now peaceful form, tears came to the ape-man's eyes, for through the anguish that his own heart had suffered he had learned compassion for the suffering of others.

Through her own tears the girl read the message upon the bit of faded yellow paper, and as she read her eyes went very wide. Twice she read those startling words before she could fully comprehend their meaning.

Finger prints prove you Greystoke. Congratulations.
D'ARNOT.

She handed the paper to Tarzan. "And he has known it all this time," she said, "and did not tell you?"

"I knew it first, Jane," replied the man. "I did not know that he knew it at all. I must have dropped this message that night in the waiting room. It was there that I received it."

"And afterward you told us that your mother was a she-ape, and that you had never known your father?" she asked incredulously.

"The title and the estates meant nothing to me without you, dear," he replied. "And if I had taken them away from him I should have been robbing the woman I love—don't you understand, Jane?" It was as though he attempted to excuse a fault.

She extended her arms toward him across the body of the dead man, and took his hands in hers.

"And I would have thrown away a love like that!" she said.

26

The Passing of the Ape-Man

THE next morning they set out upon the short journey to Tarzan's cabin. Four Waziri bore the body of the dead Englishman. It had been the ape-man's suggestion that Clayton be buried beside the former Lord Greystoke near the edge of the jungle against the cabin that the older man had built.

Jane Porter was glad that it was to be so, and in her heart of hearts she wondered at the marvelous fineness of character of this wondrous man, who, though raised by brutes and among brutes, had the true chivalry and tenderness which one only associates with the refinements of the highest civilization.

They had proceeded some three miles of the five that had separated them from Tarzan's own beach when the Waziri who were ahead stopped suddenly, pointing in amazement at a strange figure approaching them along the beach. It was a man with a shiny silk hat, who walked slowly with bent head, and hands clasped behind him underneath the tails of his long, black coat.

At sight of him Jane Porter uttered a little cry of surprise and joy, and ran quickly ahead to meet him. At the sound of her voice the old man looked up, and when he saw who it was confronting him he, too, cried out in relief and happiness. As Professor Archimedes Q. Porter folded his daughter in his arms tears streamed down his seamed old face, and it was several minutes before he could control himself sufficiently to speak.

When a moment later he recognized Tarzan it was with difficulty that they could convince him that his sorrow had not unbalanced his mind, for with the other members of the party he had been so thoroughly convinced that the ape-man was dead it was a problem to reconcile the conviction with the very lifelike appearance of Jane's "forest god." The old man was deeply touched at the news of Clayton's death.

"I cannot understand it," he said. "Monsieur Thuran assured us that Clayton passed away many days ago."

"Thuran is with you?" asked Tarzan.

"Yes; he but recently found us and led us to your cabin. We were camped but a short distance north of it. Bless me, but he will be delighted to see you both."

"And surprised," commented Tarzan.

A short time later the strange party came to the clearing in which stood the ape-man's cabin. It was filled with people coming and going, and almost the first whom Tarzan saw was D'Arnot.

"Paul!" he cried. "In the name of sanity what are you doing here? Or are we all insane?"

It was quickly explained, however, as were many other seemingly strange things. D'Arnot's ship had been cruising along the coast, on patrol duty, when at the lieutenant's suggestion they had anchored off the little landlocked harbor to have another look at the cabin and the jungle in which many of the officers and men had taken part in exciting adventures two years before. On landing they had found Lord Tennington's party, and arrangements were being made to take them all on board the following morning, and carry them back to civilization.

Hazel Strong and her mother, Esmeralda, and Mr. Samuel T. Philander were almost overcome by happiness at Jane Porter's safe return. Her escape seemed to them little short of miraculous, and it was the consensus of opinion that it could have been achieved by no other man than Tarzan of the Apes. They loaded the uncomfortable ape-man with eulogies and attentions until he wished himself back in the amphitheater of the apes.

All were interested in his savage Waziri, and many were the gifts the black men received from these friends of their king, but when they learned that he might sail away from them upon the great canoe that lay at anchor a mile off shore they became very sad.

As yet the newcomers had seen nothing of Lord Tennington and Monsieur Thuran. They had gone out for fresh meat early in the day, and had not yet returned.

"How surprised this man, whose name you say is Rokoff, will be to see you," said Jane Porter to Tarzan.

"His surprise will be short-lived," replied the ape-man grimly, and there was that in his tone that made her look up into his face in alarm. What she read there evidently confirmed her fears, for she put her hand upon his arm, and pleaded with him to leave the Russian to the laws of France.

"In the heart of the jungle, dear," she said, "with no other form of right or justice to appeal to other than your own mighty muscles, you would be warranted in executing upon this man the sentence he deserves; but with the strong arm of a civilized government at your disposal it would be murder to kill him now. Even your friends would have to submit to your arrest, or if you resisted it you would plunge us all into misery and unhappiness again. I cannot bear to lose you again, my Tarzan. Promise me that you will but turn him over to Captain Dufranne, and let the law take its course—the beast is not worth risking our happiness for."

He saw the wisdom of her appeal, and promised. A half hour later Rokoff and Tennington emerged from the jungle. They were walking side by side. Tennington was the first to note the presence of strangers in the camp. He saw the black warriors palavering with the sailors from the cruiser, and then he saw a lithe, brown giant talking with Lieutenant D'Arnot and Captain Dufranne.

"Who is that, I wonder," said Tennington to Rokoff, and as the Russian raised his eyes and met those of the ape-man full upon him, he staggered and went white.

"*Sapristi!*" he cried, and before Tennington realized what he intended he had thrown his gun to his shoulder, and aiming point-blank at Tarzan pulled the trigger. But the Englishman was close to him—so close that his hand reached the leveled barrel a fraction of a second before the hammer fell upon the cartridge, and the bullet that was intended for Tarzan's heart whirred harmlessly above his head.

Before the Russian could fire again the ape-man was upon him and had wrested the firearm from his grasp. Captain Dufranne, Lieutenant D'Arnot, and a dozen sailors had rushed up at the sound of the shot, and now Tarzan turned the Russian over to them without a word. He had explained the matter to the French commander before Rokoff arrived, and the officer gave immediate orders to place the Russian in irons and confine him on board the cruiser.

Just before the guard escorted the prisoner into the small boat that was to transport him to his temporary prison Tarzan asked permission to search him, and to his delight found the stolen papers concealed upon his person.

The shot had brought Jane Porter and the others from the cabin, and a moment after the excitement had died down she greeted the surprised Lord Tennington. Tarzan joined them after he had taken the papers from Rokoff, and, as he approached, Jane Porter introduced him to Tennington.

"John Clayton, Lord Greystoke, my lord," she said.

The Englishman looked his astonishment in spite of his most herculean efforts to appear courteous, and it required many repetitions of the strange story of the ape-man as told by himself, Jane Porter, and Lieutenant D'Arnot to convince Lord Tennington that they were not all quite mad.

At sunset they buried William Cecil Clayton beside the jungle graves of his uncle and his aunt, the former Lord and Lady Greystoke. And it was at Tarzan's request that three volleys were fired over the last resting place of "a brave man, who met his death bravely."

Professor Porter, who in his younger days had been ordained a minister, conducted the simple services for the dead. About the grave, with bowed heads, stood as strange a company of mourners as the sun ever looked down upon. There were French officers and sailors, two English lords, Americans, and a score of savage African braves.

Following the funeral Tarzan asked Captain Dufranne to delay the sailing of the cruiser a couple of days while he went inland a few miles to fetch his "belongings," and the officer gladly granted the favor.

Late the next afternoon Tarzan and his Waziri returned with the first load of "belongings," and when the party saw the ancient ingots of virgin gold they swarmed upon the ape-man with a thousand questions; but he was smilingly obdurate to their appeals—he declined to give them the slightest clew as to the source of his immense treasure. "There are a thousand that I left behind," he explained, "for every one that I brought away, and when these are spent I may wish to return for more."

The next day he returned to camp with the balance of his ingots, and when they were stored on board the cruiser Captain Dufranne said he felt like the commander of an old-time Spanish galleon returning from the treasure cities of the Aztecs. "I don't know what minute my crew will cut my throat, and take over the ship," he added.

The next morning, as they were preparing to embark upon the cruiser, Tarzan ventured a suggestion to Jane Porter.

"Wild beasts are supposed to be devoid of sentiment," he said, "but nevertheless I should like to be married in the cabin where I was born, beside the graves of my mother and my father, and surrounded by the savage jungle that always has been my home."

"Would it be quite regular, dear?" she asked. "For if it would I know of no other place in which I should rather be married to my forest god than beneath the shade of his primeval forest."

And when they spoke of it to the others they were assured that it would be quite regular, and a most splendid termination of a remarkable romance. So the entire party assembled within the little cabin and about the door to witness the second ceremony that Professor Porter was to solemnize within three days.

D'Arnot was to be best man, and Hazel Strong bridesmaid, until Tennington upset all the arrangements by another of his marvelous "ideas."

"If Mrs. Strong is agreeable," he said, taking the bridesmaid's hand in his, "Hazel and I think it would be ripping to make it a double wedding."

The next day they sailed, and as the cruiser steamed slowly out to sea a tall man, immaculate in white flannel, and a graceful girl leaned against her rail to watch the receding shore line upon which danced twenty naked, black warriors of the Waziri, waving their war spears above their savage heads, and shouting farewells to their departing king.

"I should hate to think that I am looking upon the jungle for the last time, dear," he said, "were it not that I know that I am going to a new world of happiness with you forever," and, bending down, Tarzan of the Apes kissed his mate upon her lips.

About Edgar Rice Burroughs

Edgar Rice Burroughs is one of the world's most popular authors. With no previous experience as an author, he wrote and sold his first novel —*A Princess of Mars*—in 1912. In the ensuing thirty-eight years until his death in 1950, Burroughs wrote 91 books and a host of short stories and articles. Although best known as the creator of the classic *Tarzan of the Apes* and *John Carter of Mars,* his restless imagination knew few bounds. Burroughs' prolific pen ranged from the American West to primitive Africa and on to romantic adventure on the moon, the planets, and even beyond the farthest star.

No one knows how many copies of ERB books have been published throughout the world. It is conservative to say, however, that of the translations into 32 known languages, including Braille, the number must run into the hundreds of millions. When one considers the additional world-wide following of the Tarzan newspaper feature, radio programs, comic magazines, motion pictures and television, Burroughs must have been known and loved by literally a thousand million or more.

Attesting to the unparalleled holding power Edgar Rice Burroughs maintains upon his readers are the many ERB fan clubs existing today. Established by dedicated Burroughs admirers, some of these groups publish their own fan magazines devoted exclusively to all facets of the Burroughs legend.

Interested admirers of Mr. Burroughs' literary works are cordially invited to write to the secretaries of these fan clubs for detailed information regarding membership and availability of their excellent Burroughs fan publications.

Readers in other parts of the world wishing to establish ERB fan clubs may write to Edgar Rice Burroughs, Inc., Tarzana, California, U.S.A. 91356, who will give every possible assistance.

Following are a few of the long-established fan groups:

The Burroughs Bibliophiles
6657 Locust St.
Kansas City, Missouri 64131

The Barsoomian
84 Charlton Road
Rochester, New York 14617

ERB-dom Magazine
Post Office Box 550
Evergreen, Colorado 80439

Erbania
8001 Fernview Lane
Tampa, Florida 33615